WHEN ME AND GOD
WERE LITTLE

WHEN ME AND GOD WERE LITTLE

—a novel—

Mads Nygaard

translated by Steve Schein

DZANC
BOOKS

DZANC
BOOKS

2580 Craig Rd.
Ann Arbor, MI 48103
www.dzancbooks.org

Library of Congress Catalog-in-Publication Data available upon request.

ISBN: 9781950539383
First US edition: December 2021
Cover design by Daniel Benneworth-Gray
Cover photo by Iwona Rostocka
Interior design by Michelle Dotter

Printed in the United States of America

10   9   8   7   6   5   4   3   2   1

For my dad

PART I

CHAPTER ONE

IN OUR TOWN YOU COULDN'T DROWN BAREFOOT. You had to wash up on the beach in smelly socks and underpants that kept you warm, with your sleeves rolled up far enough so everybody could see the tattoos. On the one arm there had to be an anchor, on the other, a name. The name should be of the ship you'd just gone down with. Then those who were supposed to grieve could get the news quickly.

There were a number of rules. A beached body was supposed to wash ashore with a knife in its hand. The kind of knife that didn't let go, that wanted to remain a lodger in the dead man's hand forever. That wanted to go to heaven along with the hand and slice the clouds in two. The knife wanted to see its job through to the end and give its master a chance of seeing something along the way. Or else the Earth just looked all white.

Alexander's the one who taught me all the rules. Alexander was my big brother, but one morning he stopped being that. He also forgot everything he'd said.

Alexander washed up on the beach barefoot. He had bare legs, bare arms, and lots of ocean in his stomach. Neither of his hands was clutching anything at all.

At the funeral, the whole church cried. I didn't. I peed slowly in my pants and wondered whether anyone had remembered to lay a sharp knife in the coffin.

———

Grandma lived in another town, far away. I stood out in the field, holding my breath. I tested all the corners of the world, and the wind was good. It said that Mom had stopped. Dad had finally found a cork for Mom's mouth.

I went in to say goodbye to Grandma's cows. Grandma had two. They were Christian cows. Black with pink tits. Grandma had trained them. She'd taught them to stand completely still in a long prayer, and when they were done singing milk down into Grandma's pail, they said amen and promised to hold onto their milk through the night. Satan was to be denied so much as a drop.

"Goodbye, cows," I said, and went into Grandma's house.

Grandma sat in her easy chair with God. Grandma herself was just about to die all day long. Dad said never to light a match in front of Grandma. She had dynamite inside her. She ate it every day. The dynamite was little red pills. They were supposed to go down to her heart and explode a little so it didn't stop.

"I can't hear Mom anymore," I said.

We looked at each other until Grandma told me it was time for bed. Grandma arranged my hands like they were supposed to be. And said a slow goodnight to God. Then she crawled into bed with lots of clothes on.

I lay on Grandma's old mattress. It was thin and had been on many trips. The mattress was Christian as well and liked meeting other Christians down south. Then all the mattresses lay under the heavens and prayed to God for good weather.

Even though they were good Christians, the mattresses could still get a bawling out if they got wet from the rain or pee from old ladies who couldn't just lay there with their legs crossed for eternity. At least that's what Dad said.

The next morning, the first thing I did was check whether Grandma was still alive. This took time. Grandma breathed so quietly that the flies never bothered taking off from her mouth when it opened and shut. Grandma had a lot of flies. Everybody in Grandma's town did. The town was named Hørmested. In Hørmested the people didn't collect stamps or coins, they collected cow shit.

Grandma's flesh didn't fit to her bones too well. I could take a whole lump in my hands. So I did, and gave it a squeeze. Grandma didn't say ouch, but she made a sound that was okay. So I raced out to the john to see if I still had hair on my head.

Grandma said it was possible to be scared so bad that your hair turned gray and fell off. From one night to the next. The mirror said congratulations. My hair was doing fine.

I went back to Grandma's room and got up into her bed with my soccer ball. I wasn't allowed to kick in Grandma's bedroom, or dribble either. Besides, Grandma said the day would come when God would put together a team made up of the best people on earth. God would come down from heaven and dribble around between the houses and choose the people who were best. Grandma believed she'd make the team. If that were true, the team was in for a hard time.

Grandma's feet stuck out under the quilt. The nails on her big toe were long and yellow. They didn't smell. The only smell from Grandma came from her mouth. It was Grandpa coming out of her. He was very rotten because he had been dead a thousand years.

I never met my grandpa. All that was left of him was the smell that came out of Grandma's mouth and the fine little moustache on her lip. The moustache was made of Grandpa's hair. She missed him, which was why he was still living in her head. He had been trying for years to get out so he could breathe. It had only worked for some of his hairs.

It took Grandma a long time to get up. Her legs always slept longer than the rest of her body. She had to shake them to get them going. I would have liked to help, but she said I was too strong. That I should fold up my bedding as though it would never be used again.

When we'd gotten dressed, we went to the kitchen. Grandma toasted bread and arranged my hands in a prayer. The prayer turned the bread black, but Grandma said amen and scraped the slices white with a knife.

"What are Mom and Dad doing now?"

"They're grieving."

"That's what you said yesterday. That's what you say all the time."

"It's true."

"When are they going to stop?"

Grandma looked at the coffee maker. She didn't have a TV. Grandma watched the coffee, and when the coffee was finished being made, she kept sitting, looking at it.

In the afternoon we took a trip in Grandma's car. The car was named "Chevy" and was incredibly Christian. We stopped at a farm. The farmer was rich. He had a giant mountain of cow shit. I had to look way up in the sky to say hi to the hen who was standing on top, dancing.

The farmer wasn't home, but his wife was. It was all right for me and Grandma to come in and tell her about the magazines we'd brought. They were wholesome magazines. You got healthy and immortal from reading them.

The farmer's wife made coffee and took the lid off a can of cookies. Children were hanging all over the place in the living room. They were also standing on the tables. They'd been photographed only in a good mood. Grandma sat down on the sofa. She licked her lips so

God's words would be all clean when they reached the farmer's wife's ears. I went around looking for a picture without a smile.

"And what is your name, my young friend?" asked the farmer's wife.

"Dammitall Karl Gustav."

"Oh, my goodness," said the wife.

"I come from Hirtshals. We collect beached bodies. My big brother was worth his weight in gold."

Grandma thought we should go. As quick as possible. She got mad at my feet when it was time to put my shoes back on. She refused to tie the shoelaces. She took my hand and pulled me across the farmyard. It would have been better if I had pulled Grandma instead. I was much faster than she was.

Chevy drove us to Grandma's church. We were alone there. Grandma said I should sit still and be ashamed. Grandma closed her eyes. My Dammitall gave her a headache. Dad always said I should keep thirty feet away from Grandma when I had to piss or swear. He gave me a yardstick, too, so I could measure Grandma's mood.

Grandma folded her body together in a silent prayer. I wondered what Grandpa was doing. I looked at Grandma's body to see if he were somewhere inside, knocking. If I were Grandpa, I'd try to get out through the navel. Then he'd have a real good chance of landing right in her hands. But Grandpa must have been asleep.

I set to picking my nose, both nostrils at once. It went just fine. I built a little mountain of boogers on the tip of one finger and rubbed it around till it was dry, without dropping it. That's how all magicians got their start, sitting in an empty church, next to a prayer.

Grandma opened her eyes and said she was going to take an afternoon nap. That was good, because it wasn't allowed in the church. It was okay to sit up and sleep, but not lie down, which was the way Grandma liked best. She was going to lie in her bed and I was going to be a good boy.

Before she went into the bedroom, Grandma gave me a jigsaw puzzle made out of lots of pieces. She said it was her favorite game when she was alone. The pieces were small and lay in a cardboard box with a picture on the top. You were supposed to dump all the pieces on her dining room table and hunt for the ones that looked exactly like the picture. Grandma said that doing a jigsaw puzzle was such a nice way to pass the time.

I picked up a piece. It was a sky. I picked up another piece. It was a sky with a little bit of cloud on it. After I examined all the thousand pieces, I got mad. There were only three different kinds: sky, clouds and red flowers. I put a flower piece in my mouth and gave it a spit bath. The color was gone when I took it out. Maybe the jigsaw puzzle was a good game after all. I sent seven pieces of flower to take a bath, and when they had all turned into soft cardboard, I crept into Grandma's bedroom.

I placed the pieces on Grandma's moustache, careful and quiet. Then I got her little mirror and sat down to wait. When Grandma woke up, she'd be able to see for herself how Grandpa was going to be when he fought all the way out of her head. He would be gray as cardboard, but soft and warm. And Grandma would smile. And say thank you.

Thank you so much for the cardboard, my dear Karl Gustav. That's what she'd say.

God wasn't in a very good mood that evening in Hørmested. Maybe He was tired of helping old ladies who didn't know how to be happy when they got presents. In any case, Grandma sure wasn't good at getting a lovely present above her mouth.

She happened to lift her head wrong when she woke up. The present broke. Three of the pieces fell into her mouth and disappeared down her throat. Grandpa was somewhere in Grandma's tummy. He usually opened an umbrella when food or coffee was poured down. This time, when something exciting was finally dumped on him, he stretched his arm up through Grandma's throat to grab the puzzle pieces. Grandma couldn't breathe and her head turned blue.

She coughed and crawled out of bed and set her feet on the floor. The legs didn't feel like being woken up, so when she tried to stand, they folded themselves up on the floor to go on sleeping. The rest of Grandma followed the legs. Just like that. She stopped when her neck hit her scale. The scale was made of iron and used to tell how much Grandma weighed. Now it only told how bad Grandma had hurt herself.

But the pieces escaped. They came flying out of her mouth, all wet and crumpled. I raced to the barn to her two Christian cows and lay down under the bigger one. I closed my eyes and got ready. I was lying like I was supposed to. Like Alexander. Ready to be found.

The cow stood still above me. All it did was turn its head a little. Maybe the other one was in charge. I crawled out. Crawling on your back is hard, because you have to lift your head a little. The udders tickled my forehead.

I lay down under the other cow. Neither of them had a name. Grandma wouldn't give them one. The second cow shook one leg. Its whole belly moved. It was warming up. I closed my eyes. Here it came. The hay scrunched under me. Maybe the cow was going to stamp me straight through the floor of the barn. I'd go straight through Hørmested. Down into fire and water.

The hay stopped scrunching. The cow hadn't done a thing. I opened my eyes and crawled out slowly, wanting to make sure it meant what it said. That my present for Grandma had been okay. Yes, the cow thought so. The other one, too. They waved with their tails.

I smiled and hurried in to Grandma. She was still in a sour mood. She was going to make food and pray, and that was all. We were having potatoes and steaks made out of celery root. Celery root was sour food.

While we were eating, I happened to think of Oliver from Helgoland Street. He lived in number 8 and had also been unlucky with a present. It was on Christmas Day. Oliver was bad at memorizing songs. He had to hold a songbook in his hand to remember the words. He was a little man with small hands, so he used both of them.

Suddenly Oliver's heart stopped beating. The songbook fell out of his hands, down on a skinny branch. A lot of the Christmas tree lights blew out. Then came Oliver and put out the rest. He crashed into a present that was long and not wrapped very good. Everybody could see it was a rake, and it was just the present Oliver had been wishing for. The card even said the rake was for him, but instead of unwrapping it with his hands, he used his forehead.

Oliver died twice as hard as people usually did. From a heart attack and six holes in the head. Luckily, Oliver was a man who people didn't like. He'd sat at the town hall his whole life with a rubber stamp that cost lots of money when you got it in the mail.

When Oliver was buried, the whole church sat there with wads of paper and handkerchiefs in their mouth. And every time the priest took a break, he went out behind a curtain so he could snigger in peace.

The leaves on the trees in Hirtshals didn't say much. They kept falling down and messing around in people's yards, but if you went over to Helgoland Street and picked up a leaf and held it close to your ear, you could hear it laughing its little brown ass off.

It was an incredible story. Death was good at being nasty. Who else could come up with the idea of killing a man with a present he'd been looking forward to?

I looked at Grandma. She still seemed angry.

"Grandma…?"

"Mmm."

"I know a story about a present. Do you want to hear it? It's not about jigsaw puzzles."

Grandma nodded. I put down my fork and sat up straight like a good boy.

"There was a man in Hirtshals. His name was Oliver. He lived on Helgoland Street, in number …"

"Stop," said Grandma. "Is this one of your father's stories?"

I didn't know if it was. My stories always came from a lot of different places. They, too, were a kind of jigsaw puzzle, only it was always me who decided how the pieces got put together. And I could rearrange them, even when people thought I was finished. I chose to shake my head.

"Is there beer and adultery in this story?"

Adultery was an exciting word. I had never heard it before, but it was okay for it to be in my story. I nodded and promised Grandma there would be plenty of adultery in my story about Oliver.

Grandma left the kitchen and went into the living room. Very slowly. Her slippers tried to light the floorboards on fire. Grandma stopped in front of the telephone and looked at it. My food got cold. She lifted the receiver and called someone and said they could come and get me. She said nothing else, not even goodbye.

Grandma hung up and kept looking at the telephone. I put a half celery steak in my mouth and folded my hands. Grandma could spend the whole day saying good day to people she didn't know. She got creepy when she called someone and didn't say goodbye.

CHAPTER TWO

WE HAD ALWAYS LIVED IN HIRTSHALS. We were rich there. Our house was so big that Mom still hadn't gotten around to vacuuming all the rooms. We had so many cars that sometimes I went and sat in one that wasn't Dad's.

Out in the garden was the world's tallest cherry tree. When Dad bought the tree, he got the whole town to stand there, holding it, while he ran out and bought an airplane and a parachute. Then he flew up in the sky, jumped out with the parachute, and knocked the tree into the ground with his bare hands.

We had a lot of things that were worth their weight in gold. Dad owned a boat down by the harbor that was named *Singeø*. Dad never had time to go sailing, but it didn't matter. *Singeø* could sail by itself. After it had been out in the North Sea, *Singeø* opened its belly like a cash register and a thousand tons of fish rolled out. And even though the fish were real tired, they swam right down to the bank and put themselves in Dad's account.

We never saw Dad, but we often heard him. Dad buzzed around, buying land and building houses. When the piggy bank was loaded, he took it down to the inn, cracked it open, and threw dice and beer mugs. Sometimes he came home with an empty piggy bank, but it didn't matter because in the meantime he'd gotten loaded himself.

Then he'd be hiccupping and wanting to dance with Mom. Dad liked dancing most while Mom was making food.

Our house was built on the best site in town. It didn't just have a number; it also had a name. The house was named Little Norway. Dad had built it himself out of wood, and every morning the nails bent over and bowed to him when he got up.

Mom wasn't supposed to earn money. She was supposed to stay home and be unemployed and clean house and make food and polish things. When Mom went out, it was to drink coffee with all the other lazy wives. They met often and tried to out-knit each other and practiced grabbing one another so they were prepared when their husbands fell over.

Dad only took time off when they held this party out in a field in Hjallerup. All Denmark was invited and everybody came, including the poor, who went around with rats on their shoulders. Rats were great pets for the poor. They didn't need money or help finding food. The party lasted for days, but we were only there at the beginning, for our shoes' sake. On the first day, the field hadn't been turned into mud yet. Mom didn't like parties where your shoes sank.

Dad knew exactly what he wanted to do when we got there. He rushed over and bought the large, heavy hammer that you had to pound down on top of a big thingamabob to make a bell ring. Dad kept pounding until the bell blew up in the sky and scattered like tears falling from the sun. By the time its owner was crawling around, looking for the pieces, Dad was on his way to the beer tent, singing.

There were only four things you could do in the beer tent: play accordion, sleep, be thirsty, and fight. Dad wanted to try them all and didn't stop until at least one of his eyes was turning black and blue. When Dad changed eye color, Mom wanted to go home. Mom would drive us all back to Hirtshals without saying much. Alexander and I sat with Dad on the rear seat. We took turns putting out the flames every time Dad dropped his pipe into his lap.

Mom got awful tired when Dad took time off.

The school in Hirtshals was big and tall. If you jumped out of the fifth-grade class window, you landed in a coffin. If you jumped out while you were still in the third grade, you only broke your arms and legs. I was in the second grade, so we could jump out the window without getting hurt. That made us mad.

Luckily the whole schoolyard was made out of asphalt. We played soccer in puddles of blood and our knees stuck to our pants in the winter—at least mine and Axel's. We refused to wear band-aids.

Axel was the goalie, black as coal. He was the best one in the schoolyard when it came to bleeding elbows. In class he could paint big red things without moving an inch.

Me and Axel sat next to each other. I could always borrow some blood from him. Axel was good at sports. He said that his real mother in Africa didn't go to sports. She sat on her knees, digging for water. You didn't get paid for that in Africa, and she didn't know how to ski, either.

Axel's new mom in Hirtshals was named Ruth. Ruth was white in the winter and pink in the summer. She played badminton and answered the telephone. Axel's father owned all three taxis in Hirtshals, but they didn't run very good because Axel lived in the yellow apartment buildings. Mom said they were poor. Dad said that Axel's father had lost his shirt in another business, and once you did that, it took a long time before you could lose your shirt again.

Dad also said he'd rather die than live in the yellow apartments. That you couldn't breathe over there.

Axel and them were not nearly as poor as you'd think. Axel said he had to decide himself when it was his birthday because there was no one who could remember when he'd been born. Axel had decided to celebrate his birthday on the day after the annual harbor celebration. He didn't get his presents until the afternoon since his dad always slept late with his wallet. It had gotten fat during the night because all the fishermen took taxis when there was a harbor party. The rest of the year they drove their mopeds.

"You guys aren't poor, dammit," I told Axel.

"We sure as hell are," said Axel.

"You got a lot more stairs than we do."

"Like hell we do."

"The mailman hates your building."

"He's a son of a bitch."

"My big brother's dead."

"He sure is."

We biked over to the stadium. Axel was supposed to defend the goal with no hedge behind it. So I kicked to him and Axel had to run like hell to get the ball when I missed. Our ball was named Tango and had just become world champ on TV in a country called Argentina.

It never tired Axel out, fetching Tango. He was a good goalkeeper. But when we played real club matches, he was bad. He was always running up to the other team's goal at the opposite end. We tried to knock Axel over because the referee never said anything. The ref's name was Fred and he lived in Hirtshals, so we always won. He thought it was all right for Axel to run up to the other end and refused to give Axel the red card, even though we screamed that he should. Axel was our top scorer. No goalkeeper was supposed to score that much.

Me and Axel couldn't play soccer during summer vacation. Fred and all the other referees had taken off to a desert island to eat pigs. They were tired of fish. Everybody in Hirtshals was.

Me and Axel went with Ruth and Mom to the beach. They weren't friends like me and Axel. Ruth always lay right by the edge of the water. Mom had begun sitting up in the sand dunes. She drank coffee with her clothes on. Ruth drank beer with bare boobs. They hung off her like balloons trying to float to earth.

Me and Axel didn't talk to anybody. We practiced with Tango. I stood in the middle of the beach and Axel stood by the water. The North Sea was the goal. I yelled that Tango better not get wet. If it did, I won, and Axel would have to save up to buy me a new ball. He promised—several times a day. Every summer Axel wound up owing me two million Tangos.

Axel had learned to swim when he was real little. There wasn't much water in Africa, and when someone finally found some, all the children were thrown in it so the adults could party in peace. The kids who survived were sent to Hirtshals.

Ruth was sitting on a towel, reading magazines. She wasn't afraid Axel would drown. Only when the ferryboats were sailing into the harbor. Then there were big waves and Ruth shouted that we should come over and hold onto her tits. I said to Axel that we ought to get away from there so we didn't have to, but he wouldn't.

"Sissy."

"You can't swim."

"Ruth's got balloon boobs."

"Your mom's got a hole in her stomach. You're a siss-arean."

"My mom's a real mom."

"Your big brother's dead."

"He sure is."

Ruth didn't say anything. She gave us boiled juice and sand crackers. Our teeth made noise. The waves got small again. Axel ran down to the water and spit on his palms. The ferry had washed a thousand jellyfish up on the beach, but Axel wanted to practice and jump around in them.

I went up close to Axel. I made a little mountain of sand. I put Tango on top of the mountain and ran all the way up in the dunes.

"You ready?" I yelled.

Axel nodded and spit on his palms. There was no way he'd ever be ready. My next kick was going to Norway. Axel didn't mind swimming after Tango because there was nothing he didn't dare doing.

When the sun went down out in the North Sea, Axel would be going to sleep with my big brother. It was too bad, but Axel should have shut up about siss-arean.

Mom often pointed at her scar and said she liked it. She didn't. Alexander came out of the real hole that was in front. It was easy to patch up. I got lost and tried to come out Mom's ass. At the hospital they finally gave up and drilled a big hole in Mom's belly. They dug me out and crammed me into a sucking cup. It took them days to cover the hole again.

Now Mom sat in the dunes all summer and waited for the scar to disappear. It didn't. The siss-arean stayed where it was, though ladies in Hirtshals were never allowed to go around with ugly scars—only tattoos.

I took a look at Tango and started running as fast as I could. I hit it with the hardest part of my foot. It hurt, but Tango flew off above Axel like a cloud, out past the huge rock and almost all the way to where the sea changed color. Out into the green, where skeletons walked around on the bottom, cutting grass, bones sweating.

Axel took off into the water, head first. Tango swam away. It was the wind's fault. It had changed direction because I was mad. The wind was afraid of me and tomorrow Axel was going to wash up at the feet of an old lady in Norway. She would drop all the amber she'd been collecting, poke Axel with her foot, and try to lift him. But she wouldn't be able.

My big brother weighed so much, it took six men to lift him in the church.

———

There was a cutter in Hirtshals harbor. Its name was *HG233 Sylvia*. Once *Sylvia* had been light blue all over, but her bottom had gotten brown and battered. It didn't matter much because *Sylvia* hadn't gone anywhere since her owner went blind. The owner's name was Deadeye and he was the only one in Hirtshals who could take his eyes out and make a noise with them like marbles.

Deadeye didn't mind telling folks about what happened to the real eyes. He said he'd lost them on the high seas. The accident happened while he was shaving with a razor blade. He'd been standing in sunshine and gale winds, humming a tune, when heavy seas made the blade pay him a flying visit—two times. The eyes said nothing, just "plop" and "plop" as they hit the water. Then Deadeye jumped in, but he couldn't find them.

Good and mad, Deadeye tried sailing home to Hirtshals, but since he was blind now, he wound up in England. Deadeye could tell right away that the people sounded wrong. He got so mad that he decided to just keep straight on, through town and country.

Deadeye was very strong and good at being mad. *Sylvia* had to put up with being slogged all the way round the world. A few years went by and then one day Deadeye was back, dragging his *Sylvia* along with him, right down the pedestrian street. Deadeye didn't say hello to anyone. He had a beard he could tie his shoes with and *Sylvia* looked like her whole boat hurt.

The worst thing was that Deadeye had forgotten to pull in the anchor. Not many weeks went by before he started getting hundreds of bills. They came from folks who'd had their gardens and their vegetables plowed up too early.

Deadeye had been incredibly blind and poor ever since.

"Want me to get you some beers, Deadeye?"

I got up close to him so he could smell it was me. Deadeye had the biggest nostrils in Hirtshals.

"Hello-hello, Karl Gustav. Where's your friend?"

Deadeye was real good. He couldn't only smell me, he could smell everyone who wasn't there.

"Axel just drowned."

"You don't say."

Deadeye fished around in his pockets for coins.

"You can fetch me three today."

I sprang from *Sylvia* all the way over to the grocery store. Deadeye wasn't good at getting the beer he wanted. He walked with a very slow cane. Deadeye never went anywhere without it. He also used it out in front of his house to stop cars. It wasn't a good idea for Deadeye to drive cars, mopeds, or bicycles, and that was a shame because his house was so far away from *Sylvia*.

Deadeye had to stand out by the big road every single day and joust with the cars. The cars were supposed to stop and pick him up. And quite often they did. Everyone figured it was only fair for Deadeye to be able to get down to his cutter since he couldn't watch TV like everybody else.

I walked back very careful with the beers. If you dropped a full bottle of beer, a sailor fell overboard somewhere on the Seven Seas. You might not know who it was, but it was still sad. That's what Deadeye said.

The water in the harbor was quiet. All the other boats were out fishing. When they got back—if they didn't sink—I was going to ask the skippers if they'd seen Axel out there. And Tango. It would be cool if they kicked Tango back on land from a cutter.

I gave Deadeye the beers and the three coins that were left over. He didn't say thanks. I was looking forward to us having something to eat. Deadeye always brought a lunch basket along with good things. Many of which were still alive. Deadeye had a cheese that could walk on the water and a sausage that could live in your teeth for years without really disappearing. Deadeye was a good cook and he always went around with lots of food in his beard.

Axel bicycled up. He was mad. He jumped onto *Sylvia* without saying hello.

"Why'd you just leave?"

"Deadeye wanted beer."

"Tango swam to Norway, so it doesn't count."

"How far out did you get?"

"Out until Mom was just a dot, screaming on the beach."

"Ruth isn't your mom."

"Like hell she isn't."

"Like hell she is."

"Come over here," said Deadeye.

We did.

"Open your mouths."

Deadeye stuffed a whole meatball in my mouth, and Axel's too. Deadeye's fingers tasted like potato salad. This damaged the taste of the meatballs, but we ate them anyway.

For the rest of the day we asked all the cutters that came in whether they'd seen Tango.

CHAPTER THREE

BY THE TIME HE HAD BEEN DEAD A YEAR, Alexander lived in at least four places: in heaven, in the graveyard, in his room, and in our bathtub. The bathtub was the only one of these places I went to.

Mom sat on the other side of the bathroom door three times a week, asking how I was doing. I was allowed to take a bath alone, so long as I yelled I was all right all the time. Farting and splashing around wasn't enough. Mom demanded words. She'd become afraid of many things: cars on the road, mushrooms in the woods, thunder and lightning, wild geese, unleashed dogs, Dad's paint pots in the shed, beer capsules, snakes. I couldn't even go around with nails in my mouth. Mom believed all of us were going to die all the time, including in the bathtub.

Mom had to decide how much water went in. When she turned off the faucet I took out my yardstick to see if she was just as afraid as usual. She was. All year long the yardstick said I could only be one or two inches deep.

No one was afraid back in the days when Alexander had to get clean. Alexander would fill the tub to the brim and lay down in the bottom. He was training. Sometimes I got to crouch on my knees and time him. I got to hold his watch and count out how many times the second hand went around. Alexander's hair tried leaving his head all by itself. Bubbles came out of his mouth and nose. The rest of him lay completely still. The only thing that happened were the colors. All the red would disappear. Alexander turned white and his lips blue.

Sometimes he lay there so long that small fish began swimming around with him. They swam past his ears, asking if he had a little air to spare. Alexander didn't have time to talk to them. When you're beating records, you're on your own. If you beat a record with other people you'd have to share it.

My big brother liked me best when I was his stopwatch. On Saturday we always rode up to the lighthouse. Alexander didn't lock his bike when we got there. He would eat an apple and spit out the seeds. He'd light a cigarette and put my bike over his back, then carry it all the way down over the giant rocks.

Alexander didn't care about what the wind and the waves were doing. He didn't care if the sky was dark clouds. Alexander would finish his cigarette, take off his clothes, and swim out to the spot where Norway began. Then he'd look back at me and my bicycle which were still in Denmark. Alexander would nod and I'd nod back and swing his watch in the air.

Alexander would lie on top of the water and begin beating it. He'd build a railroad track out of foam and make the seagulls scream with joy.

I biked to the water's edge and got sand in the chain. Me and the bike scrunched along as we flattened all the jellyfish so they couldn't wiggle back out and get in Alexander's way.

I watched the seconds, but couldn't keep up. Alexander's records were long ones. We ended up all the way at Munch's Seaside Hotel in the next town.

When he could see the hotel's chimney, Alexander swam up on land and shook off the ocean. I bicycled around him in circles and held the watch up in the air. Alexander knocked me over and took his watch. I sat in the sand and checked my legs to see if he'd given me some good scratches. Alexander nodded at his new record and emptied the starfish and seaweed out of his trunks.

They'd hung up a sign by the hotel. It said how warm the ocean was. Alexander always went to the owner of the hotel and said the sign was lying. The owner was a lady wearing thick sweaters. She never got mad. She gave Alexander something to write with so he could go and give the ocean its correct temperature.

When everything was as it should be, Alexander bought us ice cream cones that were the same size. We sat on the bench in front of the seaside hotel. The lady's dog stood there, looking at us. It was tall and would have liked to growl and bite, but it could see our ice cream was made out of whipped North Sea. The dog thought about this for a moment. Then it padded in to the hotel lady and reached all four paws up to her. The lady did as she was asked. She took a scissors and trimmed all its claws. Alexander didn't say a word. He just smiled, knowing everything.

In the morning we had to be very quiet. Dad had to have his three soft-boiled eggs before he could drive off to build Hirtshals better. I was supposed to have my oatmeal so I'd get stronger. Mom didn't have to be strong for anything, so she just ate four cigarettes in a row.

We tried to miss Alexander while we sat at the table. None of us had beards yet. Mom went out to the mirror all the time to see if anything new had happened.

Mom was the one who spent the most time missing. There were thousands of pictures of Alexander in our house. There were lots of me, too. We stood on the tables and on the windowsills and hung from the walls. All the pictures looked alike. They'd been taken when we were real little.

Dad said we'd been photographed by a man who did nothing but take pictures of babies. It was a crummy job. The man always went around carrying an expensive bill and a suitcase with clean clothes. The bill was for Dad to chew on and the clothes were for the man to put on when he was finished taking pictures in a flood of baby throw-up. The man wasn't happy and smelled awful. Dad said he'd never use him again. This made Mom sad because she loved photographs.

Mom started wanting a camera for her birthday. Which she got. Then she began practicing. Mom had a tall doll in the living room. The doll had no head, no arms, and no legs. Mom used the doll when she had to see whether her knitting was full of ribs. Now she went around photographing the naked doll instead. Which went fine. But every time she took pictures of me and Alexander, things went wrong.

Dad said Mom's eyes were full of bad construction, and when the pictures came back from the shop, it turned out Dad was right. Mom's eyes had only hit our feet or arms or half our heads. We looked like two sons cut in slices.

Sometimes Mom tried to get Dad to take pictures of us when he was feeling happy and loaded. But he wouldn't do it. Dad danced and hiccupped and said one could remember the things that were worth remembering, and that if Mom couldn't figure out how to do that, she'd better go over to the neighbor and borrow some eyes. Dad had forgotten everything the next day, but not Mom. She kept practicing and went to an eye doctor. The eye doctor said Dad was right. Someone had sat down on Mom's eyes when she was little.

Now, with Alexander dead, Mom often went around touching his photographs. She also rubbed soap on them and used a cloth. Alexander didn't like Mom's hands and soap. At night I could hear him talking. Complaining and wanting me to hurry outside and bring in some mud. Alexander didn't try to keep quiet. He wasn't afraid of waking everybody up. When you're dead, you get to do everything.

———

One summer day Mom was supposed to take a trip with all the other unemployed ladies in Hirtshals. The ladies were going to ride on a bus so they could sit and knit without getting in a wreck. They were also going to stop somewhere in the middle of Denmark and eat roast pork.

Mom waved goodbye. Dad decided I was going with him to work. I was happy, sitting in the car. Dad had a cold beer between his legs, like all the men in Hirtshals were required to when they drove a car. The men worked hard all the time, so they were tired when they sat behind the wheel. The beer couldn't stand there by itself. The men constantly had to use their leg muscles to hold it in place. The beer was called a ball freezer, but it could just as well have been called a stayawake.

I began measuring things with my yardstick, just so Dad knew I was ready to work hard.

"The glove compartment's eight inches."

"Great," said Dad.

"The gearshift's eleven inches."

"Perfect."

"Where are we going?"

"Out to the Cement Baker and Five-Inch."

This was real good news. The Cement Baker and Five-Inch were Dad's best men. I didn't even manage to butt my head into the Cement Baker's stomach before Five-Inch drove his wheelbarrow up in front of my feet. He knew I was the best snail finder around.

When you built a house, it was okay if lots of animals got squashed or smothered by a brick—but not snails. Every single snail had to be found and carted away to keep living somewhere else.

The house would fall apart if you built it on top of a snail, and then slowly, very slowly, all the house parts would crawl away. Dad told me this from the very first time I came along to a building site.

Dad was busy. He gave Five-Inch some money and drove away. I didn't have time to wave. I was already racing around the whole place to find out where I should start. The Cement Baker and Five-Inch sat down with a beer to keep out of the way. They knew what they were doing.

The Cement Baker hadn't always been a bricklayer. Once he'd been a cook on one of the big fishing boats, where he made white bread that was so hard and sat so heavy on a man's stomach that the boat would sink if everybody ate at the same time. Which was something the skipper couldn't afford.

The Cement Baker had no teeth left. You could never tell whether he was glad or mad. Without teeth, the Cement Baker had difficulty building a smile, but that didn't matter, because he could lay bricks like nobody's business.

Five-Inch wasn't very strong, but he was born to be a carpenter. Dad said the first thing Five-Inch did when he popped out from between his mother's legs was to measure how much damage he'd done. Five-Inch lay in his cradle for days with two fingers that knew just how much that was. If someone tried to move his fingers, he cried like hell. One day, finally, words came out of Five-Inch's mouth. The first thing he gurgled was: "Five inches." Dad said that was exactly how much Five-Inch's mom had been broke open.

The sun was shining, but it was a bad building site. By the time the Cement Baker and Five-Inch opened their lunch boxes, my footprints were all over the place but I'd only found three snails. They took up incredibly little space in the wheelbarrow.

"Come and eat, Karl Gustav," said Five-Inch.

This made me mad. I kicked a shovel. Your name couldn't just be your real name. Five-Inch had never called Alexander "Alexander."

Alexander was always Mighty Mascot. Mighty Mascot was a name that meant Alexander was in control of the Cement Baker and Five-Inch and all the others when Dad was off buying more land. The name was so cool that Alexander had been allowed to quit school. Then he didn't have to do anything but be Mighty Mascot until his dying day. He went around the building site with nails in his mouth and crawled up on the rooftops and spit his men in the right direction.

Alexander only came back down when it was time for the topping-out ceremony. This was a party for the work crew. The ceremony was held when the house's body had grown so big that it could stand up by itself. Then Dad, me, and Mom showed up with a pot full of boiling hotdogs. In the back of the car were two cases of beer with ice on top. We picked up the ice down at the harbor. The crew loved Dad's ice beer and Mom's hotdogs.

Mom lifted the pot lid so Alexander could stick his hand down in the steam and catch the biggest hotdog. He didn't say ow. He took the open mustard jar and stabbed it with the hotdog. The hotdog turned brown and Alexander took a bite that was full of fire. Then he stabbed the jar again. The whole crew smiled, as though they liked the idea of Alexander stuffing his spit into the jar. They didn't want my spit because it was called slobber. Slobber was spit's kid brother.

When the hotdogs were gone, me and Mom drove home again. Dad and Alexander had to stay and help the workers empty all the beers. I knew what they talked about while the sun went down. They talked about their names, and about how important it was to have a good one. Dad's was the best in all of Hirtshals. Dad's name was Buffalo.

The buffalo was so wild that the Indians couldn't keep it for a pet. They couldn't take it for walks, either. They could only leave it be and hope it didn't wreck everything when it rumbled across their land.

"Here! Take one with liver paste."

I looked at Five-Inch's hand and the food. The food looked good.

"I'm not hungry."

The little sandwich went into Five-Inch's mouth. It still looked good. I had the urge to tell him what I wanted to be called. I wanted to be called Big Ox. The Big Ox was king of the cows and lived in America. It could bite a train in two with its teeth and, no matter how old it was, it always went around with a long beard that never fell off.

That's what I wanted to be called and how I wanted to look, but you couldn't just say it. You had to wait until the world had decided what fit you best. It was the same for everybody. Mom hadn't gotten a name yet. Deadeye didn't get his name until his eyes got lost at sea.

The worst thing was that Axel had already been lucky.

Every time people talked about Axel, they called him Black Bastard.

CHAPTER FOUR

ONE DAY DAD CAME HOME WITH FIVE PACKAGES OF HOTDOGS. He kissed Mom on the forehead and said she should throw them in the fridge. Then he drove off again. But he promised us that in a little while we were all going to a topping-out ceremony.

Mom sat in the living room, knitting and smiling. I cut a hole in one of the packages and tied a rope around three hotdogs. They were going up in the cherry tree. I had a new way of crawling. It was called being careful. The tree almost couldn't believe it. It used to always make me bleed, which was okay, only not today. I wanted to show Dad that I didn't have to hurt myself if I didn't want to. Which wasn't easy. The branches way up in the tree only lived off air, and air doesn't fatten you up. The branches wouldn't help me; they'd only break and make blood.

I took a rest and untied a hotdog. I ate it and looked down our street. Lisa from number 5 was playing hopscotch with herself. A big car came up the street. It stopped right in front of our house. There were four men inside. They came out wearing clean clothes. Their hair was wrong, too. They used combs. Dad didn't like men who used combs. Mom did.

I jumped over the sky and in through the living room window. Mom was already standing by the door, but she would only open it a crack. She said the men could come back when Dad was home.

They wouldn't. They wanted to visit us right now. Mom closed the door and ran to the phone. I opened the door and told the men that I was home.

"We've got five packages of hotdogs in the fridge, minus three franks."

I showed them my rope with two hotdogs left. The men laughed and patted my head and walked past me. The priest was the only one in Hirtshals who patted children on the head. So we were having a visit from four priests and they all wanted to go into Dad's office.

Mom sounded wrong on the phone. The men took off their shoes. They wouldn't pay a dime to see my room; they weren't even interested. They only wanted to see Dad's office and read his papers and take them home with them in cardboard boxes.

One of the priests took a bottle out of Dad's drawer. It was Dad's amber. He didn't have the time to search for amber on the beach. He bought it after it had been melted down and put in bottles.

Mom came into the office. Her face was red. She wanted the men to wait until Dad came home before stealing his papers. The men were thin. Mom knew Dad could bash them to bits if he felt like it. Dad weighed 250 pounds and it was all muscle, except for the hair. I yelled that I could kick a guy's nose through his head. I threw my hotdogs on the floor to show I meant it.

The men rushed out of the office with all their cardboard boxes. I ran after their car until it was gone.

When I came back, Mom was going around, vacuuming. The vacuum cleaner was noisy and Mom was crying. I told her to stop cleaning. The police wouldn't like it. When they came with their dogs, the only smell they should smell had to be the thieves' feet. Otherwise the men would get away.

I pulled out the vacuum cord. Mom stopped and cried even more. I stuck the cord back in. The vacuum cleaner started up and so did Mom. I went out to the kitchen and took all five packages out of the fridge. I built a little hotdog house. When Dad came home we'd be going to the topping-out ceremony. That was the only thing we had to do. The sun was shining and the Cement Baker and Five-Inch would be so happy when Dad heaved the ice beer out of his car.

The morning was wrong. Mom was supposed to drive Dad down south. They were going to a place where Dad would get very thirsty and burn holes in his clothes. Dad wasn't glad. He was sweating, even though he'd just gotten up. He cracked his soft-boiled egg so the yellow ran down onto the table. Dad got mad at the egg so he decided to try cracking the table with his fist.

My bowl of oatmeal began dancing. I stopped it with both hands. Mom was eating cigarettes and pouring the dead stumps into the garbage can, followed by a splat of water.

"Where are you going?" I asked.

"I have to go fight it out with those dumb bastards," said Dad.

"Why are you wearing a tie, then?"

Dad wouldn't tell me, but I was glad he'd found the four men.

"Where am I going?"

"You're going to work with Five-Inch and the Cement Baker."

"A topping-out ceremony?"

Dad shook his head. Mom packed me a lunch. Without hotdogs. The five packages had disappeared, little by little. Every morning I'd got up to see how they were doing. One night, six franks disappeared. Mom never ate during the night and Dad never used to be able to eat six all by himself. I hadn't heard any chomping from Alexander's room, either. Maybe the four men had been in our house again in the middle of the night. And had drunk Dad's amber and eaten hotdogs. Maybe that's why they were dumb bastards.

I walked out to the car by myself. I didn't want Dad using up his energy carrying me. Mom asked if she should drive. No, not now, but later, Dad said. He was going to drive me out to the building site himself.

Five-Inch and the Cement Baker were standing in front of a mountain of gravel. It was a good place to build, way out by the forest where no one else lived. I was looking forward to pissing right next to the Cement Baker. He could piss a lake that was big enough for me to measure with my yardstick. The Cement Baker's piss-puddle record was two inches deep.

Dad left right away. Five-Inch drove the wheelbarrow over in front of my feet. I ran my head into the Cement Baker's belly and said to let me know when he had to piss.

Five-Inch and the Cement Baker were thirsty and tired. They had to take beer breaks all the time, which was good for the Cement Baker's pissing. By noon he'd already broken his record, but the house wasn't growing at all. Maybe it was because they were sorry they weren't going fighting with Dad. I knew the Cement Baker was sorry. With him, a trip to the grocer's could end up in a fight. Six beers and a brawl, and he was happy.

I was bored. Axel had gone to school. It had to be a pretty special day when I didn't have to go myself. I drove the wheelbarrow over in front of the Cement Baker.

"You should piss in this the rest of the day. Then we'll set a new kind of record."

I waved the yardstick and hit him in the eye by accident with the first inch.

"Ow and damnation!" he howled.

I had never gotten the Cement Baker to say "ow" before. He lifted me up and tossed me clean over the forest. Five-Inch was chuckling when I got back.

Suddenly the Cement Baker said I could be their new boss if Dad went to jail. That was a funny thing to say. Five-Inch was having no part of it.

"You keep your mouth shut around the kid," he said.

There weren't many who talked to the Cement Baker like that.

The Cement Baker took a big gulp of his beer. He burped and said nasty things to Five-Inch. They quarreled and drank another beer. The Cement Baker said the Good Old Days were over for Buffalo. That now Buffalo was going to jail.

I went and stood between them and said I was finished going to school. That I had plenty of time to make their decisions for them and they needn't worry. This was something they liked to hear. They laughed until it got dark.

Five-Inch had a wife. Her name was Kitty. Kitty had a pretty moustache and wasted no time putting another plate on the table. Then she set about pouring runny food into a baby that was hers. There were also two other small children. They got steak and potatoes and brown sauce like the rest of us.

The kids got pretty scared when I screamed that I wanted to sit next to Five-Inch. Five-Inch lifted me up in a way that wasn't good. He tried to pull my arms off. It was Mom and Dad's fault. They hadn't come home yet. Dad wasn't finished fighting with the dumb bastards, and who said I felt like being the boss when I was at Five-Inch and Kitty's?

I was tired and grumpy, but tomorrow we were going to finish building the house. And I had to get hold of Deadeye so he could bring us two crates of beer from the harbor. Covered in ice. And ten packages of hotdogs. Maybe Axel could walk alongside and make sure Deadeye stayed on the sidewalk. It wouldn't be easy, but the Cement Baker was sure to yell hooray and thank me a thousand times for arranging a topping-out ceremony. He sure would.

I looked around the table to see if Five-Inch's family could tell that things were already getting better. No one said a word.

"Who died?" I asked

Kitty looked at Five-Inch.

"No one has died. Your mother and father are coming home tomorrow, that's all," said Kitty.

I pointed at her moustache with my fork.

"You have someone you miss over your mouth who's dead and wants to get out."

"What on earth are you talking about?" said Kitty.

"Your moustache. My grandma has one, too, only it's grayer. She misses Grandpa. Yours is black. Who do you miss? A dog?"

Kitty's mouth opened. Just like the baby's. It looked dumb, and the baby couldn't understand why the spoonful of food never came. I looked at Five-Inch. Once he'd talked about a dog he liked. About how he wanted a job where he could bring the dog along. He said this, but it wasn't a good idea if you were a carpenter. Carpenters had to spend all their time on people who couldn't figure out how to do their job. This was hard work.

Five-Inch munched on his steak with sauce on his chin. I could tell by his expression that he didn't feel like talking about the dog, so they'd probably had a black one who died.

A few days from now, when I sold the house we were building, I'd give everyone in Five-Inch's family a dog. Kitty's food would taste a whole lot better if there were five dogs under the table, growling. Then the family could sit there, nice and quiet, and listen to them.

When I woke up, Mom was standing over me. She had a finger over her mouth. She whispered that Dad was out in the car. We were go-

ing home now and it didn't matter about getting dressed. Five-Inch
was standing at the door. He was only wearing underpants.

"It's okay to work in those," I said.

Five-Inch nodded. His hair was a mess. Mom whispered thanks
to Five-Inch a thousand times. She also said she was sorry, and no
to coffee. She said it was Dad who wanted to come and get me
right now, even though it was a crazy hour. The whispering was nice
enough, but then Mom tried pulling me by the hand. I socked it and
she started breathing wrong and whimpering.

We left the house fast. Dad was standing bent over on the other side of the car. He was spitting into a puddle. Dad had made
the puddle himself, because there were still some long, slimy things
hanging out of his mouth. Five-Inch yelled that he'd clean up the
driveway and that we should just make sure we drove carefully and
got home in one piece.

Mom shoved me into the back seat and thanked Five-Inch for
everything. She closed the door and sat down in front. She leaned
over to open Dad's door. Dad wouldn't get in. He stayed where he
was. He wanted to show us he was still able to throw up a lot more.

I looked out the window to try and find the sun. The sky was
dark gray. It was supposed to be a little pink just before the sun
came up, so it must still be the middle of the night. Which was
good. When Alexander was buried, Dad had already thrown up
by early evening. This time wasn't nearly as bad, and even though
Dad's head was all wet, there was no blood or black eyes. Dad had
won the fight down south and now he wanted to show us what hard
work it had been. I looked at Mom. I couldn't believe she couldn't
understand.

I got out of the car and went and stood right in front of Dad. I
wanted him to know I understood everything.

So I started clapping.

———

We sat in the wheelhouse when it rained on *HG 233 Sylvia*. There almost wasn't room for three. Our clothes were wet. Deadeye was the wettest because he and his cane were having a bad day. An awful lot of cars had passed him by without stopping. He'd stood there, jousting with them for a hundred years, and now he was mad and wanted a cup of coffee.

Me and Axel were also allowed to have coffee. We just had to promise to toss five spoonfuls of sugar in our cup and keep our mouths shut. We promised. Deadeye was bad at making coffee. His hands crawled around over everything, back and forth. Me and Axel had no problem seeing where things were. I considered pushing the sugar bowl closer to his hands.

"Shut up," said Deadeye.

Deadeye could hear what you were thinking. Deadeye could hear everything. He could tell who it was when a cutter snuck quietly into the harbor. "Here comes *HG 455 Anna Polaris* ... That one's *HG 314 Pia Petra*." Me and Axel couldn't figure out how he did it, but we both thought he ought to join some circus close to an ocean.

Deadeye had found the coffee and sugar. Now his hands were looking for the thermos of boiling water. This was difficult because it was outside in the rain with his lunch basket. He'd probably forgotten it. Watching Deadeye could make you very thirsty. He was sure to send us over to the grocery store before long. He'd already begun cursing. Then he usually wanted some beers.

"Can we turn on the windy-weather machine?" asked Axel.

"You boys cold?"

Axel said yes; I said no. Axel got to do it. He took hold of the little machine. It looked like a bread toaster and when you turned it on, warm wind came out of it. It had three kinds: one that was lukewarm, one that was very warm and one that was so warm that *Sylvia* would burn up if we forgot to turn it off. We only got to use the weather machine when it rained.

Axel took his white socks off and hung them upside down to dry. They looked pretty dumb, but Axel's hair was lucky. It was hard as a broom. Combs would break their teeth if they got in his hair. Axel's hair got so much peace and quiet that it was always in a good mood, standing straight up.

Axel blew burning hot air on his black feet. It sounded like there were sparks in the machine. I was hoping they'd grow into a little fire and be blown all over his feet. He hadn't cried one bit when I told him we were moving to another god-awful town. Axel said, he already knew. Ruth had told him all that business with Dad and jail was a major pain in the ass. And that the pain would stay there until the day he died. So Dad wasn't going to take a shit like a good man ever again.

We'd stopped being friends for a long time when Axel said that. All day long I kicked the ball past the goalposts on purpose. We played with Axel's ball and I didn't like it. Axel cheered every time I missed a shot. He ran and ran and spit on his palms so much that he managed to drink five soda pops by the time we were finished. It was a new record. I tried to get him to come with me to the bakery so we could buy ten soda pops. Then I'd make him sit on his ass and watch me drink them all in one minute.

When we got to the bakery, we could only afford four. We argued about how I could set a new record with only four bottles of pop. Axel said it couldn't be done. Five would always be more than four. I screamed back that I wouldn't let him bike home until I'd set a record. Axel said I could set a record if I smashed the four bottles on the street and lapped up all the soda pop using only my tongue. This was something we'd never played before.

I looked at the bottles, remembering a sliver of glass that had stabbed my foot on the beach. It had hurt and been hard to get out again. But feet were much more important than tongues. I told Axel I was willing to lose my tongue to set a record. Axel said that in Africa they cut ladies' tongues out. It was to make them shut up. Afterward they sat the ladies around a bonfire. They had to sit completely still and grill the tongues like marshmallows. They weren't allowed to put them back in their mouths until they were black as coal. Axel was glad his real mom didn't say much. He was sure she still had a nice tongue.

I looked at Axel. I didn't throw the bottles on the asphalt, I just let them drop. When the pieces of glass stopped tinkling, the soda pop sounded like a bunch of snakes. It sounded good and it also smelled okay. The only thing was, I couldn't figure out where to start. The pop turned into a dark stream that ran all the way to the curb and down the street to the sewer drain. I rushed over to the grate and tried to stop the river with my tongue. It didn't work very well. A lot got by, even though I tried to press my tongue completely flat. Axel laughed.

I sat watching all the soda pop run down the drain. My tongue got upset. The baker's wife came out with a broom, screaming that we deserved a thrashing, and that we'd get one next time we bought three million pieces of broken glass from her. We got on our bikes. The bottles of pop had cost two dollars. I had never used so much money on so little. I yelled to Axel that this was a record.

Deadeye wasn't finished with his coffee, but he'd found an old beer that had been sitting in the wheelhouse for a long time. This made him happy. It was a good time to take a break. I sat with my mug, looking down in the sugar. Five spoonfuls. I fished up sugar and sucked on my finger.

"Deadeye, there's something I want to know."

"Mmm …"

"Can I say it?

"Mmm…just as long as it doesn't have anything to do with what I brought for lunch today."

"It doesn't."

"Good. Spit it out, then."

"If someone claps for you, can it make you anything else but happy?"

Deadeye took a big gulp of beer and chewed on what I'd said.

"That was a hard question. Why d'you ask?"

"Well? Can you? Can you get mad if someone claps for you?"

Deadeye took another gulp. His glass eyes never moved, not even when he thought about tough questions.

"Yes," he said finally. "Once *Sylvia* was rocking so much that my cane fell overboard. I sat for days, trying to fish it up with my net. The seasons changed. The winter was hard. I kept fishing. Strange sounds blended with the song of the seagulls. It was penguins who'd lost their way. They stood on deck, chirping like women. But they warmed me up and I kept fishing for the cane. Spring arrived, and suddenly…suddenly I could smell my cane. I jumped into the harbor and swam after the smell. I had to swim under the ferry to Norway. It had one hell of a hull. I held my breath for eight hours and my beard got caught in the screws. The ferryboat gave me a shave and spit me free without a single hair left on my head. Then, just as I made it up to the surface and opened my mouth wide, my cane sailed in between my teeth and got stuck. Never before had it been so scared. I swam on my back, back to our *Sylvia*, and when we'd made ourselves comfortable I gave the cane a little peck on the cheek. And then it came…the clapping. From over on the other side of the wharf. It was a bungling German tourist who'd been sitting there all day with his little fishing pole. He was shouting 'Bravo.' He shouted 'Bravo, bravo, bravo'—and clapped."

"Then what'd you do?"

"I shouted back that he should come over on our *Sylvia* and I'd treat him to a drubbing."

"Did he come? The bungling German?"

"Nope."

Deadeye's glass eyes went out. The story was finished. He sent us over to fetch three beers. I asked Axel if he'd ever heard a better story. Axel refused to believe it was true. He'd never heard of a blind man who could beat up a man who could see.

Axel was dumb. If only Dad had heard Deadeye's story, he would have understood it right away.

CHAPTER FIVE

OUR NEW HOUSE WAS IN A GOD-AWFUL TOWN. Frogs were living in the cellar. The frogs came from a pond next to the house. The water in the pond was green and slimy. It was only to be used when a poor house caught on fire. As soon as someone saw a flame, all the people in town were supposed to run to the pond and fill a bucket with water.

I couldn't figure out how many of the frogs had chosen to hop down in the cellar, but I'm sure it was because they were going to complain to the county, which owned the house. Mom didn't complain, she moaned.

Dad and Five-Inch had no time to listen to her. They emptied the truck and decided to put the washing machine on top of a hundred frogs.

"Can't the washing machine be somewhere upstairs?" Mom screamed.

"No!" yelled Dad.

I looked at the floor to see if any of the frogs were strong enough to lift Mom's washing machine. None of them were. I really felt Dad and Five-Inch could have just swept the floor before they set the washing machine on top of a hundred frogs. Now it would be incredibly hard to give the ones that were left a decent burial. People who worked in coalmines died the same way. They stopped breathing from one second to the next and the burial only took a second, too. Those who were above ground had a hard time keeping up.

Dad and Five-Inch drank a beer every time they carried in something heavy. They weren't in a good mood. They'd had to take an incredibly long break in their building business. Maybe Dad wouldn't build anymore at all.

He had stopped wearing a nice suit and tie. After the big fight down south it had been decided that we'd give everything we owned to other people. Dad said it was the dumb bastards who were getting it all. He wouldn't say whether the dumb bastards had had the living daylights beaten out of them, but I was sure they had. I just couldn't see what they wanted our house and car and Dad's big boat for. If they could use all this stuff, they couldn't be lying somewhere down south, bleeding all over.

The god-awful town was called Rakkeby. It looked like Grandma's holy Hørmested. There was one shop and people collected shit. Me and Axel had played the boys from Rakkeby once. We won 24-0. Axel scored ten goals without getting the red card. I scored seven and got a yellow card for knocking over a player who was standing wrong.

I remember that after we'd whupped them, the boys from Rakkeby thanked us for the game. I also remember that I tried to make them not do it. You should never say thanks when you've lost 24-0. But they just smiled. Rakkeby was a creepy club.

Dad said I should come upstairs with him. He gave me two rooms to choose between—one that was big and one that was little. It was hard to decide. They hadn't said anything about where Alexander was going to live. Maybe Dad was just trying to see if I still missed him. If I chose the little room, Dad was sure to believe that I missed Alexander a whole lot. I chose the big room. Dad didn't say anything. He looked out the window. There were four soccer fields behind the trees.

"Have you seen the fields? Now you can play soccer whenever you feel like it."

That was a dumb thing to say. You could play soccer all over the world, including on the stairs of Axel's yellow apartment building and in the telephone box down by the harbor. Me and Axel had tried it all. If there was room for one foot to kick, you could play soccer.

Looking out the window was dumb, too. The grass on the playing fields was much too high in Rakkeby. I could see dandelions pointing straight up in the air. In Hirtshals the grass was cut two times a week by a man named Ginge. He'd gotten that name because the lawnmower he used was also named Ginge. The lawnmower had four wheels and a seat.

In Rakkeby they just let everything grow, so there was a good chance you'd come home from a match with weeds in your shorts. It was pretty disgusting, but it was good that Dad didn't get mad about how little I missed Alexander. I smiled at my big, new room, and Dad.

"Me and Axel aren't called sandbox players anymore. Now we're called lilliputs. Doesn't that sound good, Dad? Lilliputs?"

"Sure, but you can also play lilliput here, in Rakkeby."

I looked up at Dad. Was he wanting me to change clubs? I couldn't. I hadn't even played a farewell match in Hirtshals. That's what all the other top players did before they changed clubs. The fans had to be allowed to stand there and cry for an hour. After the match I had to wave goodbye to them. And Ginge would be waiting with the lawnmower so he could drive me all the way to my new club.

Mom yelled that Dad better come down and decide where the TV set should go. I got mad. I kicked into the carpet with my left leg. It was hard to do, and it hurt.

"There's no way in hell I'm gonna smell like shit when I play in a club!"

I'd yelled pretty loud. My ears caught on fire and my stomach filled with ice cubes. Dad stood for a moment, looking at me. Then he sat down on the floor. With his back against the radiator and legs stretched out straight. Dad had never sat like that.

I moved away from him. Maybe he wanted to train a little by himself. He was going to jail soon. In jail he'd be sitting like that all the time. I thought about joining him on the floor, but I stayed on my feet. I practiced being taller than my dad.

Rakkeby School was flat. There wasn't one single staircase, and all the windows were so low to the ground, you had to jump through the glass to hurt yourself. The roof was flat, too.

At Rakkeby School, they'd determined that whoever was the oldest decided everything. Now I was sitting in the oldest's office. He was really old. His cheeks looked leathery, like the soles of Grandma's feet. They went in and out when he talked. I got their air in my face. He spoke right down over my nose. He was mad, but didn't smell. His mouth was all clean. I'd never met a mouth like that before.

I hadn't done anything. Other than lie down while everyone else was standing up, singing. They called it "The Morning Song" and it included the Lord's Prayer. I didn't want to sing. In Hirtshals we never did.

This was a rule the old man hadn't heard of. He looked all wrong when he suddenly was standing over me in the middle of the song. He'd lifted me up by my shirt without stopping singing, then parked me upright like a bicycle and closed my hands around a psalm book. He turned to the correct page, putting his finger at the exact spot they'd come to. The man didn't need a psalm book. He knew it by heart. He was making a good job of it, so I nodded and he let go of me and went back to where he had come from, which was in front of all the rows. There he stood, completely by himself. The teachers were in a pile over in the corner, around a piano.

I had to lie down again. I wanted to lie on my back and think a little about the party in Hjallerup. It had been on TV, on the news. They were all there, including the poor folks with rats on their shoulders. The party had come right into our living room. A man got three beers poured over his head. He laughed and stuck a rat in his wet hair. It sat up there, smiling with its big front teeth. I smiled, too. And smiled at Mom and Dad. They sat, drinking coffee. But not for long. It was party time, only Mom and Dad had forgotten. It was possible to forget something like this, with Dad being on vacation all the time. Dad wasn't laughing. He stood up, sending the chair backwards and himself forward, all the way to the television. He pounded one of the buttons. The whole picture disappeared, right in the middle of beer in the hair. Right in the middle of the TV news—the most un-turn-offable program there was. Dad always had to see every minute, including the fanfare at the start and the weather forecast at the end. Dad loved the TV news, but he also loved the party in Hjallerup.

Dad stormed out of the room and down to the cellar on thundering feet. There was a crash. I raced to the window to see if Dad had come running out into the yard. Maybe he was going to run all the way to Hjallerup. But Dad didn't appear.

Mom stayed seated. Mom was still looking at the blank screen like she was guessing what was going on in the world.

"Dad just needs to sit awhile," she said. "By himself. You can turn it on again if you want."

I didn't want. And lying there on the floor of my new school, I didn't want to sing, either. Only lie awhile and think about the party, where your shoes sank and Dad bought a hammer to smash a bell and played accordion with one hand and hit people with the other. It was some party, and now it was over. This was worth thinking about.

The oldest man of all was getting tired. His cheeks relaxed. He sat down. I had nodded at everything he said.

"What was your name again?" I asked.

"Ferguson."

"Are you baptized Ferguson?"

"Yes, of course."

"What else are you called?"

"Jeremy."

"Do you only have the two names?"

The man nodded. Without a sign of embarrassment. He must have been close to a hundred years old. If I had lived that long without getting names other than Jeremy and Ferguson, I'd be in a bad mood, too.

"Don't worry, I'll find a name for you," I said. "A good one."

"Let's stick to the matter at hand. Tomorrow you're going to stand up like a good boy. With the rest of your class. You get me, Karl Gustav? You've given yourself a very bad start. At this school one can have one's face slapped if one deserves it."

"You know what?"

"No, what?"

"You can get your face slapped anywhere on earth. You can also get your face slapped without deserving it. If you want yours slapped, just let me know."

I was throwing rose hips into the green, slimy water. The pond was so slimy, they didn't even sink to the bottom. Which was fine with me. I was in the middle of writing my name. The first letter was almost done. A big B.

"What are you doing?"

A white-skinned boy was sitting by the water hole. He was new in Rakkeby, like me. They'd put us in the same class and a teacher lady had said how nice that was. The boy was wearing a white shirt and long black pants.

"What are you doing?"

"Writing my name. See?"

I pointed out my big B. The boy looked.

"I can't see anything."

"Are you blind?"

"No, but I'm going to die in a little while. My dog just died, too. Its name was Spinky."

"What did it die from?"

"Four boys were playing soccer and Spinky was chasing the ball. Suddenly he fell over, dead. Just like that. With foam in his mouth. My dad said it was heatstroke."

"Were the boys in a club?"

"I dunno."

"Do you play in a club?"

"No."

"So have you got a new dog?"

"I don't want a new one. I'm dying in a little while."

"Who says so?"

"I say so. I have a hole in my heart. I can't let myself get out of breath. Didn't you know?"

"How was I supposed to?"

"The other kids talk about it all the time."

"Over at school?"

The boy nodded.

"Are you really gonna die in a little while?"

"Yes."

"Want to play some soccer? You can be goalkeeper and stay in one spot."

"I don't like sports."

"Catch!"

I threw the ball—not hard, but not soft, either. Just a good pass. It hit him in the stomach and fell to the ground. His arms never even managed to move. It was incredible.

"How big a hole is it?"

"Like a dime."

"Why do you go around in such nice clothes when your family's so poor?"

"We're not poor. My father's an architect."

"Does he say you're gonna die in a little while, too?"

"No, he says it can take years and years…if I'm careful. What's your name?"

"Big Ox."

"What's your real name?"

"Once it was Karl Gustav, but now I'm Big Ox. It's better."

"What's your father do?"

"He's going to jail in a little while."

CHAPTER SIX

THE WHITE-SKINNED BOY WAS NAMED TIM and didn't manage to die that day. Next morning in school he seemed okay, too. I sat next to him. The teacher lady said I should stop looking Tim right in the chest. I couldn't. The teacher lady assigned us an essay. It had to be at least one page long. Nothing happened to Tim. His hair didn't even turn gray.

Later we had gymnastics. Tim still hadn't finished changing by the time the rest of us were screaming we wanted to play soccer. The gym teacher's name was George Svendsen and he wanted us to jump far and jump high and throw heavy balls that were bad for feet that wanted to play soccer.

When Tim came out on the field he had his entire uniform on, zipped up to the neck. It looked real dumb. Tim walked quietly over to George Svendsen for a chat. George Svendsen hadn't called for him or anything. I couldn't hear what they talked about, but it wasn't hooray.

When I had to jump to beat my own world record, Tim was standing in the middle of the sand, holding a rake. I ran as hard as I could. I sprang up over Tim and over the school and came down in a garden two hundred feet later, landing right on my ass like you're supposed to.

George Svendsen was standing there with his yardstick, but he wouldn't measure me because I'd stepped on the white line. Only I hadn't. I felt like arguing and fighting about it and was just about to open my mouth when Tim went over to the print of my ass and raked it away. Nice and easy—and wrong. You couldn't even see I'd been there.

I looked at George Svendsen.

"In Hirtshals it's the teacher who rakes. Don't you get money for being here?"

George Svendsen didn't manage to say anything before Tim had put his hand on my arm.

"I want to rake," he said. "I just asked if I could."

I looked up at George Svendsen. He was tall with yellow teeth. He just nodded. I walked back up the field and sat down behind the others. Every time one of them wrecked Tim's raking, he raked their assholes away again. He did it without crying or anything.

I went and took one of the heavy balls. Then I walked over to the bushes and measured off six yards with my feet. I decided it would be a world record if I could throw the ball into the bushes and never find it again.

Tim didn't take a shower when gym class was over. He put on his ugly, nice clothes and said goodbye. Now I was sure: Tim wasn't lying. He was gonna die in a little while, so I wanted him to come home with me and see my room first. He said no, but that he'd go with me over to the slimy pond and read books.

I nodded and promised I'd look at him while he read. Tim brought along a black satchel full of books. All of them were about diseases. He'd read the ones about his own disease; now he was reading about all the others he might have time to catch before he died. The books had incredibly long words.

"My grandma's sick in her heart, too," I said.

"Really?"

"Yeah. Every time she drives Chevy, she swallows dynamite pills to keep her heart going."

Tim smiled. He lay down and tried to guess what the pills were called. He tried a lot of names, but I couldn't remember the right ones, so I shook my head at all of them.

Tim was good at playing games that couldn't be won. Incredible names flew out of his mouth. I stood there, juggling with my soccer ball. When I was tired of shaking my head, I asked Tim if he'd come with me over to the playing field and stand still in the goal. He wouldn't. One read best when one was right next to water, he said.

Tim was hard to get your way with, much harder than Axel. Plus I could have fights with Axel when we both were bored at the same time. Me and Tim would have a hard time fighting. I'd have to get a hole in my heart, too, or at least some holes in my head. But he was fun to hang out with anyway. He could say things that kept buzzing around in my head, even after he'd gone home.

I thought most about what Tim said about the dog. That he'd never touched the soccer ball the day Spinky died. He'd just sat, looking at the four boys. They hadn't asked if he wanted to play. And if they had, he would have said no. They killed his dog and he just sat there. He hadn't gotten mad at the four boys, either. Spinky could just have taken a rest. That's what Tim said.

Dad got three meatballs, I got two and Mom got one. Then Dad thanked Mom for dinner. Mom said there would be meat tomorrow, too, and that was nice. Mom had begun talking about food all the time. About what kind of food could keep. And what could be frozen.

When Mom bought a package of liver paste, she cut it in three and put two parts in the freezer. She'd also begun baking our very own rye bread. It was bad. You couldn't slice it. It crumbled into a thousand pieces and Dad and me weren't ducks.

Mom cleared the table. Dad stayed seated.

"Karl Gustav?"

"Mmm…"

"Tomorrow I take a train ride. I've got to go sit in jail. Just for a while."

"How big a while?"

"Twelve months. That's only two half-years. It's nothing."

"How many soccer games is that, timewise?"

"Not that many."

"How many?"

"A hundred…if you play real good in all of them."

"That's a lot. What if I'm injured?"

"You won't be. Lilliputs never get injured."

Dad went to the living room and got his pipe. He didn't sit down in his easy chair; he came back to smoke at the table. That was incredible.

"Dad…?"

"Mmm."

"Why have you begun thanking Mom for dinner? You never did in Hirtshals."

"I didn't?"

"No. You don't fart as much anymore, either."

"But as for going to jail, you and Mother just stay home and have a nice time. And take care of each other. You have to be grown up and good to her. Will you promise me that?"

Dad went and turned on the TV. Now he wanted to smoke in peace. I would have liked to tell him about Spinky. Tim said it hadn't minded eating cat shit when it was hungry enough. Tim had seen this himself. They had three cats that shit in some sandboxes on the floor. Spinky used the sandboxes like a restaurant. No one who was going to jail could resist a story like that.

I looked at Dad. He had entered the television set. I went out in the yard to practice. Sometimes Dad came out to watch and drink a beer. If he did it this evening, I was going to tell him Tim's story. Then Dad would be glad, and when he was glad, he liked to count how many times I could keep the ball in the air. That was the game I liked best. It was okay for the ball to touch my head, my shoulders, my thighs, my knees, and my feet. Everything else was against the law.

I always liked playing this game by myself, but if Dad was there, counting, I only liked it if I beat my own record. The ball had to show off when Dad was there. Things went wrong a lot. Like the ball fooling me and reaching the ground much too fast. Then I had to get busy. Dad had to stay until things got better again. Maybe we could throw some broken glass on the lawn and make it more of a challenge. It didn't really matter. He couldn't leave before I'd beaten my own record—with a number that came out of his mouth.

I heard the door open. Dad came out, but Mom came along, too. They were just taking a walk before it got too late, Dad said. He wanted to go smell Rakkeby's cows. He wanted to practice. He was going to have to walk around himself for a year with his hands over his head to avoid flying lumps from the other shitting men.

I began counting. My voice was high and my numbers were incredibly high. I could see Mom and Dad's heads over the hedge. They were walking slowly. When the heads disappeared, I began yelling the numbers out over the hedge, out over Rakkeby. It was no record. All I was doing was holding the ball.

CHAPTER SEVEN

DAD CALLED HOME FROM JAIL every Sunday evening at eight. You couldn't call him, because Dad lived with six mice that ate all the electric cords they laid eyes on. When Dad called home, he was stretched out in a coffin with the telephone. It was pitch black down there. If Dad spoke for more than five minutes, the guards opened a little hatch so the sun could come in and roast him.

Mom had time to smoke one and a half cigarettes while she talked with Dad. This was only possible because she'd begun building them herself. She'd been given a neat machine by Five-Inch's Kitty. Now Mom was able to build a hundred cigarettes an hour and each one was different. Some of them only had paper at the tip, so when she lit one, she got a flame right in front of her mouth. It looked exciting, but Mom got scared every time. Luckily there was a pitcher of water standing next to her knitting chair.

When Mom hung up, she said Dad was fine. And the food down there was good. I nodded. Dad would say practically anything, lying in a coffin, getting thinner and thinner. It reminded me of Deadeye. When Deadeye had had so many beers that he started missing his mouth, he always said it was good to be blind. Then he never had to see everyone else sloshing and slopping around. He could get up every day and say good morning to twenty-four new, perfect hours where he made all the right decisions. There was nothing better than being alone with two glass eyes that never shattered, Deadeye said. And he probably yelled this, too—loud as hell—while he stood by the road with his cane, with the clouds pissing on him and a thousand cars whizzing by without picking him up. You shouldn't always believe a blind fisherman or a father who's in jail.

Mom said everything was going as well as could be expected. Then she sat down at the dining room table with magazines, glue, and a scissors. Each week Mom bought a magazine over at the grocer's. It was about a lot of people she knew. But there was one lady who Mom knew best. Her name was Grace Kelly. Once Grace Kelly had been a big movie star in America, but she'd stopped. She had fallen in love with a man who was born to decide everything. The man decided Grace Kelly wasn't going to play in any more movies. He also decided they were going to live forever in a country called Monaco. If Grace Kelly went along with this, the man said he would give her lots of lovely dresses and some children, so she'd have lots of lovely problems. Grace Kelly had three kids real quick and the man held his promise. The kids were full of problems. Mom kept a close eye on all this, and every time the lady's magazine had something new to reveal, she cut it out and pasted it in some books that got fatter and fatter.

Dad hadn't been gone long before Mom had filled a whole bookcase with Grace.

In school the teachers stopped sending me to stand outside the classroom door. I was never there when they called me in again. I kept my ball hidden in the trash can. It was a good hiding place. I took the ball over to the playing fields. Then I had all the grass to myself and was glad until the teacher from my next class came out and dragged me back in.

The teachers held meetings about me. They decided I shouldn't be thrown out of the classroom anymore, that I should be sent to Ferguson's office every time they'd had enough of me.

Once I got to Ferguson's office, I was given a quick slap in the face. Ferguson wasn't very good at slapping. He couldn't do it without sneezing. It looked dumb when he gave me a slapping while he had a cold. I got a red hot cheek, like I was supposed to, but Ferguson got snot all over his face.

I told him he should try hitting with his fists. It could be he'd be able to do this without sneezing. Ferguson didn't like my advice. He got mad and wanted to know if I truly wanted a fist. That I ought to think about it before I answered.

I said that nosebleeds were okay in a fight. But that you should never let your opponent know if you had a cold. That would ruin it for the one who won. You had to be pretty stupid if you liked hitting people who were sick.

After I'd been going to Rakkeby School a while, we wound up just sitting together when I was sent to visit him. Ferguson spent most of his time writing letters. He wrote to parents of children who were having birthdays. He congratulated the parents, and Tim's mom and dad had even gotten a letter where it said Tim was a gift from God. Tim wasn't exactly cheering when he told me about it, but he wasn't exactly mad, either.

One day I asked Ferguson if he'd write to my mom and dad, too, when it was my birthday. Absolutely, he said, and all the words weren't going to be nice.

"Gee, thanks a lot," I said.

"Why do you say that?"

"I like the not-nice words best."

"Like which, for example?"

"Synovial sheath membrane inflammation."

It was Tim who'd taught me that one. It had taken me a whole afternoon to be able to say the disease without stopping. Tim said he hadn't caught it yet. You could only catch it when you started pulling your willie for fun, all the time and then some.

Only males caught this disease, and it only went away when you were so old, your willie couldn't take any more pulling. Which was kind of a shame, because by then you wouldn't be able to remember you'd had the disease almost your whole life. You'd just be staring into space, never realizing you'd gotten well again.

"Who taught you that word?"

"Tim did."

"Tim who?"

"Tim from my class."

"Tim Brink? Has he taught you that word?"

"Yes. Tim knows everything about diseases and he's going around with over half of them."

"When have you two talked about diseases?"

"We do it every day. Over by the pond."

I could tell by looking at Ferguson that he didn't believe me. There wasn't anything I could do about it because he had gray hairs sticking out of his nose, and when the sun shined into his office, I could also see gray hairs sticking of his ears. His willie was dead as a doornail and he'd forgotten all about the days where he didn't do anything but pull his willie for fun.

"You say you two are friends? You and Tim Brink?"

"Yes, but don't let it get you down. I think it's best that your willie take it easy. It's just as old as you are, you know."

Right in the middle of us talking about something important for once, Ferguson wanted to fight. He didn't even have time to stand up. He came sailing over his desk, face red. Fist clenched.

Ferguson had great chairs in his office. They were comfy, with wheels underneath. They were easy to skate on; one shove with your feet and away you went. By the time I hit the wall, Ferguson was lying across the desk. I got up and went over to him.

"When you want to fight," I said, "you should always stand up first. Come on, get up, then I'll show you how."

For my birthday Mom promised me a surprise. She said a car was coming that was going to make me happy. I wondered whether the jail really could loan Dad a car so he could come home and celebrate his son.

I went out on the front steps and waited. At precisely three o'clock Tim and his mother and father came walking up. I didn't like guests that came on time.

"Can't you just go again and come late?" I said.

Mom opened the door to welcome them. She positioned herself with legs spread, right behind me. Her dress brushed my ears.

"Where the hell's the car?"

Mom's fingers pulled on my hair.

"That's enough, Karl Gustav. Gosh, it's so nice to meet you. I almost feel like I know you already."

Tim was on his way into the house with his folks when I pulled him back by his belt and told him we should stay outside.

"Can't we just go in?" he asked. "I've only got my indoor clothes on."

I thought about what Dad would have to say to a boy like this. He wouldn't say a thing to a boy who talked about indoor clothes.

"My surprise is coming in just a minute. We're staying here."

We waited. I thought it was cold, too, but I'd make a point of showing Dad I was good at freezing. Maybe I ought to take off all my clothes. My teeth were chattering already. Then a careful car started coming. It was old and worn down and didn't look very happy. But it had a black kid inside pressed against the windshield. I jumped up in the air and Axel jumped out of the car before it stopped. The world's best black bastard wheeled around and around in a muddy puddle in yellow socks, huge black shorts, and real goal-keeper's gloves.

Five-Inch got out, too, with a round present, but I didn't have time to discuss the building business. I heaved Axel with me into the house and up to my room. I changed into real clothes with soccer boots.

We ran downstairs. They were all sitting proper by the layer cake.

"Come. We're going over to play soccer," I told Tim. "Axel's goal-keeper. He's damn good."

Tim looked at me like I wasn't the one who was having the birth-day and could decide everything.

"Here!" said Axel.

Axel pulled an incredibly thin present out of his shorts. It looked like a ten-dollar bill wrapped in tin foil. I uncrumpled it and found a slip of paper.

"It's called a taxi credit," said Axel. "With one of these you can be driven all the way to the airport and fly like hell. All for free."

"My, is that nice," said Mom, and began telling about Axel and how he came from Africa but now the poor boy lived in Hirtshals in the yellow apartment buildings and his father drove a cab and things weren't easy. They were poor, and poor folks often gave gifts they couldn't afford, and in any case, no one was flying anywhere until the layer cake was eaten.

Axel dripped mud on the floor and was all smiles. Mom looked at the mud and asked Tim's mom and dad if they could get Sweden. Mom said she missed our TV set in Hirtshals. On Swedish TV they always played this pretty music before the programs started. They played it through the morning and part of the afternoon. It was incredibly beautiful to clean the house to, Mom said.

The only thing I wanted was to make it over to the field and shoot past the goal and see Axel run like he was supposed to. I looked at Tim. He looked at Axel. Everyone looked at Axel, and it was my birthday. I stuffed Axel's present down my underpants and ran out on the field with my soccer ball. Whoever wanted to play could come when they felt like it.

Axel was on my side, I could tell. He threw himself onto the grass because it was wet, and if we threw ourselves hard enough, we came down to dirt and mud and nice-all-over. Axel was my friend. Axel was a whole town. Hirtshals had come to my birthday.

We played real good. It didn't matter that Axel refused to catch the ball anymore. He would only box it away. He was training at his new sport and said that everybody in the boxing club had shorts that were so long, you could use them as a snot rag when you got a bloody nose without taking them off. You just yanked them up to your face. Axel also said I should stop calling him Axel. Now his name was Floyd Patterson. I'd never met Floyd Patterson down in Hirtshals, but the name was great.

"Lucky bastard!"

We got in a fight and Axel made a big deal out of his new rules. Now we couldn't mess around in the mud, we had to dance around each other with fancy little steps and spit in each other's face. This was much too neat, and the sun was already going down because I was born in November.

We went home, arm in arm, after I'd been hit in the head a thousand times. We checked out our bumps and bruises under a lamp. I always won at that.

Mom and Five-Inch were alone and, my, what a sight we were, Mom said. Tim had left the house a long time ago. Mom said that hadn't been nice of me. The poor boy had sat all alone, moping. Mom never said people got bored—they moped. Like the poor dead birds that were buried in a clock, and every time another hour was gone they came to life for a second and said cuckoo. You couldn't die worse if you were a bird. I said Mom should shut up. Five-Inch bit his lip.

"Can't Axel damn well sleep here?" I asked.

"I can't. I gotta go to training. We're up in the sports hall. We got beautiful shorts."

It made me sad when the car drove out to the road and away. In the dark you could never see if Axel was waving goodbye.

Tim was good at being mad. Once he started, he couldn't stop. After my birthday he acted like I'd gone. Disappeared. In the classes where we sat next to each other, he only looked at the teacher. And at recess, when I stood in his way, he looked to the side. After school he just went home.

In December came the snow. I built a snowman over by the pond. First I built Tim as a big boy. Then I got a saw in the cellar and sawed him in half. He wasn't very good at standing by himself after that. I had to make him a huge clubfoot.

Brown leaves became his hair. A stone, his eye. A little broken stick became his mouth. For a tie I used an old rope. I looked a long time at my construction. I was satisfied, but not quite. I was missing his hole in the heart. It had to be there, too, because Tim should know I believed in his dying in a little while.

I searched a lot of places. It wasn't easy to find something that looked like a sick heart. In the end I emptied my pockets. There was an old balloon that had popped. Now it only had its knot and a little stump left. It was perfect. The balloon stump wouldn't stay in place by itself. I found a big nail in the cellar. That helped. In the end, the snowman looked exactly like Tim.

Next day in school I said to him that he could come over to the pond and see for himself. I said I wouldn't get in his way, and if he wanted, we could build a snowman that looked like me. It didn't have to be bigger than him.

It made me glad when he came. Tim had so much clothes on, I could only see his nose. The jacket was zipped all the way up and stopped above his mouth. I couldn't hear what he said. He was a mumbling jacket.

Tim stood a long time, looking at himself. I was just about to say how nice I thought he looked, but I didn't manage to. Without saying anything, Tim kicked his head off. It went into a thousand flakes. Then new sounds came out of the jacket. It sounded like he was crying. He wasn't allowed to do that. It made him short of breath.

I zipped his jacket down fast. He was coughing and panting. I didn't know what to do. I just wanted to give him a present that was better than the one he had given me for my birthday. Which was a book on diabetes. It was thick, but it wasn't good for anything when I unwrapped it after he'd gone home. It was only good for something if he was the one reading it. He was supposed to lie there, next to our pond, and read aloud and teach me words I could use in Ferguson's office.

There was only one thing to do: I kicked the rest of Tim to pieces. I kicked until the ground was completely black.

Tim sat down in the snow and looked out over the pond. I made a lot of snowballs and laid them at his feet. He didn't throw them, but he stopped being out of breath. I would have liked if he had said something. I was willing to wait. But Tim just sat there.

"You shouldn't be afraid to die," I said. "It doesn't hurt that much. The last thing a person does before he dies is wave farewell."

"That's not necessarily so," said Tim.

"Yes, it is. You wave to the people who are watching. That's the very last thing you do."

"Then what if a person's all alone when he dies?"

"You never are. Not even way out at sea, when you drown. There's always someone standing on the shore, watching."

"I won't drown. I'll just fall down dead in the middle of a lawn. Like Spinky. He didn't wave at all."

CHAPTER EIGHT

ALL WINTER TIM LAY IN HIS BED with a lot of old and new diseases. He almost never came to school and I wasn't allowed to visit him because his mom read him fairy tales all the time. It was to make it easier for him to sleep, even when it was light outside.

I couldn't understand. If I had an animal that was going to die in just a little while, I'd keep it awake—morning, noon, and night—so it could play as much as possible. I'd even build a bonfire so the animal could go camping before it was too late. But Tim was supposed to sleep.

Sometimes he called and asked how it was going at school. It was hard to give an answer, so I mumbled something and Tim began telling about the fairy tales his mom had been reading to him. Tim liked the ones with the unhappy endings best. His mom didn't. Tim's mom's name was Kirsten and she had nice dirty hands and feet. She made pots and bowls out of clay and sometimes she got to display them over at the grocer's, so people in Rakkeby could look at them and leave again, saying they cost an arm and a leg. No one bought Tim's mom's pots and bowls. That was why she didn't like fairy tales with unhappy endings.

I wasn't bored much without Tim. I went and trained over at the fields. In Hirtshals they always took down the goal nets in the winter. The nets couldn't stand frostbite. They didn't know this in Rakkeby.

Here the nets were allowed to freeze to death, but when I was training I always went from goal to goal and kept the nets warm.

I had four soccer fields to myself, with no kids to get in the way.
I always aimed for the posts. When I hit them, the ball came back.
That was a pass. I loved receiving passes from the posts. Sometimes
the passes were real lopsided and sometimes they even wound up
behind the goal posts, but I ran after all of them anyway. When you
played soccer on four fields, all alone, you had to run after all the
passes that came your way.

One day, when the snow had hidden all the blades of grass, a
combine harvester drove across the playing fields. It was big as a ferryboat. I couldn't see who sat in the wheelhouse; it was full of smoke.
The combine harvester stopped a ways from me and a little window
opened so the smoke could come out.

The man stayed sitting inside. He was smoking a pipe. There
wasn't a sound in Rakkeby Stadium. I began juggling the ball in the
air. And counted as loud as I could. It went incredibly well.

"56-57-58..."

At 59 I heard the cab door open. I wanted to look, but when
you're juggling, you have to keep your eyes on the ball. I kept on.

"75-76-77..."

Now I could smell the man and see his feet. He smelled like cow
shit and his feet were big.

"So you're the one called Karl Gustav," said the man.

"Shut up. 83-84-85..."

I had never made it over one hundred. I started thinking wrong.
I began thinking about next Sunday. If I got over one hundred, I
could tell Dad I'd beaten my record. But now I couldn't remember
how far I'd gotten. Counting. Maybe I'd already passed a hundred.

"Where am I?"

"104-105-106," said the man, and kept counting.

I made it to 116 before I dropped the ball. I threw myself at it in the snow and dribbled around a little. The man smiled. He had a red moustache and red hair that didn't use a comb. He said he was manager of the soccer club in Rakkeby. He'd heard about some boy who ran around out here, playing all alone. It was a shame, he said, because there was a master bricklayer in town named Mogensen whose business was going so well, he wanted to give sweatsuits to all the boys who could play soccer. And if I gave him my name and phone number, the man with the red moustache would call me when practice started. Then he took out a yardstick and measured how tall and wide I was. He wrote all the numbers down on a dirty brown slip of paper.

"Well, what do you say?" asked the man.

"How do they look, these sweatsuits?"

"They're green and white. They say Mogensen Masonry on the back, and under his name there's a trowel. You know, one of those things that…"

"I know all about trowels. I'm a builder myself. But my sweatsuit has to be yellow and black."

"Why?"

"Those are the colors I play best in."

"Are you from Hirtshals?"

"Yeah."

It was cool that he knew this. The man knew his soccer. I took his pen. It was a pretty big deal, and very professional, to sign a contract on the spot. I wrote down my name and telephone number.

I liked the idea of the trowel on the back. Sponsors were one of the most important things in soccer. In Hirtshals we'd had Hirtshals Fishmeal Factory on our stomachs, which could be hard for your opponents to read if you ran as fast as I did. But a trowel on the back… that was good.

"You heading home now?" asked the man.

"Why?"

"I can give you a ride."

"I could use a ride."

The man with the red moustache said to hop onboard. He also gave me his name in case we became separated in the harvester. The man's name was Siegfred Tightwallet.

We drove back and forth in Rakkeby. I pointed at a lot of streets I'd never been on before. Some of them were so small that we hit the sidewalk on both sides. The curbs gave in to us; cracks appeared in the street. And Siegfred Tightwallet just smiled and smiled.

I led us to Ferguson's home. If Siegfred Tightwallet leveled Ferguson's house to the ground, I was willing to change clubs.

I was standing with my back to Dad when he got off the train. I wanted him to see the bricklayer's trowel before anything else. Mom was standing with her front to him. Her whole body was trembling and she had lipstick on. She shouted hooray. Dad lifted me above the treetops and turned me around in the air. When I landed, I got a big, black beard in my face. It was scratchy. You almost couldn't recognize him. I pulled on the beard to see if it was real. He showed me his teeth. All of it was real. Dad had been missing me so much, he was bearded all over.

Dad piggybacked me across town. My mouth was in his ear. I yelled all about how I was doing as a professional and how I'd been to practice five times and scored 56 goals.

Siegfred Tightwallet was no fool and went around with a fat wallet in his back pocket. After every practice he was head sponsor of a soft drink contest. Whoever kept the ball in the air longest won. I had five bottles of pop standing on the living room table; Dad would get to see them when we got home. I'd only drunk a little out of one of them, but it was only because I'd been juggling the ball in the air so long that day that some of the others had already taken a shower by the time I was done. Siegfred Tightwallet had never seen anything like it. He said it was incredible, and when a coach said something like that, it was okay to open your trophy bottle and take a sip.

Mom walked alongside me and Dad. She was smiling with tears in her eyes and asked Dad if he was hungry. Of course he was hungry. He'd been eating shit a whole year. I yelled to Mom that she should shut up. Dad stopped in the middle of the sidewalk. My cheek suddenly started stinging. Dammitall. Right in the middle of being carried through town.

But at least it was good that Dad was better at slapping than Ferguson. Dad's slaps made your teeth creak. I didn't get mad, just quiet. Ever since Dad went to jail, I'd said shut up to Mom hundreds of times. She never said anything back, just looked at me like I was someone else's son and there was no doubt she'd be getting her own back soon. Which she did, so long as she kept quiet.

When we came in the door, it was time for steaks. The food was ready. I took Dad by the hand and dragged him over to my trophy bottles. I told him the winning number of juggles for each one. They were all over a hundred, except for one. But it had been windy as hell that day and Siegfred Tightwallet still hadn't learned to pump up the ball the way I wanted it.

Dad lifted up my green trophy, the one I'd drunk a little of. He flicked off the cap with one finger, which was pretty cool, because I had banged it back on with a hammer.

"Did you save them so I could see them when I came home?" he asked.

"Yep."

Then Dad said he was sorry. Don't worry about it, I told him. In school I'd gotten so many slappings from Ferguson that half would have been plenty.

"Who's this Ferguson?"

"The school principal. That's all he's called."

"And he hits you?"

"All the time and then some."

"Only slaps?"

"Yeah. I tried to teach him how to use fists. He's no good at it."

"Shall I go down there and slap him clear to China?"

"You don't have to."

Dad lifted me up to his beard. He carried me in to the dining room table that had been missing three plates all year. I was so happy when Mom came with all the food, I wasn't hungry. That's about as happy as you can get. Dad drank beer; Mom drank milk. And I took the green bottle of pop that Dad had opened. There weren't any bubbles left. I drank it in one, long gulp, so Dad could see how thirsty I got after playing a hundred matches all alone like I'd promised.

I lay awake in bed that night. I could hear Mom and Dad talking. Their bedroom was right next to mine. I'm sure Mom was talking about food. Dad was talking about me. About how incredible it all was. Dad's voice was loudest, but Mom's said the most. Then they started getting noisy together and our county-owned house did some heavy breathing.

It had been so long since Mom and Dad had gotten noisy together. In Hirtshals they used to feel like it sometimes, even in the middle of the day. After they'd been noisy, Mom would hum to herself while Dad snored.

That's how it was now, too. Dad snored bulges into the sides of our county-owned house. Mom hummed a little, but then she got quiet. She was wondering why she hadn't grown any beard. She'd been bad at missing Dad. I'd been best. I was the only one Dad said sorry to.

In our county-owned yard stood an apple tree that never got any-where. The apples wanted to become something in life, but they just stopped growing as soon as they showed up. When Dad got out of jail, he didn't want to just keep sitting in the cellar. He wanted to be outside, and after walking around with a garden chair a while, he set it right under the tree that had never gotten anywhere.

I got Tim over so we could talk about it. Tim wanted to do this standing at a distance. He was scared of people who'd been in jail. He'd heard that the guards sat the wimps on top of a stove that was turned up all the way, and they had to sit there until their asses were melted fast to the hotplate. This made me mad, and I said we could just go ask Dad to see his, under the light. Tim screamed not to ask Dad about anything whatsoever.

Finally we agreed to stand over by Mom's clothesline.

"Well, what do you think?" I asked.

Tim was by far the best when it came to diseases, but sometimes he knew about other things, too.

"The apple tree's in the shade," he said.

"Yeah, but so's the pear tree and the plum tree. And they give tons of fruit."

"Where does he go when he has to pee?"

"My Dad doesn't pee, dammit, he pisses."

"I beg your pardon."

"Dad always pisses right by where he's sitting. He only pisses some-where else when Mom's out on the terrace with ladies from the church."

"Where does he piss then?"

"He goes and pisses right where the ladies are sitting."

Tim gave up and opened his school satchel.

"Look at this one. It's all about sexual diseases."

I looked at the book, but I liked talking about Dad better.

"Dad has wet hair. See?"

"Mmm…" said Tim, and pointed at a willie that was blue.

Dad was looking up at the flagpole. It stood in the middle of our yard and teetered when the wind blew. Today it wasn't moving, but Dad looked like he was mad at it anyway. Then Dad noticed me.

"Let's see if I can hit the knob on the top," he shouted. "Give me the ball!"

I made a good pass to Dad. It wasn't perfect, but that was because I tried to hit him in the belly so he wouldn't have to stoop for the ball. Dad looked up at the sky. The flagpole had a red knob on the top. It wasn't very big.

"Shall I throw it or kick it?"

I looked up. The sun was carving into my head.

"You might as well throw it," I said.

"It only counts if I hit the knob right in the eye. The ball can't touch the pole first."

Dad was a true sportsman. He thought up rules that made it harder for himself. Dad had gone to jail and grown a full beard. Now Dad had gotten out of jail and immediately placed himself under a difficult sport.

Tim closed the blue willie and crawled in under the pear tree to be safely out of the way. I smiled and positioned myself close to Dad so I could fetch the ball if he happened to miss.

He did, and by quite a bit, too. I went and got the ball. Dad threw again. Another miss. He tried with both hands. He tried kicking the ball up. He walked around the pole and threw from different spots. He tried to dodge the sun. I looked across the sky, trying to find some clouds that could help him. Dad got wetter and wetter.

His shirt was sloshy. Dad started talking to himself. This was a tactic, a good idea. I looked at Tim to see if he was watching, but he'd begun reading again. We got mad at each other. Dad didn't notice. He kept throwing. Faster and faster.

Dad had been storing up energy in jail; I could see it. Wires started appearing out of his head. They came when he was seeing something through to the end. Then Dad turned into a machine. He became electricity and lightning.

I sat down. Spectators were one of the most important things in sports. Mom yelled out the window that it was time to eat. She stood a little ways back from the window, watching. She wasn't smiling. She was incredible. I waved her away with my hand. Dad would have an even harder time hitting the knob if he also had to worry about Mom's food getting cold.

"Go in and eat!" Dad yelled.

"No, no! We're staying here to watch."

"Go in and eat! Now!"

Tim waved from over by the hedge. He was heading toward the fields. It was a detour even though Tim never took detours. I went in. Mom poured potatoes and sauce and meat onto my plate. She said I could eat wherever I wanted. I could also turn on the TV. I sat down at the dining table. If I crouched down a bit, I could see the top of the flagpole. I put meat in my mouth. My eyes kept going up and down. Sometimes I could see Dad's wet hair. And I could watch the ball all the way up to the knob, but—nothing doing.

When it got dark, I sat up in my room and kept watching. With the window open a crack, I could hear how things were going. Beer being swallowed, the ball hitting the ground. And an ocean of swear words.

At least the apple tree that had never gotten anywhere was down there with him.

CHAPTER NINE

RAKKEBY SCHOOL HAD THESE EVENINGS where the teachers finally got to say something. They were called parent-teacher meetings. Me and Mom walked over to the school. We didn't stick together. I was twenty yards in front. When we got there, I held the door for her. Mom never had much energy when there were parent-teacher meetings. On our way down the long hallway, she wondered quietly whether the teachers might have something new to say this time. They wouldn't, I said.

Mom had to talk to our Danish teacher and math teacher. It was a lady and a man. The lady said my spelling could be a bit better. That at least I ought to be able to spell my own name when I handed in a paper. The man said the way I did math was incredible. Incredibly wrong. And that it would be a good idea if Mom and Dad could do some number exercises with me.

Mom was good at letting the teachers speak their piece. Sometimes she looked up from her knitting, but otherwise she didn't interrupt.

When the teachers were finished, Mom took a little knitting break. Then she told the teachers what she was knitting and who she was planning to give the sweater or socks to. Now it was the teachers' turn to give Mom a chance. She asked the lady and man whether they knew the family she was knitting for. The teachers never did.

They sat there, feeding Mom a big, fat lie, because in Rakkeby everyone knew everyone.

Mom didn't get mad. She began telling about the family she
knew best of all.

"Have you heard? The prince's youngest daughter is starting to
make pop music. The prince doesn't like the idea at all. And Prince
Albert…he's been seen in bad company. Time and again. The only
one they don't have any problems with is Princess Caroline. But she
is also the one who absolutely resembles her mother the most. I've
always said so. Don't you agree? That Caroline is the spitting image
of Grace Kelly?"

The teachers looked at each other. Then they got busy. Suddenly
they had to find the custodian so he could give Mom an invoice and
tell her what I had wrecked since last time.

Mom looked at a bill for a desk. Which wasn't fair, because
I hadn't wrecked the desk at all, just borrowed thirty shavings
or so. Everybody said it smelled much better in the classroom
after wood chips began flying from my pocketknife. Instead of
the stench of sour lunches, the classroom suddenly smelled like a
circus. I'd done everybody a favor—including the desk, since no
one had ever paid it a compliment before. But the custodian said
it had to be replaced.

Mom wasn't stuck together at all when we walked home.

One evening there was a knock on the door. Dad shook his head and
lifted the right cheek of his ass. Dad was good to his chair. He never
farted right down in it. Sometimes he lifted the left cheek, so the
fart shot the lamp and made the light bulb brown. But usually he
lifted his right one, to blow Mom out to the kitchen for some fresh
coffee. This time she was blown all the way to the knocking door. I

followed behind. Outside a man was standing in an orange garbage man's overalls. He pointed up in the dark.

"Look! They're up there! They've been there several minutes. They're flying in circles. They're happy."

I stuck my head out and looked up in the darkness. The sky was pitch black. Mom called Dad. The man was jumping up and down. He was glad and kept pointing up in the black air.

"Our garbage can's over there," said Mom.

Mom didn't like the man. That was too bad. She ought to like people who could see things in the sky other people couldn't. The man laughed.

"I didn't come to empty your garbage. I just came to share the sight with someone. It's not every day one moves to a town with UFOs. I'm your new neighbor. My name's Valdemar. My wife's name is Eleanor. Eleanor just popped down to Hjørring to get a roast chicken."

Dad came out. He lifted Mom out of the way and looked at the man's forefinger and followed it up into the sky. When Dad could see that our new neighbor was hopping and dancing and pointing at pure nothingness, he said he could come down in the cellar and have a beer if he felt like it.

The man would like to join Dad in the cellar, so long as it was okay if he ran back and forth to see if the UFOs were still circling outside. It was. Valdemar was sat down at Dad's cellar table. He kept on talking, mostly about people who put diapers in the top of their garbage sacks. This happened too often. If he could have children of his own, he'd be considerate enough to bury the diapers. That was the least a person could do, he said. But he couldn't have kids, not a single one. Then he told about his wife, who had eggs and ovaries in her belly. It was one big mess down there. Eleanor had been a hairdresser, but she'd had to retire suddenly. Her breasts were too heavy.

She couldn't trim folks' bangs without standing wrong and it hurt. Valdemar stood up and showed how Eleanor used to cut folks' hair in Hjørring. He used my head to demonstrate and leaned down on me so much, it was easy to tell how heavy Eleanor's boobs were.

"And that was the end of Eleanor's shop," Valdemar said.

Dad hadn't even taken a sip of his beer yet. He just looked at our new neighbor as if Valdemar was the best thing that had happened in years.

Then Valdemar remembered his UFOs. He ran out to look for them, beer in hand. Some beer splashed onto the floor. Dad didn't get mad; he just grinned. So I grinned too. The cellar was warm. Dad wanted to be friends with Valdemar.

A while passed. Dad sent me out after fresh beers. I ran into Valdemar.

"They're gone," he said. "Disappeared…just like that."

The sky had stolen Valdemar's voice and given him a new one. A feeble one.

"Talk about the UFOs! Keep talking about the UFOs!" I whispered.

Valdemar went back and sat down with Dad. He didn't have anything more to say. He stared into space, mouth closed. Something happened with his eyes. They got full of puddles. Big splashes started raining down on Dad's table. His mouth was still shut, but sounds came out between the lips. It sounded like Valdemar was crying.

Dad began muttering. His cellar was used to lots of kinds of weather, but not rain. Dad got up and walked back and forth a little. Folks usually behaved when Dad stood up. But it didn't help. Dad went and stood by the cellar window and looked out.

"The UFOs are probably just in Hjørring, getting gas," I said.

Valdemar said nothing. I got mad and went over and stood next to Dad. We looked out the window. We couldn't see a thing. Absolutely nothing. We just heard a crying garbage man.

Mom would be coming down the stairs soon. To hear a little about Valdemar's wife. But before she got that far she'd smell the spilled beer. Then the floor would have to be washed. And she'd know it was Valdemar who spilt, because Dad could fall off a roof with a beer in his hand and not spill a drop.

Two car headlights came sailing in on the other side of the hedge.

"Oh, god, it's Eleanor," cried Valdemar. "Let me just borrow the faucet."

Valdemar was already standing by the sink with his head under the water. It looked like he was brushing his teeth with his fingers. Water was spraying everywhere. After Valdemar had gurgled and spit out three times, he said thanks for the beer and ran out the cellar door and up the stairs. Me and Dad watched him run over the lawn, crouched down and orange.

"Why'd he wash his mouth, Dad?"

Dad didn't know. Now Dad wanted to sit alone awhile and think things over. My head was spinning, too. Valdemar had done a lot of things wrong, but he'd been an exciting visit.

Mom was sitting, talking with Dad while I practiced on the living room floor. Dad said I should come in to them. That meant we were moving again. Or else Grandma was dead. Mom smiled. Dad cleared his throat.

"Your mother has gotten a job. She's going to look after a clothes boutique in Hjørring. She's going to be selling clothes to ladies. Lucky it's not you or me. But that's the way it is."

Dad got up and went down to the cellar. I went with him. I did stretching exercises with my back to Dad.

"How many hours will Mom be gone?"

"All week long, except Sunday."

"Who's gonna make food, then?"

Dad didn't answer. He shot a beer cap at the ceiling. I moved my stretching exercises closer. I wanted Dad to know I wasn't the type who just changed jobs. I was going to play professional till I died, and when Rakkeby got it together and sold me to a bigger club, then everything would be good.

I wondered whether Mom would be allowed to smoke in her boutique. And what if she had to work evenings? Then Dad would have to go over to the school and talk with the teachers and the custodian. Dad wouldn't talk to them about Grace Kelly. He'd stomp them. And end up in jail again. Then I'd have to make food myself. Or maybe I'd have to go live with Grandma in Hørmested.

Hørmested had the worst club in the whole world. This was a fact, because Hørmested was in the same league as Rakkeby. We'd beat them 17-2, and even Tom Snot had scored a goal. It was an awful win.

I went to the phone and dialed. A lady answered.

"Give me Tim!" I said.

"Is it very important, Karl Gustav?"

"Yes, it's incredibly important."

Tim's mom was gone again.

"This is Tim Brink speaking."

"Can you smoke in a dress shop in Hjørring?"

"Cigarettes?"

"Yeah."

"No, it's forbidden."

"When do they close?"

"The dress shops?"

"Yeah."

"In Hjørring all shops close at six. Except the post office; it closes at four o'clock."

Now I felt better. As long as Mom could still keep coming to the school meetings, it was okay for her to stand in a dress shop and smoke her cigarettes out the window.

"Tim!"

"What?"

"I got a job for us. It's important."

"What's it got to do with?"

"Flying saucers."

We sat behind a bush and got ready. I warmed up my hands. I had to throw perfect. It wasn't going to be easy, but the weather was good. There was no wind and the moon was a big flashlight, shining right down on Valdemar and Eleanor. They still hadn't scraped enough money together to buy curtains. That was good. We could see them right through the window. They were in the middle of eating dinner. In a while Valdemar would stand up from the table, walk through the room, and sit himself down in front of the TV. We had to catch his eye while he was taking those few steps.

That afternoon me and Tim had bought the biggest plates the junk dealer had in stock. Twenty for two bucks. They were plastic, which was a good idea, because it could well be we'd have to toss them past Valdemar's windows a few times. No one knew how good he could see, and I had a hunch his eyes weren't exactly normal.

Tim was cold and started talking about a space ship that had crashed somewhere in America. The spacemen had survived, but the crash had given them terrible headaches. The Earth was hard as rock when you hit it at the speed of light. Especially in the desert.

Ever since then, the spacemen had been cooped up in a top-secret cave, along with all the other things the American president needed more time to understand. So far it had taken seventy years.

"It's a waste of good minds," said Tim. "I really hope they let the spacemen play chess, at least."

"Shhh!"

"Big Ox?"

"Yeah?"

Tim took a plate and held it up to the moon.

"How's there supposed to be room for a spaceman inside this?"

"Shhh! They have dogs!"

"They have dogs?"

"Yeah, shhh!"

"What kind?"

"I dunno. Now shut up!"

"Try and explain what we're doing again. Just once more."

I shook my head. What a dope.

"The man in there is Valdemar," I said. "He's married to the world's biggest boobs, and it's true 'cause I've seen them myself. The boobs have wrecked the whole family, but Valdemar loves UFOs. He believes so much in UFOs that he can see them, even though they aren't there. So we're gonna give him the real thing. Then he'll run right over to Dad and drink a lot of beer. If he can keep from crying his eyes out, they'll be friends by midnight."

"That's a pretty strange way to become friends."

"Yeah, but that's how it happens sometimes. Just like us. We only became friends because I thought you were gonna die in a little while."

I adjusted my captain's armband. It had a habit of falling down when there was too much on my mind. Even though the mission had to be top secret, I wanted to look right because very soon I was going to make Dad's life much better to be part of. I loaded my hands with plates. They were blue, yellow, and red.

"What color's best, do you think? You decide."

Tim scratched his chin. With mittens on.

"Yellow's the most conspicuous," he said finally.

"Conspicuous?"

"Yes, conspicuous."

"That's a damn good word, Tim."

"Thanks, Big Ox."

Now something was happening. Valdemar was standing up.

"Here we go!"

I jumped forward a step and positioned myself like an Olympic plate thrower. Valdemar was about to get a whole swarm of happy UFOs. But then he walked away from the TV and completely out of sight.

"Goddammit!"

Eleanor didn't move. We could see her hair. She just stayed sitting where she was. Valdemar came back. Leaned over the dining table and picked up some kind of pot. And disappeared again.

"What the hell's going on?" I said.

"He's clearing the dinner table. We can sneak over to the kitchen window and throw them from there."

"Why the hell should we do that?"

"In case the man washes up."

"In case the man washes up?!"

I ran across the lawn, not caring if anyone saw me, dropping almost all the plates. Over by the kitchen window I could hear whistling. And see Valdemar standing in front of the sink. The whistling made him look like he was kissing and he had a dishtowel over his shoulder.

Inside the house a dog began to growl. Tim came running up beside me. He had all the plates with him.

Valdemar spotted us. He waved with the sponge. Smiled.

"Should we throw now?" Tim asked.

"No, Valdemar's no good for this. He's a lady."

CHAPTER TEN

FOR HIS BIRTHDAY, Tim wished for a long bicycle ride. He wanted to cycle up to Skagen. Tim had read in the newspaper that there was a movie theater in Skagen that showed porno films at eight o'clock in the evening. This was incredibly early and folks all over town were upset about it. A fat lady from the local church had been in the newspaper, holding up a sign that said the theater was really disgusting. Tim said she had high blood pressure. He could tell, even though the picture wasn't in color.

I asked Tim how his own blood pressure would do, up in Skagen. The bicycle ride would take hours, and what if he died, right inside the theater? Tim said we had to cycle really slow, and he wasn't at all sure he could make himself wank off if there were too many people. He'd rather wait until he was back home, in bed.

Tim had been lying to me. For a hundred years he had just seemed like a little boy who raked our assholes away at the long jump pit, when I'll be damned if he hadn't already broken a thousand records with his willie. For a whole year he'd jumped the gun without telling me. He was afraid I would be upset. He actually said so.

As if that wasn't enough, Tim told me he'd gotten so good at it, he could explode without losing his breath at all. This made me really mad and I went home and practiced till my hands fell off.

After a few weeks I was okay again, and it was all right now for him to have his birthday present. Tim said he'd pay for the tickets if only I'd cycle up there with him. It was rare you could make money by giving someone a birthday present. And if I had to choose between eating a gingerbread man at his place and blasting my rocket off at the movies, I knew where we'd be going.

We met over by the grocer's. There was a sign that said SKAGEN: 35 MILES. That was a long way, especially when we had to bike home again. Tim's bicycle and its ten gears were all shined up. Mine was old and the seat had rusted fast in position from the days when I was shorter.

By the time we reached Ilbro, the rain began. Not a mile further, yelled Tim. He was catching a cold and maybe it was better if we saw porno some other day when the sun was out. We argued. Tim was wearing the wrong clothes, long black trousers with a belt. I just didn't get it. How could a boy who read ten books a day be so dumb when he had to dress properly for his willie's sake? There weren't even pockets in his pants.

I didn't want to quarrel, so I kept bicycling slowly with Tim following along. He had use for me. In the newspaper they'd said that you had to be sixteen to get into the theater. This was because the movie was in German. We'd discussed how we were going to get through customs and decided I looked the oldest.

The movie's name was *Ficken*. It was a short title and didn't sound like much, but when Tim looked the word up, it got much better. The film that we'd been willing to cycle a thousand miles to see was called "Fuck." Or "A Fuck." Or "Fucking." During our bicycling breaks we discussed which sounded best. I was the one doing most of the talking. Tim just stood there with his cheeks slightly red, breathing as quietly as possible.

We made it to Skagen a little before eight. The sky was full of holes. Rain poured down on us, but the theater's name was Palace, and in palaces full of pornography, wet clothes didn't mean a thing. At the entrance, Tim's face turned beet red.

"I need a glass of water," he said.

"What for?"

"I have to take my pills. I've got a fever."

On the other side of the street was a fine little hotdog stand, and its manager was willing to sponsor a glass of water. Tim took a little plastic glass out of his jacket pocket. He petted the three pills and swallowed them, one by one instead of all at once. I looked at the hotdog man. He thought it looked wrong, too.

"Thanks for the water," said Tim.

"The money," I said.

Tim handed me his birthday present. I started preparing myself. I told my shoulders they had to rise up to my ears and look old. Then I started walking with long, plodding steps.

The man in the palace ticket booth looked me down in the eyes. He smiled and asked how old I was.

"Twenty-eight."

The man leaned back and slobbered at the ceiling. Then he called out, toward the back, whether the cops were in town that evening. Nope, came the reply. I couldn't see what this had to do with *Ficken*, but who cared? Me and Tim got the tickets. We were told to sit in the last row and leave as soon as we were done. The man laughed and said it probably wouldn't take long. I was just about to mention how much we'd trained, but Tim tugged on my sponsor sweatsuit. We went into the darkness.

It wasn't filled up inside, and nobody who was there liked each other much. People sat very apart. I thought Tim was sitting too close to my left hand, too, so I moved a seat away. Tim nodded; he was right-handed.

Then the movie began. No commercials. A slow warming up

would have been nice, but the German fickers didn't have time for that. The very first picture was a lady sitting on a sofa with a machine between her legs. The machine was red. It looked like a willie without balls and sounded like Dad's shaver. The lady sucked on the machine and did some kind of strange training with her tongue. Then she spread her legs and showed us lots of nice, black hairs. The machine took a dive into the woods. This was pretty incredible, because we'd just seen a man standing out in the kitchen. He was wearing a white apron, but nothing else. Then, luckily, the lady's machine broke down and she became whole again, so we could see both the living room and the kitchen. The family had hardly decorated their house at all. The lady looked mad. She shouted something in German to the man in the kitchen. I leaned over to Tim.

"What'd she say," I whispered.

"'Won't you bring me some new batteries, my love?'"

"I don't believe a damn word."

"Really, that's what she said. I swear. See? Now the man's taking two new batteries out of the drawer."

I had a look. It was true. Two large batteries. The lady was sitting on the sofa, still mad. She tried licking her boobs, but they weren't big enough. She wriggled her tongue around in the air and the man came over to her. He said something that sounded sad. I didn't bother asking Tim, because I knew what he'd said. He'd said that her tongue wasn't in shape and she should be ashamed of herself. But then he started feeling sorry for her. In one quick swing of the body he tossed both the batteries and apron the hell out of there. But what was totally incredible was his willie. It was two miles tall. It was so tall, the lady had a hard time dealing with all of it.

I started getting pissed off at her. She could just get up off the sofa, but she wouldn't. She tried reaching with her tongue again. I looked at Tim to see if he was just as mad as I was. He wasn't. He was practically lying down on his seat, his whole body tight as a guitar string. It looked like he was using every small muscle in his arms to hold himself up. His little rib cage rose and fell, rose and fell.

I looked up at the screen. Now the lady was sitting on the floor while the man tried to get his entire willie to stay in her mouth. He didn't want to spill on the carpet or the furniture, because she looked like a lady who never cleaned house. After the man sprayed her all over her face, she wanted to take a nap.

Suddenly we were somewhere else. Now there was another lady with three men. She was down on all fours like a dog. There almost wasn't room enough for all the men. My head was on fire. I was in a frenzy all over, including my willie, who stood up in the sponsor sweatsuit and screamed to high heaven. He wanted some attention. I gave him all I had.

On our way back to Rakkeby we didn't talk much. Somewhere in the dark Tim said it had to be a miracle that he was still alive.

CHAPTER ELEVEN

WHEN YOU BUILT A HOUSE, a lot of things had to be level. When things were level, you could trust them. When things weren't, they fell apart. Dad had said this a thousand times to his men in Hirtshals, and now I said it to my coach, Siegfred Tightwallet. He had cut Rakkeby Stadium's grass all wrong.

I was lying with my snout in it. My left eye, the best one, could see one dandelion after the other. Some of them were even gray-haired.

I'd called him the evening before to get him to fix the field. Tightwallet's mom took the phone and said her kid was out slaughtering pigs, but that he'd be in soon to have a plate of pork chops. I could call again, she said. I told her she ought to kick her son out and over to another farm because it wasn't professional, having a coach who lived with his mother. And that she also ought to quit calling him "kid." She said goodbye.

I stood up and patted my sports bag. My sports bag's name was Puma. It held my life. There was beautiful old dirt in it. The dirt smelled of conquered territory. Then there were my good-luck underpants that Mom got to wash only when we lost. And there were my good-luck socks that she had to darn right away when I dribbled holes in them. My captain's armband was already sitting on my upper arm. Tightwallet had bought it in Hjørring at the beginning of my career for two sacks of grain. The captain's armband was red and made itself at home on my arm—also at night and in school. A lot of people thought it looked strange in the winter, but I didn't care. Real team captains took their job seriously all year round.

Our team wasn't that steady. We could win matches 14-7 or lose them 1-46. It was farming's fault. Almost all my teammates had fathers that were farmers, which meant we could only produce our strongest team in the winter and summer. In the spring and fall there was sowing or harvesting. The farmers' sons were supposed to help. Right in the middle of the soccer season.

Siegfred Tightwallet understood this. If a player said he couldn't come because he had to go to a confirmation or a funeral, he was off the team for good, but when the farmers' fields called, Tightwallet gave the players a slap on the back and wished them well.

I was stuck in the midfield with reserve players like Potato Pete and Tom Snot. Their dads weren't farmers. No one knew who their dads were, or why they played soccer. They never kicked the ball, they didn't sweat, they didn't run, they didn't tackle, they didn't know the rules and they cheered wrong. I was on bad terms with them even when we won. Often Siegfred Tightwallet had to run onto the field and break us up.

It was sports week in Rakkeby. Siegfred Tightwallet had arranged a match with my old club. He had also bought a used trophy we could play for.

The town's men were drinking themselves drunk in the beer tent. Their wives stood outside, looking at the suckling pig roasting over glowing coals. They discussed the potato salad and hoped the men would remember to eat some. Otherwise the beer would hit them too hard and then they'd start fighting. Which was okay, just not during sports week. During sports week all Rakkeby was supposed to get along nicely and buy lottery tickets, where first prize was a side mirror for a tractor. According to Siegfred Tightwallet, this was something everybody could use because there were always bunches of kids running alongside the tractors while they were plowing. And if a cheap side mirror could save the life of just one of them, there was no reason to buy a bigger, more expensive first prize.

Folks nodded to me and I nodded back. Not because I wanted to; it was part of the captain's job to say hi to everyone. The players' bus from Hirtshals came sailing up to the clubhouse. It was black and yellow. Axel was on it. It had been a long time since I'd talked to him. He jumped out and saw me right away. He smiled.

"Our bus has a toilet inside. I just spermed all over it."

I swore to myself. Hirtshals was a major club. In Rakkeby we sat in two sad junk heaps when we had away games, and if one of them crashed, half the team died. That was pretty careless, because the rules said if you came to a match with only eight men you lost automatically.

The ref that day wasn't professional. It was Siegfred Tightwallet's cousin from a village half a mile outside Rakkeby. His name was Leo Lopside. His one leg was shorter than the other. He ran without being level one bit. And besides that, on the most important day in the club's history he'd forgotten his heads-or-tails coin.

"Y'don't happen to have a coin on you, do you?"

I was standing in the midfield circle with the captain from Hirtshals. His name was Toby. They called him Puff because he'd begun smoking when he was six. Puff could tackle a horse head-on, and before it knew what was happening, it was lying on a frying pan like a fillet nobody wanted. Puff had an open cut over one of his eyebrows. If he'd been in a fight yesterday, he was going to be good today.

Puff turned around and yelled to his troops that the ref was a prize idiot. Leo Lopside smiled through it all and used a long and a short blade of grass instead of tossing a coin. He could just as well have heaved two boogers out of his nose and seen who ate his quickest.

The match was very even, without any big openings. At half time the score was tied, 4-4. I hadn't scored yet, but I'd nailed the crossbar on a free kick. That was cool.

At half time we got much too much food. It was Siegfred Tightwallet's fault. He hadn't rinsed out our drinking bottles well enough. Which was a bad mistake, because now they were full of ants. The ants loved the taste of old grape sugar and were experts at finding our bottles in the locker room. They'd probably been partying all week. The ants were overweight. I yelled that something was crunching in my teeth. Siegfred Tightwallet yelled back even louder that nothing was better for soccer players to eat at half time than ants, because ants knew how to work like no one else, and that was exactly what we were gonna do when we went back out on the field.

When Siegfred Tightwallet was done yelling, he ate a whole bottle of ants, just to show us how good they were. Then he said there was something we had to see. Tightwallet squatted down in front of a dirty towel. The towel was hanging over something very pointy and tall.

"Are you ready?" he asked.

Everyone nodded. Tightwallet pulled away the towel, nice and slow. The trophy appeared. He blew the dust off. The lid on the trophy sat crooked.

"This is what we're playing for. Now get out there in the second half and plow them under. Let's go!"

Behind Tightwallet I could see Dad come walking out of the trees toward us. There were already lots of spectators with draft beers in their hands. There was no way Dad was going to get through the second half without something in his hand. In jail they hadn't given him anything at all to drink. Ever since he came home he'd been working at loading himself up again.

Leo Lopside blew the whistle to start the second half. Dad came walking along like a dazed buffalo. I ran straight at Puff and tackled his knees. Puff didn't notice. No one noticed. I played with bad feet. I was planning to dribble, and only dribble. Not to pass the ball one single time. Instead I lost it and toppled over and rolled around to get a free kick. I wanted our medic out on the field. Our medic was Tightwallet. He was supposed to come storming out with the club's entire collection of first aid. Which consisted of a wet sponge. I wanted Dad to see me being treated with that wet sponge. To see how I could stop a whole soccer game. How everything came to a halt when a man was down.

Leo Lopside didn't see anything, or else there was nothing to see. Puff and Hirtshals didn't play good, either. The match ended 6-6. Overtime ended 1-1. So it all had to be settled with penalty kicks.

I couldn't breathe. I couldn't hear what was being said. All I saw was Siegfred Tightwallet pointing at me and four others. We had to go down to the other goal. Down to Axel, who was hopping up and down, socking the crossbar and smiling.

I didn't want to kick. I watched while Axel flew through the air and boxed one of our kicks straight to hell. Axel didn't shout with joy. He just spit on his gloves. Our goalie stopped one, too. We were still even, and stayed that way until Puff kicked the ball over the goal, over the hedge and all the way over the silo, the highest building in Rakkeby.

Tightwallet ran straight through the hedge without taking the loophole. He came chugging back with drops of blood in his red beard and handed me the ball. My hands were wet; I couldn't feel my legs. Axel smiled. I took a long time setting the ball in position. My fingers couldn't make it lie still.

"Don't worry, I'll fetch it when you miss," shouted Axel.

Everyone could hear it. Everyone knew what it meant. I tried running fast at the ball, but my legs chose to walk. I hit the ball, closed my eyes, and fell over forward. I'd slipped. It was the grass's fault. The dandelions' fault.

I landed on my side, my cheek plowing the grass. I opened my eyes. The ball wasn't up in the air at all, like it was supposed to be. It was just rolling. Axel watched it. A silent roller. His eyes got wide; he could just scoop it up. I heard screaming.

When the ball finally reached Axel, he jumped to the side. A random flying fish jump, like he'd done so many times down on Deadeye's *Sylvia* when we were bored. He pretended a flying fish had flown by. A thousand flying fish. He was still pretending. Nothing ever scared Axel.

The ball rolled into the goal; it just managed to reach the net. Then it died. Axel was lying on his back by the one goal post. He plucked a blade of grass and put it in his mouth.

Axel lay there on the ground and stopped being my friend.

Mom came home from work at sundown. She parked her bike and began making food. She'd peeled the potatoes in the morning. Now the meat only needed frying and the sauce to get thick. Dad was sitting in front of the TV. He'd decided it was better eating dinner in the living room.

Mom's food was good as ever and was much easier to eat when you held the plate in the air right under your mouth. Then you could shovel it straight in with a fork.

When we were finished, me and Dad set our dishes on the coffee table. Mom smoked a cigarette and told how many dresses she'd sold and who'd been in the boutique and what had been going on out in the street in the meantime. Mom spoke right across the coffee table and into Dad's right ear.

All evenings went like this. Mom did the washing up. Then she knit a while until she fell asleep in her chair. Dad woke her up just before he went to bed. Then Mom got up and did some cleaning where she thought it was needed. She didn't use the vacuum cleaner; it made too much noise at night. Instead she crawled around the floor, plucking up dirt with her fingers.

I sat in front of the TV, fighting to stay awake. Mom didn't look tired, but it would be real nice if she went to bed. I didn't like touching myself when Mom and Dad were lying right next door. It was better down here in the living room.

I was the luckiest boy in the world if the television showed a movie where men took the clothes off of women. But now, with Mom selling dresses all day long, she cleaned house so late that all there was left on TV was a goodnight picture. It never moved and there were never any naked ladies. It showed a red sky, a lake in the woods with a swan, or some dead trees under black clouds.

I dozed until Mom said goodnight. She crept upstairs to Dad. She was good at not making noise in the john. She didn't flush after she peed. I could only hear her toothbrush and the water giggling on its way through the plumbing. Finally I heard their bedroom door open and shut with hardly a sound. Then I pulled my pants down. It was hard to wake up my willie. He had gone to bed, mumbling that red skies and wooded lakes and dead trees turned him off.

We sat there together, missing the German fickers.

CHAPTER TWELVE

SUMMER VACATION DIED and the custodian wasted no time raising the school's flag. Me and Tim were shifted a step to the right. We got older, one step a year. Ferguson was the only one left in place, grinning from ear to ear. It was hard to say what he'd been doing all summer. But he sang in church. Every Sunday he stood between the priest and the folks from town. The priest came from a long ways off, but many of the farmers had put in nine long years at Rakkeby School. They'd just followed Ferguson to a new place.

Mom thought Ferguson sang beautifully. Every word was so distinct. No matter where Our Lord may have been, He could hear everything without straining Himself. When Mom came home from church she always said what a stately man Ferguson was. "Stately" was a rare word. It meant that you had no problem going down to Monaco and getting a pat on the back from the prince.

In Ferguson's office nothing had changed. I sat on my chair while Ferguson trotted back and forth. He was mad—at himself, too. His slap was loose. It had taken him almost two hours to notice that the flag had dropped to half-mast.

"I've been thinking about you all summer long. I don't understand you, Karl Gustav. Your mother comes to church every Sunday. She sings with her eyes closed. She immerses herself in the psalms. But you...you just want to trample on everything. Why, Karl Gustav? Why?"

I got mad. We were supposed to talk about me and him, not Mom. I got up and looked out the window. The custodian had spent all summer making an animal farm for the youngest kids with two rabbits and a guinea pig. He'd made their water dishes of wood so they could get a splinter in their tongues every time they lapped up the last drops.

"Mom got a job. I don't think she'll be coming to church anymore."

"Sure she will. I've had a talk with her, you know. She prays that you'll be better. Did you know that? You are with her in church every Sunday. She sits there, wringing her hands, because you make life so hard. She prays that you'll stop."

I turned around.

"You wanna fight, or what?"

"No, we are not going to fight. And we never have. We may have nudged and pushed each other a bit. And besides, now it's stopped. You must tell me why you're the way you are. Is it your brother? Is it him? Wasn't his name Alexander?"

The whole school got quiet. My heart ran a lap. It was beating all over, mostly in my head and hands. I had been waiting for years for Alexander to show up, come pouring out of someone's mouth. Like Dad, sitting under our county-owned yard's tree and suddenly starting to tell about all the times him and Alexander came home from a building site. A long time after I'd gone to bed, but the car would wake me up. And I'd crawl to the window and look out at the yard. They'd always be sitting on the bench where I could only see them as dark shadows. But I could see the tip of the cigarette burning. It went back and forth, from one hand to the other, one mouth to the other. They'd just built a house and had to sit down and think it over a little. In total, complete darkness. With one smoke between them. And I'd open the window quiet as I could to hear what they were talking about. But they never said a word. Just sat. Alexander still had construction between his legs. He could still feel the roof's peak beneath him, a whole other place in Hirtshals. And there wasn't one spot on that house Alexander hadn't touched. He knew every time he cycled by the house with its new owners that the nails would bend over and bow in a greeting of creaks and groans. Alexander didn't have to brag because he knew Dad understood everything. So they sat on the bench in Little Norway, the house where it all began. There they sat. Without a sound.

That's how Alexander was supposed to come out of someone's mouth.

I stormed Ferguson, head first. My forehead hit his belt buckle. It was hard and cold, but it gave way. Ferguson piled into the door. The door helped by holding onto him. I used my arms, my legs, my knees, my feet, my teeth. I didn't want to get past him, I wanted to get through him—tear through him. That's what I wanted. Nothing else.

I sat in my room, waiting like Dad told me to. My window was as open as it could go. I wanted to be able to hear the ambulances. I touched the bump on my forehead. My belt-buckle bump, built of steel. First it was just red with blood on it—a nice bump, but not that incredible. Now it had gotten big and blue. When I pressed it, it answered inside my head for a long time.

The custodian had come bounding into Ferguson's office to save him. Everyone had gotten blood on himself. It was squirting out of Ferguson's nose like tomato soup. Then the custodian dragged me all the way home. I didn't resist that much. We were headed in the right direction.

Dad came up out of the cellar. The custodian let go immediately. Dad looked at me like I was home from school too early. But the war wasn't over yet. There were still plenty of explosives in me. I yelled what had happened. I didn't prettify the story one bit.

Dad listened. His ears grew big and his eyes little.

"Go up to your room and wait."

And then Buffalo took off toward the school, with the custodian running ahead to warn all of Rakkeby to run to its basement. Buffalo was on the loose. He had been hibernating for some time, but now his son had awakened him.

I looked at the sun. It had moved. At least a few feet. Dad was taking a long time finishing what I'd started. Maybe Ferguson was hiding. Or maybe Dad was sitting in Ferguson's office, waiting for him to be able to stand up again.

Then I heard the cellar door being slammed shut. Its glass window breaking and falling out. The county's house jingled. So finally it must be ours; Dad had just taken care of that, too. Yes, Dad was his old self again. I spit on my palm and slapped it onto the bump so it would look fresh. Then I rushed downstairs to the cellar.

Dad was standing with a beer. He didn't have a scratch on him. Red in the face, but otherwise nothing. I nodded.

"Are The Good Old Days over for Ferguson, then?" I asked.

"What is *that*?" Dad bellowed. "What by the Seven Gates of Hell is *that*?"

Dad pointed at the table, at a pile of slips of paper.

"Look at them! Pick them up!"

I took the top one, remembered it right away. It was for the guitar. You had to sit completely still with it and only use your fingertips. The music teacher said strings and fingertips went together. And that you had to give things time to work. Lots of time. If we were lucky, we'd be able to play guitar by the time we left school. It wasn't true. If you bashed the guitar into a desk, it played louder and better. I had demonstrated this for the class, but the guitar wasn't made out of wood from Norway. One blow and all the guitar's belly flew out in splinters. It cost $89. That was expensive for just making one sound. Dad thought the sound was expensive as hell. Dad thought everything was expensive as hell.

He screamed that I was going to sit in my room for a week and think over why he'd had to stand there in front of a fucking wimp as the only man in the whole world who didn't know his son had been destroying the entire school.

I went over, stood closer to Dad, looked straight into his belly. He raged past me into the storeroom next door where we had Mom's apples and his beers. I heard him shoot a capsule at the ceiling. I stayed put.

Dad didn't come back in. I went upstairs to the bathroom. I borrowed Mom's mirror, a little one. It was only to be used on faces. I set it up against the wall by my bed. I lay on my stomach and looked at my bump. Somehow I couldn't see it anymore.

Tim was feeling so well, he went to school. But he didn't dare visit me. He was sure the county-owned house was going to explode. I didn't hear Mom and Dad quarrel over my bills. Not a bit. Instead they were noisier than ever in the bedroom. I lay in my bed listening to them. They were married to each other, but they sounded a lot like the $89 guitar. I couldn't understand how Dad could be in the mood.

Afterward Mom talked a little. Dad's voice was there, too. He sounded like a motor having a hard time starting. Like *Sylvia* when Deadeye tried getting her going once in a while. He just wanted to see if she still could. It made Deadeye glad when she finally began singing. Then he turned her off again and proposed a toast to her trusty body.

I missed Deadeye. Even though he didn't allow you to speak much, sometimes you could give him an important question. Right now I would have liked to know if a father could save up his being mad over his son's bills. For later. For the bed, where he'd then tell his wife what he thought about it all. With his body.

But I didn't think it was like that, because Mom's voice wasn't like she was being squashed flat under a mad buffalo. Mom's voice sounded as usual. Full of fresh knitting-needle talk.

Tim dared only call on the phone. He talked about Inga with the glasses. She was the ugliest girl in the school, and Tim thought he was crazy about her, even though this was impossible. On Friday the phone rang in the hallway. Tim had something new to tell.

"I'm the luckiest boy in the world. Wanna know why?"

"No."

"Goodbye, then."

"C'mon, just spit it out!"

"Not if you don't care."

"I didn't say I didn't care. Say it!"

"Inga can't swim."

"Is that good?"

"You betcha. 'Cause I can't either."

"So…?"

"We got swimming in gym class. We were down there today. By bus. It was only Inga and me who couldn't swim. Isn't that fantastic?"

"We have swimming?"

"Every Friday for a year. How about you, Big Ox? You know how to swim, don't you?"

CHAPTER THIRTEEN

I'D BEEN LOOKING AT THE RED TILES FOR A WHILE. They were very clean. I couldn't see one single ant crawling around, hunting for grape sugar. I couldn't even see a little clod of dirt. Hjørring's public swimming pool was an ugly place.

The boys from the soccer team acted like it was no big deal. They were all there. Potato Pete and Tom Snot were already under the showers, soaping their crotches. They were using these blue sponges that started foaming as soon as they got wet. It wasn't honest soap, but Tim said everybody had to wash themselves before they got to continue on to the big flooding. It was a rule.

Tim pulled off his T-shirt.

"Just wait till you see Inga in a bathing suit," he said.

But I didn't hear him. My eyes were on Tim's chest. A scar ran from his throat down to his belly button. It was long, white and thick.

Tim popped in under the shower. I followed.

"What's that?" I asked, touching the middle of his scar.

"My operation. You know. I told you."

I ran my finger up and down the scar. It could be Tim had talked about an operation, but he'd never shown me his scar. Tim smiled like everything was just fine. He'd merely gotten a lightning bolt in his belly. It had torn him in two and knocked a hole in his heart, but what the heck. Tim had gotten sewn up and immediately hid every-thing behind lots of clothes so everyone could keep thinking he was a nobody. Tim was one big liar.

Inside the pool area I saw Tom Snot and Potato Pete sprint over to a tower with a ladder that went right up to the sky. They wriggled up the ladder like salmon. At the very top there was a diving board you could run out on. Tom Snot was first. The board gave way under him, but he continued all the way out to the edge. Then he jumped as high as he could, straight up in the air. He landed again on both feet. The tip of the board had turned into a trampoline. Tom Snot jumped into the air. Way up under the sun he did a somersault. Then he straightened out, arms pointing down toward the ocean. Tom Snot was a spear. There was a little plop as the water swallowed him whole. I leaned forward. Down in the depths I could see a dark blob. He'd never come up again. All swimming would immediately come to a halt. Tom Snot would be dead in no time.

Then the blob began to grow. Something big broke the surface, swept all the water aside. It was a fist, and in the fist a pair of swim-ming trunks, waving. Then came Tom Snot's head.

"C'mon, girlies. Poppa's ready."

Another door opened at the same time and they filed in, wearing little, tight bathing suits. They sounded like birds. With beady eyes that immediately began peeping at Tom Snot's swimming trunks. The only thing on their minds was to stick their beaks in him. They wanted him, were willing to fight for him. I could tell.

That was the end of the world's worst soccer player. Tom Snot could be called Tom Snot no longer. My stomach began tying knots, and I started looking for Tim. He was standing right behind me, mouth open.

"Look, there she comes. The last one. With the glasses. Oh boy, is she beautiful."

I didn't see her. All I saw was a grown-up with muscles and a whistle around his neck.

"Okay!" he shouted. "Eight lengths to warm up. Let's go!"

Everyone immediately began doing what the man said.

"Aren't you going to wear some cork, Big Ox?"

I turned toward Tim's voice. I couldn't see him at first, even though he was standing right behind me. He was wrapped in cork—arms, legs, and stomach. Inga with the glasses was just as corked up.

Tim handed me a bunch of belts. They didn't weigh anything. I couldn't tell what they were for. Tim started helping me without even asking first. I knocked his hands away.

"Come, Inga. Let's go in the water. Karl Gustav doesn't want any help."

Tim went with Inga down a long flight of steel stairs. Then, incredibly, they let go of the railing with both hands and stepped out onto the open seas. They could touch the bottom. Tim was in water up to his stomach. Inga was up to her neck.

Then the man came over to me.

"You're new. Can you swim?"

I wasn't able to talk to anyone. I went to the stairs and took hold of the rail with both hands. I turned my back to the water. With eyes almost closed, I let my worst foot sink down a little. The water was cold and alive. The man was standing over me. I could smell him. He smelled heavy. I felt myself being pressed a step down. Now both feet were underwater. The stairs had little holes. They were sloppily made. They were far from finished being built and could easily collapse. The man left. Go home, I begged. But he came back with cork. Three slabs. He jumped into the water, much too close. He busted up the sea and it landed all over me. I wasn't ready at all.

The man handed out the slabs to me, Tim and Inga.

"Now just go out there and lie on the water. It's incredibly easy. Go!"

The man pointed out over the waves. I began walking into it. I weighed so much, the ocean floor kept giving way. It sank deeper and deeper, disappearing more and more.

Now I was in the ocean up to my neck. I could see an edge. There was a pipe, a marvelous pipe. The cork slab wanted to go to it.

"Away from the edge!" I heard.

I turned myself around. The man's voice was strong. He blew waves toward my mouth. I made a wrong step and swallowed. The water wasn't clean; there was something in it. I tried turning around, wanted to run back to the edge and the pipe. My feet slipped. I fell. My fingers couldn't hold on. The slab of cork said farewell. I floated downward. My ears screamed in the darkness, my teeth crunched. Alexander was in my mouth. He was trying to fight his way out. I opened my mouth as wide as I could. The ocean poured in. It didn't hurt. I could drink it. I filled myself up. Everything got soft. And warm. I almost felt like seeing how it looked. Maybe Alexander would be there, right before my eyes.

Then it started hurting. The sea tore at me, slung me around. I could feel the ocean floor. It was made of ice. There were voices, all talking at the same time. About color. About shit. About smell. About a broom in the corner. I was supposed to fetch it. I curled up. I coughed through closed eyes, out through my nose, out through my stomach.

"Big Ox, if you'd just move…just a little."

I stayed where I was.

"I fetched the broom."

I smelled myself. Tried to roll away from the smell. Tim began scrubbing.

It was running out of my trunks. I climbed to my feet. Headed toward the door with my hands between my legs. Dripping black. Tim followed behind, using the broom where my hands weren't big enough. He followed me into the showers. He said nothing.

On the bus home, Tim sat down next to me. That was all he said.

At one minute to seven me and Puma went through the hedge. We knocked on the door. Valdemar was there right away. He was wearing his best suit with his dog in his arms.

"It's so nice that you can help us. And you've got a sports bag with…what's in it?"

Eleanor stepped up behind him in a green dress and red lips.

"Get that dog off your clothes," she said.

Valdemar set the dog down and pulled a bag out of his pocket.

"This is pigs' ears. If you give Curly a pig's ear, you'll be friends for life."

I looked at the dog. Curly was little with big ears. Its life was a secret. No one had ever had anything to do with Curly.

Sometimes Valdemar asked Dad if Curly could come along for a quick beer in the cellar. Curly couldn't. Dad didn't like dogs that yapped at night, and this was something Curly was good at. Curly barked anytime, day or night, and for a long time. Including now, where Valdemar was down on his hands and knees, kissing his dog goodbye.

When Eleanor and Valdemar had driven off, Curly took a furious walk around the living room. I sat down on the floor and called to it. It didn't come. I opened the bag of pigs' ears and held them out.

Curly just kept on. Round and round, all the way out along the walls of the room. It dragged its belly across the floor. Wild-eyed. The dog looked nuts. Maybe it was mad because I'd gotten three bucks for being there. Valdemar said Curly was a little bit bad at being home alone and usually took the whole house apart. And that Curly also ate Eleanor's shoes. When it had gotten all the juice out, it spit out what was left.

Valdemar said him and Eleanor weren't equally glad about owning Curly. I already knew this. You could hear them quarreling all over Rakkeby because Eleanor had a voice that could force the sun way up in the sky. A lot of times you could hear Curly's name in her screaming.

This always ended with Valdemar going for a drive. He did this without Curly because Curly also liked biting the car's back seat.

I looked at Curly. It was still going around in circles. The big ears stuck straight up in the air. Curly was a dog in a state of emergency. Someone in a state of emergency isn't interested in eating pigs' ears.

I opened Puma and checked my things. Boots, shin guards and good-luck socks. I'd forgotten my good-luck shorts, but that didn't matter. I changed clothes, taking my time. I zipped the sponsor sweatshirt all the way up to my chin and turned my back so Curly could see my trowel.

Finally I picked up my captain's armband. It didn't want to go on my arm, just be petted a bit.

Siegfred Tightwallet hadn't called to have it back yet. He hadn't driven around in his combine harvester looking for me, either. I knew this because I'd spent a lot of time biking around town to see how much he missed me.

I never ran into him. This hurt, because Siegfred Tightwallet had often told the story about Rakkeby's top scorer, Charlie Bob. It was just before the biggest match of the season—the local showdown with Hundelev—and Charlie Bob hadn't shown up.

Everyone in Rakkeby piled out onto the streets to help look for him but no one remembered their stretching exercises. From one minute to the next Rakkeby was full of pulled muscles and sprains. The whole town was an injury. The only ones who weren't searching were the players from Hundelev. They just stood around, wide-eyed, smelling victory.

Five minutes before kickoff, Siegfred Tightwallet found Rak-keby's most important player. Charlie Bob was lying in the darkness of a barn on top of a naked milkmaid. Charlie Bob was all worked up and using his energy wrong. Tightwallet got really pissed off. He tore Charlie Bob off the naked milkmaid and gave his top scorer such a whupping that Charlie Bob started running like hell to escape the pain. He ran straight through Hundelev's defense and scored without cheering, then raced to the sideline where he begged Tightwallet for the wet sponge for his butt. No way. Charlie Bob had let his team down. Charlie Bob had let down all of Rakkeby and the whole county.

I closed my eyes and tugged at my upper lip. I was going to miss Siegfred Tightwallet. He could figure out a tactic that lasted much longer than a soccer match. Sometimes the tactic went to bed with me at night and dribbled its way into dreams full of milkmaids and big showdowns with Hundelev.

I lay my captain's armband back in Puma. I took my soccer boots and tossed them across the room. They hit the wall and fell to the floor. This made Curly bark like crazy. Curly could hear a thousand times better than humans. Curly could hear screams that hadn't been screamed yet, the ones that were waiting in the throat for permission. Curly could hear that my Good Old Days were over.

One day Ferguson came and fetched me from class. I hadn't done anything. In his office, he didn't want to slap me, or even bawl me out. The only thing he wanted was to look at me. And smile. He smiled and said there must have been a miracle. All the teachers said so. That I had changed. That they almost didn't recognize me anymore.

Ferguson opened his lunch box. He found himself a plate, opened a drawer in his desk and removed a napkin, knife, and fork. He started with an open egg sandwich with slices of tomato and mayonnaise. There were some chives standing on the windowsill. He asked if I'd cut some for him. He handed me the scissors. I shook my head. This was hard. My body was no longer to be trusted. Ferguson cut some himself. Smiling. It sounded like big snips of hair.

Ferguson munched and smiled away. In the middle of a mackerel salad sandwich with onion rings, he took a piece of paper and laid it on the desk. Now we were going to write a letter, he said. We were going to write to Mom. And congratulate her.

He told me to take my chair and sit next to him. We were supposed to celebrate together. He pulled me close to him. We were leg to leg. Then he began writing. Hand and pen flew across the white paper, word by word, line after line. The sentences squirted out of Ferguson.

After he'd written his name at the bottom, Ferguson raised his pen with a sigh. He held the paper up and shook it a couple of times. Then he folded the letter and stuck it in an envelope. He guided the top of the envelope over to my mouth. My tongue couldn't resist. It came out and licked clear across the letter.

My tongue was Ferguson's taxi driver. It drove straight to the spot he'd always wanted. To where all the other nice children sat and waited, smiling and watching without saying a word.

PART II

CHAPTER FOURTEEN

RAKKEBY HAD A HEDGE THAT WAS FAMOUS. It was the hedge in front of the community center. Every Friday the hedge came along to the party. It stood there, calm as a cucumber, and took on a flood of folks who emptied themselves however they felt like.

The hedge got watered so much, it could easily pack up all its branches and sail away. But it stayed put. And every spring it budded and flowered and smelled as lovely as ever. The hedge received a lot of praise for this.

All the couples in Rakkeby had met each other right there, and even though they'd quit going to parties, they still often walked past the hedge where it all began. And each time, what happened was that the lady pulled the man's fists out of his pockets so he wouldn't look bored and lazy. Then the couple had to walk hand in hand all the way past the community center and remember everything about that night where the wife got frisky for the very first time.

One evening in May, a girl was standing by the hedge, bent over, throwing up. Her name was Gina. I didn't know her at all. I just knew she'd quit school. And there were people going around saying she'd had some wine bottles stuck up her.

I went and stood next to Gina and took a piss. When Gina stood up again she had stuff stuck in her hair. I let go of my dick and tore off my shirt without unbuttoning it. The buttons made a neat sound, bouncing through the darkness. I handed Gina my shirt and said she could keep it.

Gina yawned at me and dried herself off and asked if I'd come home with her. We walked over the railroad tracks toward the woods. She dried herself off some more and tossed my shirt into a ditch. Gina was lurching a little, but she was a head taller than me. Out in the middle of nowhere she squatted in the grass and peed and the ground said thanks.

Gina lived on a very old farm. The barn's windows were broken. A little horse was tied to a post, asleep. The horse was so small, it could fit on the backseat of a car. It was a practical horse if you had to move.

There was garbage strewn around the farmyard and clothes lying around the laundry room. There were clothes everywhere, except in the living room. Gina's mom was sitting on the floor eating from a dish of cold, thick buttermilk. She crushed a toasted biscuit in her hand and sprinkled it over the buttermilk and the floor. This didn't matter, because the floor was already covered in newspapers. They didn't have a TV set, but they had daddy-longlegs on the walls and hedgehogs on the floor. There were cardboard boxes standing around with dishrags on the bottom. Inside the boxes were water dishes and plates with green fruit I didn't recognize. Some of the hedgehogs were asleep on the dishrags; others were taking a walk in the living room, claws crackling on the newsprint.

I didn't know much about hedgehogs, but I could see they were one of those kinds of animals that saw toilets everywhere. The mother didn't say hello, but it didn't matter. She could see I was good for her daughter from the moment I arrived, shirtless.

Gina lived in the attic. You went up a ladder and opened a hatch. There were no lights up there. Gina struck a match and got a candlestick.

We traveled out in space and reached a mattress. Gina lit more candles. There was a chair next to the mattress and an alarm clock on the chair. It was late. Gina had no rugs on the floor. She had creaky planks of wood and lots of straw that you could put in your mouth when you wanted to think hard. If a fire broke out, we'd die quick. That's how all bedrooms were supposed to be when you'd never been in bed with anybody.

Gina pulled off her clothes and lay down.

"I'm ready," she said.

"Why does your mom eat cold buttermilk at night?"

"No idea."

"Is your dad sleeping?"

"He's dead."

"How many hedgehogs have you got?"

"A real lot."

"What's that green fruit?"

"Avocado. Can't we just fuck and quit talking?"

"Okay…"

"C'mon. I owe you for the shirt."

Gina yawned again.

"Don't you have anything we can drink?" I whispered.

Gina had red wine. In a bottle without a cork. The wine was called Voilá.

"Just drink out of the bottle."

I had a pain in my neck. I was sitting wrong. With my back to her. I wanted to be lying on my belly with my face just over her pussy. The wine tasted like hell.

Gina started messing with my pants. All I could see were her hands. I wanted to take hold of them and lift her up so I could see her better. Once Gina's fingers dug deep enough, things happened fast. She dried the sperm off on the blanket and lay down on her back.

"You can just sleep here, if you want to."

Gina blew out the candles. I couldn't keep up. Porno never told you about ladies that turned off the light. I was sure Gina thought the sperm shot too soon. In porno, things were supposed to take about nine minutes. If Gina wouldn't mind using her hand again, I'd give her all my clothes and everything else I had.

I could hear a dog barking somewhere close by. I could also hear the sound of the mother's spoon, shoveling up the cold buttermilk.

Gina had fallen asleep. I crawled closer to her mouth. She smelled of vomit. I felt like kissing her anyway.

I worked my way down next to her, pulled the blanket up and lay there, fidgety. My hand swept over the planks and straw, searching for the box of matches. I wanted to be able to see something. I couldn't even remember what she looked like.

Gina was making a lunch. She wasn't stingy with the butter. She popped a slice of salami in my mouth. Gina's mom was sitting on the floor in front of a barred cage. She stuck her nose right against the bars and said sounds to a hedgehog.

The hedgehog didn't answer. It was in shock. It still had drops of water on its quills. The hedgehog had just been given a bath. The mother used a deep dish and filled it to the brim with chamomile tea. It was an incredible idea. So was the pink bow around the hedgehog's neck.

Gina handed her mom the lunch pack.

"And if you drink yourself drunk, I'll kill you."

We all looked at Gina. The mother nodded. So did I. The mother was on her way to a pet contest. It was something that the saints arranged each spring. Gina said the saints prayed to all the gods in the world that her mother wouldn't show up. But she did, with lunch pack and bowed hedgehog.

Gina's mom collected prizes. Victories hung in the bedroom over her bed. They were called favors and had to do with training horses. In the old days they'd had a lot of horses. Now all they had was the practical horse outside, but it wasn't nearly as practical as I thought. Gina hadn't allowed her mom to take it to the pet contest because the horse always wound up standing alone in the dark, whether it had won or not. Gina said her mom always ended up drunk when she brought the horse along. So Gina had suggested her mom try her luck with a hedgehog.

The mother put the lunch pack under her blouse. It looked like she'd latched it to her bra, something I'd never seen before. Now the food would get warm. I was just about to say so when Gina put a finger to my mouth. She thought it best that me and the mother didn't get to know each other.

The mother set the cage on the back of her bike and cycled off along the potholed, gravel road. After the hedgehog fell off two times, she decided to walk.

"She's all right, your mom."

"We'll never see that hedgehog again."

We stood at the window a while. I kissed Gina on the cheek. Gina's lower lip was big and broken. I was the one who'd done it, but no one said anything. The mother hadn't noticed, and Gina could stand everything. She smiled at my kiss and smiled at the horse outside. It had yanked out its post. It could run the hell away if it felt like it, but it stayed standing where it was.

"Shall we go up and keep fucking? Or we can take a walk with Little Horsey."

"Is that its name?"

"Yeah."

"How about when it grows up?"

"Little Horsey will never grow up."

I was sore and needed a break. We went out barefoot. The grass was wet. Little Horsey wanted to join us on a walk around the old farm. I told Gina what I'd do when her mom died from drinking. I'd build the farm up again. Nothing big, just a little castle. Gina nodded. We could do it all. We were free to do anything.

I'd had a nightmare. Alexander was holding my head, hitting it. When I woke up, I socked Gina. When she got a candle lit, her chin was red and wet. The lip had broke. I caught her and tried to make everything good again.

Afterward we were quiet. I got worried. Gina said I should raise my head. She pushed the pillow in under it. She shoved a foot between my legs and then fell asleep with her mouth against my neck.

When we'd been lovers for nine days the alarm clock began ringing at a quarter past three in the morning. Then Gina sat up and smoked a cigarette real fast. She had to be at Hotel Garni in Hjørring by four o'clock. She made beds. She said she could change a double bed in half a minute.

"You need to get a job, Karl Gustav. Why don't you go by the mink farmers' on your way home? They're always needing someone, and you're good at skinning."

"Skinning?"

"Skinning off the fur, that's the most important. You just have to remember to wear steel gloves. If a mink gets hold of your finger, it doesn't let go. And the throat…it's best it doesn't get hold of your throat. Then you have to stand still and wait for the man with the air rifle. And you can't shout for him."

"The air rifle?"

"It's good, hard work, Karl Gustav. Your fingers fall apart. You won't even be able to unzip your own pants. That's the kind of man I want. See you later!"

Gina disappeared through the hatch and down the ladder to go to Hjørring on her moped. The wind combed her hair and her mouth smoked cigarettes along the way.

All the beds had to be made, including the ones that hadn't even been used. The manager went around and patted them all on the ass, but a regular job was more important than anything else. That's what Gina said.

I crawled around a little with my nose down in the mattress and pillow. I was smelling out old times. All the ones Gina had had without me. I thought I could smell some men in the mattress. But not the pillow. The pillow was my pal. And the birds. The birds were there before the sun came up. They sat on the roof because it was full of rust. The rust helped the birds keep their footing. They stuck their beaks down through the holes when they felt like it and whistled for the day to get underway.

When it rained, me and Gina lay there getting wet, nice and slow. Gina liked rainy weather, but not the wind. In windy weather, the sheets of tin on the roof tried leaving home. They squeaked and screamed. I liked the way they sounded, but Gina said it was the worst sound in the world. When the wind started howling, Gina's body grew a fence, and all she wanted to do was lie under the blanket and keep everything else out.

I got up and looked for my clothes. Downstairs the hedgehogs were going around, yawning. The lights were never turned off in the mother's section of the farmhouse. Gina's mom had trouble sleeping, and in the dark it was impossible.

Outside I poured a pail of water for Little Horsey. Little Horsey could drink five gallons a day. I watched the drinking for a while before starting to walk back toward town. The road was totally empty. The cows stood still. The mink farms lay side by side. Long, flat prisons with tin roofs. The animals were never permitted a walk in the yard.

They were born behind bars in Rakkeby and ended up on some lady's body out in the world somewhere. If the mink could decide, it would be the other way around. Which was probably why they went for the throats of all the men Gina had known. I hoped they kept it up.

In front of one of the farms a black watchdog was trying to break its chain. It yapped and jumped and kept getting thrown to the ground, never learning a thing. Gina's smell was strong. The dog could smell everything we'd been doing. It would do anything to be in my shoes.

Whistling as I walked, I finally reached the finest place in Rakkeby. My party shirt was still lying in the ditch, just where she'd tossed it. A beautiful spot. It would get cold when winter came, but a shirt only had room enough for one miracle. I could never touch it again. If it was lucky, someone else would pick it up. I said hi and walked on.

When I got near the school, Dad came bicycling with his rolling toolbox behind. The box was made of wood and the wheels were from an old baby stroller. The box was welded to the bike. Now they belonged together. Dad had already done what Gina said: found himself a job.

It started with the bench out in front of the grocer's. It needed painting. Dad got ten dollars and two cold ones for it. Without fiddling around, Dad painted the wood he himself sat on and sometimes fell off of.

The grocer was satisfied. His cash register had hardly lost any weight. He told everybody about Dad's cheap paintbrush. That was something folks liked hearing about. Soon Dad became a traveling odd-job man. He built garages and horse stalls, woodsheds and terraces.

Dad came home to Mom's food with crumpled-up dollar bills in his breast pocket, and one evening when he was in a hell of a good mood, he called the dress boutique and said Mom wouldn't be coming back. Mom dropped her knitting. When Dad shuffled off to bed, she waited for his snoring. Just as soon as it started coming through the ceiling, Mom called her boss and said sorry and how were the rules about quitting a job real fast and he certainly shouldn't think it was because she didn't enjoy being there.

Mom moved home to the kitchen. Her chin got stuck out and her eyes got popeyed from trying to sneak a peek at the thickness of Dad's wallet all the time. Dad's wages went up and down a lot, and sometimes they didn't go anywhere at all. Folks in Rakkeby liked to talk about the improvements they wanted made, but when push came to shove, the improvements apparently could wait. Not that it hadn't been nice, having Dad out to look at what needed being done. Then Dad would bicycle home with his rolling toolbox, in a mood that sent him straight to the cellar.

But this morning Dad looked like he was cycling off to something with meat on its bones. There was smoke coming out of his pipe. This only happened when he was in a good mood.

Now that Mom could no longer tell about all the dresses she'd sold and what was happening out on the street in the meantime, she didn't talk nearly as much. But they were doing better. Dad was, at least. You could tell by the toilet upstairs. When Dad had work, he began hitting the middle of the toilet bowl instead of making a mess. It was incredible that you could shit better from building sandboxes and making nice stalls for Arabian stallions, but that's how it was. Dad sat on the can just as much and just as long as he always did, but now he hit the bull's-eye.

When I got home, Mom was ready on the porch. She ran her eyes up and down my body to make sure all parts were in good shape. My eyes got the same treatment. She stuck out her head; we were standing nose tip to nose tip.

It was Prince Albert's fault. The prince had confessed to having smoked some hash at a party in Monaco. And the magazine that told the story was afraid Prince Albert was going to the dogs. The magazine had given Mom and everyone else's parents some good advice. Every morning they were supposed to stop their child on the porch and look deep in their eyes. Hash made it so the child couldn't blink. If the eyes stood completely still like a shiny window, the parent was supposed to call an ambulance immediately. Mom held her breath. I blinked like crazy.

"Thank God," said Mom, and went in to see to the coffee.

CHAPTER FIFTEEN

THE SCRAP METAL DEALER'S NAME WAS LEFTOVER. Leftover couldn't sit still, but his blue overalls could. Leftover said he'd had them on for fifteen years and three months, nonstop. And they still hadn't gotten dirty.

"Look!" he said, pounding himself in the chest.

Leftover was right. The cloud of dust got up from his desk and didn't have the slightest thing to do with the blue overalls.

Leftover wrote everything down. He had a whole bookcase with folders that were full of all the good business he'd done, starting at the age of seven when he'd sold a sick parakeet to a raging, drunk vagabond. One dollar and twenty-five cents. And just for my information, the filthy bum had regretted it like hell ever since.

"And the parakeet. You know what happened to it?"

I shook my head.

"It didn't even make it out of town before it..."

Leftover stuck a finger in his throat and made an ugly noise. After that he laughed and laughed. When Leftover laughed, his gums took over from his teeth. It wasn't that pretty a sight. But this wasn't my problem, especially if I happened to be sitting across from my new boss.

Leftover's office was large and super modern with a walkie-talkie system and a telephone with an incredibly long cord. At the end of the office there was a half wall you could lean against and look out over Leftover's mountain of old rubbish that was worth its weight in gold. The yard was full of containers. They stood there, scattered about like silver treasure chests, each and every one filled with goodies that folks didn't want.

If I got hired, I'd have to learn how to sort stuff. This wasn't easy, Leftover promised. It could take seventy years of training, but that didn't matter because I was a little shit with my life before me.

"I have a motto. You might as well learn it now. 'One can't make an omelet without breaking eggs – except for here.' You can try repeating it."

I said it real fast to show I'd be on time and a good apprentice.

Leftover was shaking his head when the phone rang. He grabbed the phone and took an important walk around the office while he told about a generator that was in the prime of life.

I stood looking at two globes with lights inside. They took up the best places on the desk. One of them had a hole in the South Pole, but that didn't matter, said Leftover. The globe with a hole in the South Pole was only used for keeping warm the one hanky Leftover had been using the last six years and seven months. It was blue and made out of something that couldn't fall apart. After Leftover sold the generator, he took the hanky and blew his nose. He must have had a little cold because, when he spread out the hanky over the world like a tablecloth, it didn't take long before it started sputtering. That had to be snot.

"Where were we now?" said Leftover.

"You didn't like my motto."

"I sure didn't. You said it much, much, much too fast. Plus it's my motto, not yours. It took time, getting it right. It's a good, old saying with a twist. Without the twist, it wouldn't be worth a pot of piss. Here!"

Leftover picked up a weapon and held it toward me.

"What is it?"

"A weapon," I said.

"Golldangle me, no, boy! That ain't good enough. This here was my pappy's old saloon rifle. And I ask you: is that good or bad?"

"Is what good or bad?"

Leftover heaved a sigh.

"If I sell it—God forbid—would it be good or bad that it belonged to my pappy?"

"I dunno."

"Is it something I ought to tell the buyer?"

"Yes."

"Hell's bells," said Leftover.

The hanky had begun smoking. Leftover turned it over. He also rotated the globe.

"You must never lay a handkerchief over the Equator. Remember that!"

I nodded. Leftover took two sugar-free orange sodas out of a crate. He opened them with the saloon rifle. I was real impressed.

"You're making a hell of a mistake, Karl Gustav. That this lovely toy belonged to my pappy is *my* business and no one else's. No one else in the world."

"What should I say then, Leftover?"

"No, it isn't at all as easy as folks make it out to be…"

Leftover sat down and threw both his legs up on the desk. He used a large shoe size; the shoes sailed silently between two worlds. A pair of swallows darted above us. They did a somersault in the air, then flew in an arc over all the goods in the barn and out through the gates of Leftover's empire. I followed them with my eyes.

"This is where it's happening, Karl Gustav. It's your future we're talking about, and it isn't looking good. Well, back to Pappy's saloon rifle. What you gotta do is, you gotta—golldangle me—give the rifle a good story. You have to say the weapon in your hand once helped an unhappy man shoot his wife and three kids somewhere down around Silkeborg. And afterward, when the unhappy man tried shooting himself, his hands were shaking so much, he shot himself in the foot. Right in the worst place. A source of permanent shame. That's how you wanna sell my pappy's saloon rifle," said Leftover, and sniffed all his words up his nose with a satisfied grunt.

I gave a nod. Leftover rinsed his mouth out with sugar-free orange soda and planted a thick finger on the globe that didn't have a hole in the South Pole. He twirled it around until the finger hit the Andes Mountains. It was here something happened once that explained everything worth knowing about modern recycling. With his entire body Leftover demonstrated how an airplane had crashed in snowdrifts so big, they put out the fire in the motors. There was a fair amount of survivors after the crash, but also a fair amount that died. When the fire went out, people started freezing. They also got hungry.

"They got just as hungry as all the children in Africa put together, and there wasn't a living soul in the whole world who could dream of sending so much as a crust of bread to the Andes Mountains. The plane had landed in an unholy place where it was minus a hundred degrees. The mailman had never been there. You start to get the picture?"

I nodded again. Leftover smiled and explained that luckily there'd been a wise man onboard. Teeth chattering, the wise man had made a suggestion. They ought to start burning the dead people's clothing. This was an idea the other survivors weren't crazy about. At all. They argued for a few days, but in the end it was the cold that decided. Many of the dead had jeans on.

"And that was golldang lucky," said Leftover.

Because it was as if jeans had been created to keep bonfires alive in the Andes. They could smolder forever without going out. They were worth their weight in gold. The survivors kept warm for a few days, but the smoke was very black and heavy.

"Incredibly heavy," said Leftover, and shook his head. "All the survivors were forced to look the other way, right at the row of people lying dead on the ice, naked as the day they were born. The bodies were blue from top to toe. When the smoking jeans were on their last legs, the wise man made a new suggestion. That they begin warming up the dead over the smoldering fire. Then, at least for a moment, the dead would get the right skin color back. The dead would appreciate this, no doubt, because who wanted to go to heaven wearing the same color as heaven itself? They'd be invisible and just disappear into thin air."

Leftover stuck his head down close to mine.

"So: would you vote yes or no to the wise man's suggestion? Think it over well. Your future depends on it."

I picked all the paper off my sugar-free bottle. I thought about Gina. It was for her sake I was sitting here. That was something I had to remember. I was supposed to get a job so she could say farewell to Hotel Garni. Gina didn't need pats on the ass from anybody but me.

"I would vote yes to the wise man's suggestion," I said.

"Good, my boy. Come with me!"

We crawled down a ladder from his office. Leftover said he hadn't built stairs on purpose. The customers who were the most bothersome were those who had trouble walking or else were totally handicapped. Rakkeby was teeming with cripples who did nothing but complain all the time, and some even brushed up on their complaining before they wobbled into town. All scrap metal dealers who were worth their salt had offices you needed to be in good shape to get to.

Once we got outside, I hoped we'd talk about my pay or look at the silver treasure chests, but no. We were going to talk about what happened in the Andes Mountains after the wise man's suggestion had been accepted.

"It started smelling like meat, get me? And little by little the blue bodies took on a color that looked like beef. The bonfire started up again slowly. The wise man knew this would happen, of course. He said to all the others that they should close their eyes and think of their favorite restaurant. They shouldn't think that these were dead fellow travelers, being barbequed before their eyes. And you know what the wise man did while the others tried looking the other way?"

I shook my head.

"He sharpened his pocketknife on a stone."

Leftover folded his hands on his belly, threw back his head, and started laughing like mad. The fat under his chin lapped back and forth. He couldn't stop. I was missing the point. I couldn't see this had anything at all to do with modern recycling.

I broke in. "Do I have the job, or not?"

Leftover stopped at a container and patted it on its side.

"No, for the love of rust, you do not. But you can read this till tomorrow."

Leftover pulled a book up out of his pocket. It was tattered and thick, but incredibly good, Leftover promised. The book was written by the wise man when he came home from the Andes Mountains without having lost so much as one pound.

"If you want to get anywhere near being hired, read this tonight. Tomorrow at eight in the morning you come back and tell me what you've learned from it. It's that simple."

I waved goodbye, disappointed. It was harder talking your way into a job than I'd figured. Especially when you never got to say anything. I couldn't see the point in quitting school, either, if I was just going to get homework from a junk dealer instead.

But that night I went to bed with the book anyway. All 356 pages. I let them whirl through my fingers, pausing now and then. I was just about to put the book down when I noticed something. The book's first page was blank. There was nothing on it—not even a little page number in the corner. This made me stop and think. It must have been a building defect.

Next morning I went over to Leftover's.

"Here you are," I said. "Here's the book and an empty page. The empty page was right at the front and was going completely to waste. I tore it out so the book can get on with the story."

Leftover looked at the naked page a long time.

Then he said, "Karl Gustav, it's lunchtime in four hours. How many fried eggs can you eat?"

CHAPTER SIXTEEN

THE SCREAM WAS LONG AND DIDN'T STOP. I put a hand over my mouth. The scream wasn't mine. It started running down my back. And down the stairs. Out in the hallway I bumped into Dad. He was leaning over the banister, naked.

"It was just the chimney," he yelled.

I leaned out over the banister too. I could hear rummaging in the kitchen.

The scream was gone. Now it sounded like the faucet was being torn out of the sink. Then the coffeemaker started up. Dad smiled and went out to the john. His pissing didn't sound afraid. I went down to Mom to make sure.

Mom was standing in her panties and bra by the coffeemaker. She was watching how the coffee made itself. For Mom, there were two calming sounds in the world: coffee being born and the queen's New Year's speech. When both were happening at the same time, nothing bad could come of us. The rest of the time, anything was possible.

Mom's arms and legs were splotchy. She was a little shaky.

"It was just the chimney," I said, and looked up at the ceiling to see if there was a hole.

Dad came downstairs. He went out in the yard. After a little while he came in and banged eight bricks down on the kitchen counter.

"Oh, God, is the house falling down?" asked Mom.

Dad shook his head and opened the fridge. He took a beer. Dad looked like a man who had kissed off sleeping anymore that night. This was a good time for a talk about the future.

"Dad, I'm dropping out of school."

Dad didn't say anything. He went and sat down at the dining table. I followed him.

"And why is that?"

Dad wasn't too impressed with my claim that I'd be the best scrap metal man in Denmark. I'd never collected anything. I'd never found anything. I'd never looked for anything. And I couldn't patch a tire on my own bicycle. Dad didn't think junk metal was my calling.

And what was worse, Dad had heard that Leftover didn't drink or smoke. Which was true. Leftover lived off fried eggs, sausages from some pigs in the neighborhood, and sugar-free orange soda. People like that weren't to be trusted, Dad said. They were fanatics, and it was precisely fanatics like this who were behind the destruction of Jerusalem and every disaster since.

Mom came in with fresh-brewed coffee. There was still a cold mouthful left in the bottom of the thermos. She drank that first.

"But you can't just quit school," said Mom. "It's going so nicely now. There are never any problems at the parent-teacher meetings anymore. You've become so polite, and your grades have improved."

"Grades have improved?" said Dad. "What's that supposed to mean?"

"Nothing, Dad."

"Spit it out, boy."

"It's just that suddenly I'm getting these other grades. A little higher. But they've made a mistake. I never say a word in class."

Mom nodded eagerly. She explained to Dad that the teachers had finally discovered I was growing up. Ferguson, too.

"We've even received a letter from him." Mom went to get the blue cookie tin.

The cookie tin was full of songs for festive occasions from the old days in Hirtshals. Songs about rich families that Mom and Dad once knew. The letter from Ferguson was lying in there, too. I'd never seen it. Dad unfolded the letter. He already didn't like it. He could smell my tongue on the envelope. He got all red in the face.

"Pious!" he bellowed. "It says here that my kid's gotten pious!"

Dad jumped in the air. He hammered his knee into the edge of the table. Mom's coffee sloshed over.

With a snort, Dad went out to get the telephone book. He tore through the pages. When he found what he was looking for, he dialed the number. Somebody answered. Words, spit, and curses spewed out of Dad's mouth. The telephone receiver got soaked.

When Dad was done raging, he thundered off to the cellar. Mom leaned over the table and reached for the letter. Dad had splashed beer over the words. As she picked it up, all the blue letters melted together, never to be read again.

Mom took a look at the blueness.

"It's all right," she said. "I know the letter by heart."

We watched Tim's mom sitting in the middle of a thousand vases that looked exactly the same. She was working. She had red nail polish on her toes, the one foot tramping and tramping, clay slurping in her hands. She never said anything, but she looked a lot, especially out the window. In the garden stood a brand-new, wood-built house that Tim's dad had drawn on his lopsided table. The house looked very nice and square, but not many people had seen it, even though Tim had painted signs and spent a long time pounding them into the ground along carefully chosen roads around Rakkeby. The signs said that Tim's mom was a potter who lived in the area and had her own showroom in the garden. The signs didn't tell how much Tim's mom longed to sell something, but you could tell by the way she looked out the window. The red toes were by far the most alive part of her body.

Tim was sitting in his office chair, rotating around. He liked sitting with his mom. There was also a mattress where he could lie down, close to her feet. He often took a nap while his mother made un-sellable things. Tim really liked how it sounded. Slurping clay and the singing of whales were Tim's best sounds in the world.

I went into Tim's room. There were airplane propellers hanging from the ceiling. There were magazines under his bed that doctors had written.

I lay down on the floor. Tim's floor was a kind of home for me. Before Gina chose to throw up at the exact right moment, I used to drink myself drunk over at the community center, then stagger to Tim's house and knock on his window. He was always awake, waiting for news about Inga with the glasses. Had she been there? Who was she standing with? Did she drink, and if so, how much? What clothes was she wearing? Did she take any off? Did she dance? Did she dance with the same person more than once? And then—after Tim had taken his pills and quickly made up a bed for me and plumped up his pillow and turned off all the lights—came the last, all-important question, quavering through the darkness: Did she kiss anyone?

I flipped through one of Tim's magazines, stopping at an article about bats. It was in English.

"Tiiiimm!"

The office chair came creaking over with Tim on top.

"What's this say?"

"Good article. Well written, too."

"Yeah, right. But what's it about? Just the important stuff."

"The scientist behind the study was born in 1946. He grew up in the countryside where there were a lot of calcium mines. That was how…"

"The bats. What's it say about the bats?"

"Don't you want to know anything about the scientist?"

"No."

"Just the results?"

"Yes."

Tim sighed. "The investigation showed … Are you ready?"

"Yeah."

"That if a male bat is kept from mating, his brain begins to grow. The head simply gets bigger. Seven times out of ten, it ends in a cerebral hemorrhage."

"Jesus Christ."

"Yeah. Something happens to the males that get to mate as much as they like, too."

"Like what?"

"They get bigger testicles."

"Their balls grow?"

"Yes, they get bigger testicles."

"Does it really say that?"

"Yep."

I smiled and closed my eyes. I saw myself hanging from Gina's ceiling by my claw tips. With her lying naked on the mattress, looking up at two hairy balloons. If she didn't grab out after me, I'd fly away and explode in the air into thousands of unborn bats.

"So, do you understand why I subscribe to these magazines? The stuff's exciting, you gotta admit. Isn't it…? Isn't it…?"

I was listening to the wind outside, the trees rustling. It would be nice if Tim also knew something about ladies who couldn't stand wind, but the doctors never wrote about things like that. The doctors were just like Tim. They only knew about things that were good for thinking about, not doing something about.

"Have you shot any more cats lately?"

I nodded.

"How many?"

"Seven or eight."

Tim shuddered. He didn't like Leftover. He wouldn't even come and visit me when I was standing out in the rain, waiting for a possible customer with the saloon rifle over my shoulder to take care of the wild cats that were always bedding down in places Leftover didn't approve of. The cats especially liked the used baby buggy department. Leftover sold an incredible amount of baby buggies. This was because folks in Rakkeby had children as soon as they met each other in the community center. The quicker folks got married and had children, the sooner they could celebrate their silver wedding anniversary, and this was something everyone went around looking forward to. The brand-new parents could never afford a brand-new baby buggy. It cost an arm and a leg. This was fine with Leftover, but the wild cats weren't. At all. They shed hair like hell, and even the poorest mom in Rakkeby wouldn't go along with having her baby lying in a big, fluffy forest of cat hairs.

So it was one of my most important duties to shoot anything that purred. I did what I could, but I had inherited all Mom's eye mistakes. I never hit a damn thing.

"Are you really planning on keeping that job? With him?"

"Yeah."

"Then we'll be cut in two."

That was a strange way to put it. But my half was bigger anyway. I made money and had a wife. Tim wanted to go to high school and then on to the university to become a doctor. He thought I should become a hospital orderly. It would be easy, he said, even though I couldn't spell or do math. Tim promised he'd help me get through hospital orderly school. We could share an apartment. And in the evenings Tim could read aloud from his textbooks while I lay on the sofa, scratching some lady behind the ears. It didn't matter how dumb she was. That was up to me.

There used to be a time when I liked hearing about Tim's dreams. I could put myself right in them. He was going to earn a fortune in no time and not know what to use it on. Then I could be his boss and give him an allowance for the books he wanted. But now it didn't matter.

We lay there a while without saying anything. We were good at it. Tim had no problem lying down all day, getting up only once to go to bed.

"I heard something about Gina," he said, suddenly.

"Oh yeah? What?"

"They say Gina's father isn't really dead."

"Who says?"

"They all do. They also say Gina's mother gets picked up out in the woods. By hermits. They drive her off in a car. They do a trade. She gets some schnapps and they get..."

Tim stood up and opened the window. He always did this when we talked about Gina. It got too warm, too dirty. Then I was the movie theater. Showing him my latest film with Gina was about as good as it got. I loved bringing him along, down into the cave. And describe what I'd done and said, and what I wished Gina'd done and said. Tim believed it all. I had faithfully brought Tim along into Gina's body, and then he had to ruin it with news like that ...

I got up and left, slamming the door. Walked into Rakkeby, full of all the little houses with the little, long-nosed people who were always searching for the spot where things smelled the worst. Just as soon as they found it, they hurried home again, smiling. Hurried home and opened the windows, hurried home and called everyone they knew and traded stories. And now the story about my mother-in-law had even reached Tim.

Gina's mom could choose the most secret tree in the woods and it wouldn't help. She'd bicycled out there after the pet contest. She hadn't won. It turned out Gina was right. We never saw the hedgehog again.

The mother didn't come home for six days. Then she waltzed into the living room with a bag of coffee and ten avocados. There were overturned hedgehogs on the floor. Gina had refused to feed them. If one was lying in the way, you could just walk around it.

She looked like the tiredest mother in the world, Gina's mom, but she wouldn't go to sleep. She began throwing dead hedgehogs into a black plastic garbage sack. After clearing them away, she sat down on the floor to be nice to the survivors.

She peeled the avocados with a knife and spread the slices around all over the place. The newspaper floor turned light green. The mother filled the water dishes. Her hands were shaking. Her whole body was. Her head was pumped up and so were the bags under her eyes. No one in the world could have told what color those eyes were.

One evening Dad didn't come home to our county-owned house at dinnertime. We were having leeks with meat. Mom was looking forward to dinner. She looked forward to dinnertime every day. The food tasted extra good because the leeks were something Dad had gotten at work. A whole sackful of them, and even though some of the ones on the bottom had seen better days, they could easily provide us with dinner for a whole week. We'd been using an incredible amount of toilet paper and I was pretty sure Dad was sitting on a john somewhere.

Mom was only a little nervous. But then it was time for the news on TV. It was full of accidents and the weather forecast promised rain. By the time the news was over, Mom was convinced that Dad way lying at the bottom of a cliff with a broken back.

"Dad's doing some work for that insurance salesman. Do you know him, Karl Gustav?"

I did. The insurance man had lots of money and marble pillars at the foot of his drive. The insurance man had just been holding a garden party with live music. That was pretty incredible, but most incredible were the three taxicabs he'd bought to wait all evening for the guests who managed to make it out to the driveway before they toppled over next to the pond full of goldfish.

"I don't think it would be right, calling," said Mom. "Can't you just pop over to Eleanor and Valdemar and see if he's there?"

It was a waste of time. Dad had only been over at Valdemar's one single time, and that was before their dog got run over. After the traffic accident Dad would only talk to Valdemar down in his own cellar. Then, when Valdemar started crying, Dad could go upstairs and watch television until the worst had passed.

I went through the hole in the hedge. Valdemar was in the kitchen, washing up. He didn't seem different, but he was. Valdemar had been on a trip to the funny farm just after Curly died.

Valdemar was still having a hard time understanding how he could have such bad luck. A couple of months before the accident, he'd discovered why Curly was yapping around the clock. By spending all his days off with the dog, Valdemar noticed that it barked every time a motor vehicle drove by.

So Valdemar figured there was only one thing to do. He had to find a new house to move them all into. Somewhere so deserted that no motor vehicles would be able to find it.

But unfortunately they didn't manage to move before the night Eleanor finally had enough. Curly was barking and Eleanor ran downstairs, past the dog leash that Curly was supposed to always be attached to. Then she opened the door. The dog almost couldn't believe its own eyes, and before Eleanor had a chance to react, Curly charged out the door, yapping, straight in front of the first moving car he could find. The car didn't even have time to brake.

Valdemar had heard the hollow thump and ran in his underpants all the way out to the road. He lay down next to his dog. And he must have still been lying there when Eleanor came knocking on our door in the middle of the night. Asking Dad for help carrying Valdemar back to bed.

Dad didn't like Eleanor. At all. Dad always said Eleanor was the type who paid too much attention to other people's marriages. Not only that, she interfered in them.

For example, she was capable of coming down to our cellar to get Valdemar to come home. This wasn't only a case of interfering in Dad's marriage, it also destroyed the taste of the beer. Dad called her Mean Elly.

Still, Dad got up on the night of the accident. The next day he said a crying garbage man in underpants was one of the worst things there was. And he hoped to God that Valdemar wouldn't get himself another dog.

"Have you seen Dad?" I asked.

"No."

Eleanor came out to the kitchen.

"Have you lost your father?" she asked.

I nodded. Eleanor smiled.

"I'll bet he's sitting in some bar down in Hjørring."

"No, he's not," I said. "Dad would never pay more than a dollar and a quarter for a beer."

"It'd be nice if you knocked first, next time you come over," said Mean Elly, and went back to lie on the sofa.

I took off on my bike. The insurance salesman lived in this new neighborhood where houses shot up from one day to the next. Six people were standing between the marble pillars, wide-eyed. The insurance man was waving his arms and pointing at a bonfire that hadn't been lit yet.

"Here I am," he was going. "I pay all my taxes and I hire a man to do a little handiwork...wanting to help the poor soul...and then suddenly I see...out of the clear blue...he's knocking down the playhouse with his bare fists. Ashley Gwendolyn's playhouse, razed to the ground in no time. Think, if she had been home...if she'd *seen* it...I'd never be able to look her in the eye again."

I nodded to the flock of wide-eyes, not waiting to see if they nodded back. I just kept cycling. Around and around between all the new houses.

It was a long night. Mom paced back and forth in the living room. Monaco was spread out on the table. Mom was cutting and pasting. She'd turned off the food and made one plateful instead. Which was now in the refrigerator, so Dad could eat when he came home.

Morning came. I got up earlier than usual. Mom was going around in a cloud of cigarette smoke. She breathed with a little squeak, as though a mouse had made its nest in her throat. Then Dad came bicycling up the road, doing figure eights.

"There he is," I said.

Mom flew to the door. With me behind her, only not flying. He wasn't going to be looking like the same old dad. Smashing a playhouse with your bare fists makes you look terrible.

But as Dad came up behind the hedge, he didn't look changed. The pipe sat in his mouth like it was supposed to. Maybe he looked a little confused, but that was probably because in the meantime he'd rode his bike right through the hedge, leaving the rolling toolbox stuck in the branches.

Dad reeled straight to the cellar. Mom stood in the doorway, arms flapping.

I ran outside and followed Dad's route; Mom took the cellar stairs. Dad had turned on the radio. He was humming. With the reddest eyes in the world.

Dad popped open a beer and looked at Mom.

"No matter what you say, I forgive you," he stated.

The music vanished and a very serious voice began speaking on the radio. The voice told there'd been an accident. Down in Mom's Monaco. A car had driven off the road. They'd rushed the princess to the hospital, but there was nothing they could do.

Dad stumbled up the stairs. Mom stayed standing where she was. I rode over to Leftover's.

CHAPTER SEVENTEEN

OUTDOORS IT WAS SPRINKLING WITH SNOW and inside the old lady was putting a piece of toffee in her mouth. There were enough to choose from. She had emptied the whole bag and unwrapped all the candies. Now they were lying in one long, straight row on the table. The chocolates were already melting.

The old lady's name was Agnes. She didn't care about her heating bill. The radiators were throbbing in my head. Agnes didn't sweat. She was ready, munching candy, and had just told me about her good-luck stone. It was gray and smooth. She had gotten it from her grandson once, when the whole family had gone camping. Over time, three of Agnes's children had gotten divorced, but the fourth one would soon be celebrating its copper anniversary. This was thanks to the stone, she said, and tonight it was going to bring her luck as well. Agnes was sure of it.

Agnes was going to be playing walkie-talkie bingo for the first time in her life. I was supposed to show her how. But now, sweating away, I was having a hard time understanding why I had to sit with an old lady in the evening when I'd said yes to being a scrap metal dealer's apprentice in the daytime. But Leftover wouldn't budge on the issue. During the day we sold scrap metal and when it got dark we went into the entertainment business.

Leftover was convinced that walkie-talkie bingo would be a gold-mine for both of us. In no time the game would turn into a craze and take Rakkeby by storm.

Leftover had bought a big batch of walkie-talkies from Army Command in Hjørring. Now they had to be distributed among the unfortunates of Rakkeby who sat all alone every evening, dreaming of taking part in some game. It wouldn't cost the unfortunates much.

Agnes had gotten herself a walkie-talkie system—with an antenna, a magnetic pole, playing pieces and five bingo cards—for only $189.95. Tonight's first prize was ten dollars, but that was only because Agnes was playing solo, Leftover said. She was a test case and wouldn't have any objections, especially if we didn't tell her.

Leftover had explained it all to me that afternoon during a strategic planning meeting in his office. Agnes was going to be the test case because she had such an incredibly hard time walking. Every day Agnes made the short trip over to the grocer's or up to the rest home. No matter where she went, it took her four hours each way. Leftover had written this down in his folder with the things that were worth remembering.

Agnes was just as good at stopping and gossiping with folks as she was bad at walking. There was no limit to the number of people Agnes managed to chat with in the course of one trip into town.

If Agnes got herself a full bingo card in the early evening, all Rakkeby would know by the next morning. For ten bucks Leftover had opened up a new, incredible market. Soon all those with difficulty walking, hearing, and seeing would be able to sit at home in the comfort of their living rooms, playing walkie-talkie bingo.

I'd grumbled a little bit about the ten dollars. That I thought it was a crummy first prize and I wouldn't swindle some old lady I didn't even know. Leftover couldn't have agreed less. You didn't send a manned rocket to the moon without first trying it out on some dogs that needed airing anyway.

"Don't you remember Balalaika, the Russian space dog?" he'd said.

Now I looked at Agnes.

"Goodness gracious. My teeth are gone," she muttered.

Agnes took a piece of toffee out of her mouth and held it under the lamp. There was no trace of teeth. She opened her mouth all the way and felt around with her finger.

"They must be up at the rest home," she said.

"Ladies and gentlemen, are we just about ready?" came Leftover's crackling voice through the walkie-talkie.

I pushed a button on Agnes's walkie-talkie.

"Karl Gustav here! Over."

"Yes. And …? Over."

"Agnes says she left her teeth at the rest home. Over."

"She doesn't need her damn teeth to play walkie-talkie bingo! You're her guide dog. Tell her that! Over."

Agnes stuck her nose right up to the walkie-talkie.

"I will not play without teeth," she warbled.

"Karl Gustav here! Over."

"Well? Over."

"She won't play without teeth. Over."

"Then you better find them for her. I'll keep the line open. Over."

Agnes had begun stacking up the little blue bingo pieces. She'd been given exactly seventy-five. It wasn't enough for five full cards, but Leftover had decided she'd only get one prize the first evening. Leftover had written down which numbers she needed. Then he would sit in his office and steer the excitement.

"Can you remember where you left your teeth?" I asked.

"Right next to the piano, I think."

"Okay. I'll be back in a little while."

Outside the snow was falling in big, soft flakes. The air in Rakkeby's empty streets was ice cold, but I kept sweating. Mom and

Agnes knew each other, both from the rest home and church. They sang in the choir. Mom wouldn't be glad when she heard that Agnes had spent $189.95 to win ten bucks.

Something had happened to Mom since the traffic accident in Monaco. She couldn't sleep. She'd walk around at night. And she'd stopped smoking from one day to the next. She looked all wrong. The mouth got smaller; it was missing smoke. And on top of it all, she'd begun calling Grandma up. A lot. Every day, a thousand times a day. That was something Mom hadn't done since Dad was in jail.

Mom began living inside the telephone receiver. It had nothing to do with reporting the latest news, because Mom never had anything to say. She just sat and listened. To Grandma at the other end. Hørmested's end. God's end. And when she said goodbye and hung up, quiet as a mouse, Mom took out the Bible and began reading aloud to herself.

Dad knew what was wrong. And he also had the solution. Mom just needed to start smoking again. One ought never give one's body a shock if one could avoid it.

Dad had even bought a pack of cigarettes to show he meant what he said. Mom didn't like Dad's solution. The cigarettes disappeared without a trace.

The rest home's doors rolled apart. An old lady was sitting on a chair, doing a crossword puzzle. The lady was using a magnifying glass and was curled over like a somersault, frozen in midair.

"Do you know where Agnes's teeth are?" I asked.

The lady shook her hair.

"What about the piano? Where's that?"

The old lady pointed with a long, crooked finger.

"Thank you!"

The piano was standing in a big empty room. Agnes's teeth had fallen onto the floor, under the piano. I got down on my knees. A big gray ball of dust had decided to give Agnes's teeth a kiss, and now they wouldn't let go of each other. I tried blowing them apart. It didn't work. I rolled my sleeves all the way down and without touching them with my fingers, I stuffed Agnes's teeth into my pants pocket.

I came back and knocked on Agnes's door. Nothing happened. I opened the door and brushed the snow out of my hair before I went in.

Agnes was dozing in her chair.

"Agnes, are you awake? It's time to get up and win ten dollars."

Agnes's mouth opened. A piece of toffee rolled out between the lips. That had to mean she was awake.

"Listen, Agnes, would you mind just sticking your hand down in my pocket?"

It was cold as ice in the office. The swallows didn't like coming anymore. They'd headed south. Leftover was sitting like an icicle with a bright red nose. A nose that had been blown a thousand times in the course of the morning. You could tell by the hanky. It was steaming away, covering most of the Pacific Ocean.

On the floor stood a row of thirty unsold walkie-talkie systems. They looked real quiet. Maybe they were never going to say another word. Leftover figured that's how they were going to end up. He said it was a catastrophe and a damn shame. The walkie-talkies were all from a company called Midland. They were the real thing. Leftover said Midland had won the whole Korean War by coming through crystal, golldang clear, and if there hadn't been so damn much jungle in Vietnam, Midland would have won that war, too.

Leftover looked to see what time it was. He had three clocks in his office. None of them had been in the military, but all three were good at marching in step. At the strike of twelve noon, Leftover put a match to his gas burner. He sighed and turned the flame way up.

With a bent saber that had once belonged to Genghis Khan, he cut a fat slice of margarine and scraped it off into the frying pan. The margarine sputtered and hissed, but Leftover never said ow. Leftover had thick skin over his whole body. On the other hand, the lawn of golden hairs that ran up his arm often caught on fire. Then Leftover had to get busy. The overalls couldn't get hurt, no matter what.

Leftover opened the carton of eggs. He picked up six and knocked them out. The eggs came from a farm where the hens could go into a cozy camping trailer and press, nice and easy, without having to rush. Every single egg was born peacefully. Many of them were so glad and thankful, they gave you two yolks for the price of one. Usually when this happened Leftover did a little dance. Today it happened two whole times, but there was no dancing. Instead Leftover poked holes in three of the yolks with the tip of his saber.

"How about a hotdog? Aren't we having any hotdogs today?" I asked.

"If I were you, I wouldn't mention hotdogs. Not ever."

I bowed my head. That morning Leftover had been up at Agnes's with a bouquet of flowers. A brand new one. An hour later he was back, nose running, and with a wallet that was $189.95 lighter. And between his hands—like a little, sick baby—he was bearing walkie-talkie system #31, totally and thoroughly unused. He set system #31 on his desk between the two globes and said I should study it carefully because that's what the worst business deal in the history of the company looked like. It was what happened when you mixed business and pleasure. I should be thoroughly ashamed of myself, he said. Especially the part of myself that was the source of the shame.

Leftover turned off the gas and scraped three fried eggs over onto my plate. He dipped two fingers into the mustard jug and spread a thick layer over the eggs. Leftover never used utensils. Knives and forks spoiled the taste, he said. It was better to eat with your hands, and if you were lucky, maybe there was still some used taste left on the fingers that went with fried eggs and mustard.

Leftover said there was nothing in the world he liked better than touching things. That this was very important if you wanted to be an expert scrap dealer. And that Agnes's teeth were nothing compared to some of the things Leftover had had his hands on in the course of time.

Once, long ago, Leftover had discovered what a great natural resource was lying there, steaming, after a cow had given birth. He started driving from one farm to the next, collecting afterbirths. He hung them out to dry in the open air, and when the flies were done, the idea was that the afterbirths had turned into the finest pillowcases money could buy. Folks would sleep like a dream and feel newborn when they woke up the next morning.

The only reason the experiment didn't work was because the afterbirths ended up being so tough that even a leather sewing machine couldn't get a needle through. Leftover was still sorry about that one, he said. But Agnes's false teeth...? Boy, oh boy, had I ever behaved like a randy bandit.

Leftover shook his head and ate his eggs while he hammered numbers into his electronic adding machine.

"Let's see...if we don't get the walkie-talkies sold, you owe me... bumala-bum-bum... The flowers cost five-fifty...that makes a grand total of...$6,116.50. Sorry about that, Karl Gustav, but it's going to be a hell of a long time before there's any weight in your pay envelope."

I tasted the figures. They were high. So high that money stopped having any meaning. I was thinking more about the stories that were already leaking through the hedges out in Rakkeby. First there was this man who'd destroyed an innocent child's playhouse and the next second sonny boy is being accused of sticking an old lady's hand down his pants. Mom was going to be lucky if they didn't stone her in church on Sunday. And Gina. What if Gina had heard the story?

"I didn't do anything, Leftover. Honest. I just didn't want to touch her false teeth with my hands. If you had to go get my teeth out from under a piano, you wouldn't want to use your hands, either, would you?"

"What about dentists?" yelled Leftover. "They spend all their time doing nothing but poking around in people's gums. What's that make *them*? High-price whores?"

Leftover folded up a batch of fried eggs and tilted back his head. Held between two fingers, three eggs were swallowed at a gulp. I got up and took a sugar-free orange soda without asking.

The saloon rifle was standing there, waiting for me. The sky over Rakkeby was dark. Snow crunched under my feet. We followed the tracks I had made that morning.

Me and the rifle weren't exactly friends, but it was cool it was there.

CHAPTER EIGHTEEN

OUT AT GINA'S THE WATER PIPES GOT LUMPS IN THEIR THROAT and the lumps froze to ice. The water couldn't run anymore. The radiators stopped, too. Down in the living room there were bowls on the floor. They were full of snow, trying to defrost. The hedgehogs couldn't figure out how to drink snow.

It wasn't like Gina's mom hadn't tried to show them, down on her knees, licking up the ice. The hedgehogs watched, but they couldn't get the hang of it. Gina's mom didn't get mad. One by one she lifted the hedgehogs up and thrust them carefully into the icebergs, so at least they got some snow on their snouts. Then the mother blew on the snow until it melted. She said it was incredibly important that they got something to drink.

Gina's mom belonged to a club that did everything it could to help hedgehogs, not only in Rakkeby, but in all of Denmark. The club published a newssheet for its members. It was called "The Hedgehog Herald." Gina's mom sent in hedgehog drawings she'd made herself. It made her incredibly glad when the mailman delivered a newssheet with one of her drawings.

But now the snow had closed the roads. The mailman simply couldn't get through. After Gina's mom had given all the hedgehogs a washing, she went out on the main road to find the mailman.

Me and Gina went up in the attic and did what we usually did.

Way down under the blanket. I was naked; Gina was wearing woolen socks that went all the way up to her pussy and a sweater that reached from her neck to her knees. On her hands she had mittens.

The entire farm was so quiet that I could hear Gina's eyelashes when she blinked. They scraped against the sheet. Gina had long eyelashes that she was proud of. She said they were the best thing about her whole body. They were so fine and big and special that once a butterfly had landed on them. Gina had been lying in the grass, her mind somewhere else, when suddenly her one eye sprouted butterfly wings.

When she blinked, the butterfly took off. Gina must have had a pretty good memory, because it had happened when she was real little.

Gina took good care of her eyelashes. She began each morning by removing sleep from them. Both the corners of her eyes and the lashes. She sat completely still and worked with two fingers. Sometimes she worked so hard, a fingernail hit her eye. This made her look like she'd been crying all night, which she never did. Gina said she couldn't even remember the last time she'd been sorry about anything.

In the attic there was something important for me to do every morning, too. Down at the far, dark, peaked end of the room there was a nice-sized hole in the wall. Some of the stones had decided to fall out. The ones at the bottom. The wall had grown an open mouth, even though Gina found a board to keep it shut.

In the morning it was okay for me to pull the board aside and take a leak in the snow. The way the hot stream curved through the air was incredible, and sometimes, when I'd had enough beer the night before, I could manage to write a whole G in the snow. Then I made Gina come over and take a look. At first, of course, I did it mostly to get her turned on, but she got much more than that. She got to hearing wedding bells, and my G in the snow became an early—but very welcome—morning gift. Gina said the morning gift was essential when two people had just gotten married. And I'd better remember it, too, else she'd divorce me the day after.

Gina had already planned most of it out. The gown was going to be white, with a long veil. On the walk up to the church, the veil was going to drag along the ground and make a sound like a trickling stream.

The church couldn't be in Rakkeby. It had to be further out in the country, somewhere where you couldn't buy schnapps at ten o'clock in the morning. The wedding party was to be held in the woods, just the two of us. On our wedding night, we weren't going to sleep one single second. We'd lie looking up at the stars, and when one of them shot itself down and disappeared into the treetops, we'd make love. For the first time ever. All the rest of the stuff we'd been doing didn't count. It sounded a little sad and wrong, but I loved hearing about our wedding.

There were only a few minor details left to take care of. If we got married while Gina was still a head taller than me, she would have to stand before the priest in bare feet and a hairdo that was incredibly flat. On the other hand, I'd be wearing cowboy boots and hair sticking up.

Husbands that were lower than their wives always ended up seeing UFOs and washing the dishes. Gina had said so herself.

A couple of times a week she checked my hands to see how they'd been coming along over at Leftover's. Gina wasn't satisfied. My hands still weren't rough and worn. I still wasn't tired enough to sleep the whole night without having nightmares. And every time I woke up in the middle of the North Sea, she got the remains of my arm thrashing right in the head. This she was tired of.

"Karl Gustav!"

"Huh?"

"How about going down to Little Horsey and knocking a hole in the ice?"

"Naked?"

"I don't care, as long as you do it."

"Then I will," I said. "Nude!"

In the laundry room there were a pair of pink slippers. They fit fine. Outdoors they got white. The snow came up to my knees. Little Horsey was standing in his stall without shivering. I took the shovel and chopped away at the black tub. Bits of ice sprayed the air. The water broke through and washed up over the thick crusts like a life raft. Little Horsey jumped onboard right away, thirsty as hell. The horse poked its muzzle down among the rocking ice floes and swilled life back into himself. Little Horsey was someone you could figure out. He was actually the only form of life on the whole farm I could help without having to wonder whether I was doing the right thing.

There was the day when I'd tried it with the hedgehogs. They'd needed something to drink, too. I took a quart of milk and poured into all the bowls with a generous hand.

The hedgehogs were really happy. A chorus of sip-slurping singers sang through the room. I waved my arms, realizing how cool the laws of nature could actually be. Somewhere stood a cow, eating grass. Then a woman came along and tugged the milk out of the tits. The milk made its way over to the grocer's and ended up in my hand soon after. Now I was standing in front of a full orchestra, conducting how glad we should be.

Then Gina's mother came out of the bathroom. At the sight of this delightful drinking binge she began to whimper. She got down on all fours and crawled around the floor. Every single bowl got tossed out the window. Not just the milk—the bowl, too.

By the time she was finished, the hedgehogs had begun hissing. They were on my side, no doubt about it. Many of their faces were still dripping milk. They were almost dislocating their tongues, try-ing to catch the last drop.

With weird, rubbery steps, the mother came toward me.

"You must never…" she gasped. "You must never…"

I backed away, into the wall, the mother in pursuit. With her eyes fixed on me, she didn't bother avoiding stepping on the enraged hedgehogs that were scuttling about. Gina came into the room. She spun her mother around and popped her upside the head. The cheek said smack and the mother and a lamp toppled to the floor. Gina took my hand and hauled me up to the attic.

Under the blanket I told her about the milk.

"Mom is right. Hedgehogs can't tolerate milk. They puff up or something. The hedgehog is the stupidest animal on this planet."

"Then shouldn't you go down and say you're sorry?"

"No," said Gina. "Mom was drunk."

Leftover was planning a business trip to Mosbjerg, fourteen miles away. There he had a cousin who also was a scrap dealer and had plenty of irons in the fire. The cousin had gotten himself an idea. He got one every day, said Leftover, but this one actually wasn't so bad.

In the course of the winter the cousin had figured out that dog sleds were going to be the next big craze. There were indications that winters in Denmark were turning arctic, and instead of just letting oneself be buried in snow, one could just as well cash in on the cold.

Leftover had been turning a similar idea over in his own mind. In the newspaper he'd read that Americans had invented a brand-new job. Filthy rich dog owners who couldn't be bothered walking their hounds could hire a complete stranger to do it for them. It was a funny idea, but not in America. America was the land of opportunity. And sooner or later, all that was invented in America came to Rakkeby.

Out by the cousin's there already lived a family from Turkey, and Leftover had heard that Hjørring County was looking for space for an alarmingly huge family from Mongolia. Then it wouldn't be long before Denmark was swarming with Mongoloid children with fathers who didn't know how to make a living. These were the kind of people who God created to take Danish dogs for walks.

The cousin had already built a bucket that could hold twenty dogs at a time. It had wheels, so it was mobile in all kinds of weather. When Leftover got to Mosbjerg, they were going to try it out. The bucket would be filled with twenty mongrels the cousin had been allowed to borrow from a man who lived off selling sick dogs to folks who didn't know better.

The first evening in Mosbjerg, Leftover was supposed to attend a ball with his cousin at the community center. And I was absolutely not supposed to get into my head that it was in order to invite some lady home, no, sir! It was because Leftover loved to dance. He loved it so much, he'd taken off the blue overalls. Now he was dressed in a gray suit with gold tie—all of it brand new, from a dead person's estate. And he'd gotten more gold in the bargain in the form of an old Danish championship cup in jitterbugging.

Leftover sat himself up in his truck with the big crane in back. The prize cup he put in the cupholder next to the steering wheel. This was to get in the mood, he said, wriggling his fine, incredibly polished ballroom shoes.

Fetch me the saloon rifle, will you?" he said.

"You bringing that along?"

"Of course."

"What for?"

"For the dogs. In Greenland it happens all the time…the mutts get their legs caught in something. And if I know my cousin, what he's built is going to be a pile of crap. It's for the dogs' sake. A limping mutt'll give anything in the world to get it over with. Self-respect, my boy, self-respect."

"Then what am *I* gonna shoot with?"

"You're not. Today you're going to sell like you've never sold before. And remember: if you're getting somewhere with a customer, you call me. What's the number?"

I stuck out my hand. Leftover had written the cousin's phone number on the palm of my hand with a gold-plated pen that had belonged to a famous tattoo artist up north. Leftover couldn't remember the tattoo artist's name, but it was important as hell that I remember to call if there was a customer ready to buy for over twenty dollars.

I followed Leftover out to the road, just to enjoy the sight. Leftover tried to play a tune on his squeeze-bulb horn. I looked at the thousand skid marks on the main road, just before and just after Leftover's side road. The black stripes had been made by cars that didn't know Leftover never looked when he was backing up his truck. Once a person on a moped buzzed straight into the crane truck's belly. The driver got a cracked-open skull. Leftover got nothing more than a little dent.

In the end it was Leftover who got compensation. Folks said this was because Leftover had run back to his house after a bottle of liquor and emptied all of it down the throat of the man with the broken skull. When the moped driver woke up in the hospital, he was one of the worst drunk driving cases ever recorded in the county.

Up in the office I tossed my cap onto a globe, took over the boss's chair, banged both legs up on the desk, and called Gina. The phone was answered immediately.

"You stay away from here, Harry! You hear me?"

It was the mother's voice. She didn't sound glad. Then the line went dead. I tried again, but there was no answer. Who was Harry?

Probably some man from the phone company. Gina's mom was always getting visits from all kinds of companies that said she owed them money. Even the grocer from Rakkeby had been out there one day. He refused to leave before he got something that was worth just as much as the money she owed him. But in the end the grocer couldn't find anything he wanted.

I tried calling Tim. He was in school. Finally I called up Mom.

"Mom, I'm here at the office. What are we having for dinner?"

"We're having meat rissole."

"Fine. I'll try to be home by dinnertime. It depends a little on a lot of things."

I hung up. Blew dust off the desk. I turned the globes around until they were in the right position. I put Africa in place. Australia, too. Then I took a well-deserved break with a sugar-free orange soda.

The world stood still. I looked at the telephone. Asked it to ring. If only I could sell a generator, just like that. I grabbed Genghis Khan's saber and slashed the air.

By now Leftover was rumbling around in Mosbjerg's forests. Living the life. Maybe the only reason he'd hired me was so he could get away once in a while.

For a hundred years Leftover had sat in his office, knocking eggs out into the frying pan. And when the sun went down, he'd lock the front gate and shuffle over to the world's smallest house that contained nothing more than a little john, a little kitchen, and a little living room with a sofa that could turn into a bed.

In the days when Leftover's mom was alive, the house had been twice as big. Leftover said he had lost his way when she died. I was sure this was true because his nose always started crying when he mentioned his mother.

Elvira died of a blood clot in the brain. After that the house was much too big, which Leftover didn't like. Little by little he removed

Elvira's bedroom and laundry and bathroom with its giant tub on lion's paws. Leftover said he was the only man in Rakkeby who'd built his house smaller. He carried all the surplus bricks the few yards over to the beginnings of his great empire. It may well be his mother was dead and his childhood home halved, but Elvira could still help her son with his junk business.

The bathtub on lion's paws guarded the entrance to the container area. In the bottom of the tub stood a plant. It was a palm; it had to be a palm. Elvira had always dreamt of a trip to a warm land. Anywhere in the world, just so long as there was a palm tree she could sit and crochet under. Leftover said it was the saddest thing that had ever happened, that he never got his mother flown to a country with palm trees. Elvira didn't ever make it further than a nursery in Sønder Harritslev, and even though the nursery had plants as far as the eye could see, it wasn't good enough. That was something mother and son both agreed on as they drove home in the crane truck with a little baby palm riding on the seat between them.

Now the palm had grown up. It came almost to the top of the bathtub. In a few years it would be able to look out over the edge. It was all thanks to Elvira. Every time it rained, Leftover rolled his eyes heavenward and thanked his mom. The rain wasn't provided by Our Lord, it came from Elvira because she knew how her son always forgot to water the palm.

"Hello …?" came a voice from somewhere out in the empire.

I flew out of my seat and over to the ladder. In the car radio department stood a man I'd never seen. He was wearing a fancy hat. I leapt down the ladder and led him out into the light so I could better judge how rich he was.

"And what is the gentleman looking for today?" I began.

"Where's Leftover?"

"He's in Mosbjerg to shoot dogs and dance the jitterbug."

The man nodded and picked his nose.

"And you are…?"

"I'm the assistant president. What does the gentleman wish?"

"When's Leftover get back?"

"Not before tomorrow.

The man had a full beard and green rubber boots. I was disappointed, but didn't show it. Rich folks never wore rubber boots; they had people for that.

"What the hell do you want, then?"

The man answered by pointing at a tractor lawnmower we'd just gotten in.

"How much you asking for that?"

I assessed the lovely machine. Leftover had driven it all the way home from Tornby, up over a mountain that was a whole 272 feet above sea level. Leftover said it had coughed a little just before the summit, but the rest of the way the tractor had tried to swerve over every sprig of grass it could get its blades on.

"Four bucks with tax," I said.

This gave the man a start. His fingers bristled. The nails were black. The man was probably a poor gardener, ready to be taken up the butt. The man heaved a wallet out of his back pocket. A damn thick one. Like a Bible. He opened the wallet and suddenly I was staring at the Garden of Eden. I made a gasping noise. If the man held the wallet up in the air, all the money that had ever been lost by other people would begin crawling through the mud and weeds in hopes of coming home. Home to the Garden of Eden, home in the back pocket of a man who had suddenly stopped being a gardener.

The man handed me four bucks and fished a little card out of another compartment in his wallet. He laid the card on the tractor seat. I really wanted to see what it said on the card, but the man quickly moved on, pointing at things. Scooters, toilets, off-road motorcycles, shower cabins and bicycles—all things I'd hauled out that morning to show the customers that never came. And now, suddenly, like magic, I was doing some serious wheeling and dealing.

I remembered a little bit about something to do with calling Leftover, but I knew my boss would never forgive me if I told the man I needed to hold a telephone meeting right in the middle of everything. So I walked along, throwing incredible prices around. The man took the hook every single time. With no haggling. I collected the dollar bills in my clenched fist, and the man kept on sprinkling his little cards around. The cards were professional, I had to give him that. They were sticky on the bottom so the wind couldn't blow any deals away.

When we reached the end of the empire, the man turned and looked at me.

"Why don't I just buy it all? Lock, stock, and barrel. What do you want for this whole dump?"

Strange spots started dancing before my eyes—small golden ones—but I had my answer ready. An amount was already balanced on the tip of my tongue. It had been ready for a long time. Now it finally jumped off.

"$6,116.50."

The amount almost knocked the man over. I could see I had the upper hand, so I said, pointing, "And that's not including the bathtub over there. It's Elvira's palm grove. And you can't touch the office upstairs, either. Just the walkie-talkies. You can have them as part of the bargain, but not a golldang thing more."

The man rubbed his mouth nervously. Then, taking big, rubberboot steps, he walked to his car, which I hadn't really noticed yet. It turned out not to be just a car; it was a crane truck, and it looked pretty new. The man came back with a stack of papers, full of long, complicated sentences, but down at the bottom there was just a line. Here the man wanted my autograph. He also handed me a ballpoint

pen, but that wasn't for him to decide. I left him standing there, confused, while I sprinted across the empire, up the ladder, and over to
Leftover's desk where the famous tattoo artist's gold-plated pen lay in
waiting. Now its time had definitely come.

Down on one knee, with the contract lying on the grass, I wrote
my name better than I'd ever done before. Then I revealed the golden
pen's secret. It had a lady inside. When I turned her upside-down, the
lady lost her clothes. The man didn't seem impressed.

In the afternoon I watched people work. The man knew lots of
other men with crane trucks and the empire was shrinking incredibly
fast. Just to try something new, I sat in a nice folding chair and ate
fried eggs. I'd just bought the folding chair back from the man. For
$5.75.

When the sun was finally about to set, I was left sitting alone
with Elvira's palm grove. Where the containers had been standing
were now brown squares of ground. The crane trucks had hoisted
the containers up like Lego blocks. By tomorrow the brown squares
would begin turning green. Every single liberated sprout of grass
would be thanking me for the fresh air.

I cycled out to Gina with the folding chair over my shoulder and a
fortune in my pocket. We were going to go to bed together. Tonight
there could be nothing to hold her back. Gina would open herself
like a smiling car ferry and let me sail her around the world.

Little Horsey was standing on the grass like he was supposed to.
He blinked at me and said life was good. Little Horsey loved springtime. Me and Gina had been celebrating the day he got turned out to
grass. Gina had spread out a blanket and served coffee with aquavit
and butterscotch candies. This was something she did every year, she
said, but I was the first man who'd been allowed to come along.

The sun shined down over us. The wind was still. Everything was so beautiful and quiet that I came to tell Gina the story about Agnes and the walkie-talkie bingo. Gina was good at listening. She understood everything. She laughed so hard, she got a bellyache and the mother came to the doorway. Gina howled that I should tell the story again; Mom had to hear it, too. And suddenly we were out on the grass, all four of us, laughing. Little Horsey ground his teeth and snorted with delight, and Gina took off her blouse and lay topless, getting red. Then she ran inside, fetched ten dollars and—incredibly enough—said the mother could bicycle to the grocery store and pick up lots of cake and avocados. Gina didn't say a word about killing her if she came home drunk.

When Gina's mom was gone, I got to kiss Gina's nipples. They didn't taste nearly as good as I was expecting, and Gina didn't like it much, either. But I got to. Gina'd rather give me a hand. This time the hand was good, better than ever. I could open my eyes and see what she looked like after. There was no blowing out candles. We were lying in the greatest light there was. Gina's face was completely naked. Dark and pretty. And when the mother came back a little later without at all having stayed away for days, Gina went and got a knife and cut the cake. What a day.

Now I biked over to our hole in the peaked wall to see if Gina was watching the sunset. She wasn't in the hole. The hole was covered by the board. I jumped off my bike and unfolded the chair. There was an old car parked in the yard. It was black and the front wheels had stopped in the middle of a turn, as though the driver had been considering driving straight through the house. It made me smile. It had to be a man, come to rake in some debt. That was fine by me. I took my bundle of cash in my hand and got ready to do some business for Gina's mom.

The farm was quiet. In the living room the hedgehogs crawled slowly around on the newspapers with their eyes pointing down, as though they'd taught themselves to read. I made my way to the attic. It was empty and dark. I took away the board. The sun had painted the treetops red. Faintly I could hear the festivities starting up over at the community center. It wouldn't be long before the hedge where we met would begin sailing through the night. Maybe Gina'd gone over there. Maybe someone had already told her what had happened. That today her man had beautified Rakkeby. That he'd turned junk-filled containers into a park. This would make Gina proud. She'd want to mark the occasion.

I jumped back down from the attic and was on my way out the door when I saw the mother's feet in the kitchen. With the pink slippers lying in front. I stuck my head in the door. Gina's mom was sleeping. It looked like she'd had a nosebleed.

I heard a weird jarring sound. And splashing. I stepped over the mother. The sound was coming from the bathroom. More jarring, more splashing. And a voice.

I bent over and looked through the keyhole. I couldn't see Gina. I could see a man. He was old. With a fat moustache. Sitting with his hands clasped behind his head, saying nothing. I could see his one foot. It was raised up high. It had soapsuds on it.

The water was warm. Steaming. The voice was coming from Gina's mouth. She was telling a story. I couldn't make out the words. But she sounded exactly like herself.

The man's big toe was pointing right at me. The big toe smiled. It said I ought to run along.

CHAPTER NINETEEN

DAD WAS BICYCLING out in the middle of the main road like he was a car. Every single vehicle that passed him honked its horn. Dad never wavered. He waved at the pissed-off motorists.

One of the wheels on Dad's rolling toolbox had gone crooked. Every three feet, the wheel left the asphalt. It looked like the whole toolbox was about to turn over on its side.

At a grocery store Dad stopped to do some shopping. He came back with ten cold beers, a coke, a pack of Lucky Strikes, and a box of matches.

He handed me the cigarettes and the matchbox.

"Start smoking," he said.

We bicycled on. I had a hard time keeping up. The cigarette pack gnawed at my nipple. It seemed like Dad thought I was getting just like Mom. He didn't want me going to the doctor. It was better that I try his medicine. Dad figured it wouldn't be long before I started walking around at night. It would be good for me—and Mom, too—if we took some walks together. Then we could go around and smoke and not be able to sleep. And think about all the people who were dying like flies all around us.

We were on our way to God's Hørmested. I hadn't been out there since Alexander drowned. I couldn't even remember if I'd seen Grandma since. Grandma wasn't a person you saw. She lived only in the telephone, together with Mom. They shared thoughts about God. Grandma always had the most thoughts. Now she was dead.

As we swung into the winding gravel road, Dad slowed down. The farmhouse was gone. Charred bricks lay spread around in little hills. The fire trucks had left. Only the wide tire tracks in the slippery earth told of sirens and firemen.

The grass around the little black hills looked like burnt confetti. The flames had eaten themselves all the way to the dung heap. Here the fire had stopped. The flies were still soaring around, confused. Arguing in the air.

Dad parked his bike up against the old pear tree. I could remember that tree; I'd sat in it myself. It was a tree for moping in.

"Jesus H. Christ," said Dad, and cracked open a beer. Silently he walked around the destruction. I climbed up in the tree. The leaves were black and bone dry. But the leaves on the branches farthest from the fire were still green and juicy. The pear tree was confused, too.

Dad yanked charcoal boards out of the ashes and made a pile.

"They're still damn warm, but they'll do just fine. I'll build us a bench."

I thought I'd heard wrong, but Dad took his saw out of the rolling toolbox. He started cutting up the warped, black boards. The most charred stumps he threw back where they came from.

I leaned against the trunk, opened Dad's cigarette pack, and struck a match. The noise was loud. I blew the flame out fast. I got clammy all over. I remembered when Grandma hadn't been able to take any more. Remembered when she'd gotten up in the middle of eating, grabbed the phone, and said they could come and get me. I'd just told Grandma a story. A story she hadn't liked.

She'd stood by the window and said they could come and get me. I'd really wanted to know who "they" were. It could be a thousand different people. It could be the police, to haul me off to jail. It could be the priest in Hirtshals, who wanted me to come back and wash the floor after Alexander's funeral.

"They" turned out being mostly Dad. Grandma stayed standing in the doorway. Not a word was spoken. I went and sat in the car next to Dad. I wanted to hang onto Dad's neck all the way to Hirtshals, if that's where we were headed. I put on my seatbelt, locked myself to the car.

Now the man who came and got me then was going around humming, with nails in his mouth and a hammer in his hand. He was building a bench. It was the only thing to do, he felt. Grandma's death wasn't that big a deal. We bicycled out to it; we looked at it. We could stand it.

I remembered how Grandma used to arrange my hands properly for all the prayers and I remembered her nickname for God. It was Jehovah. Jehovah sat up in heaven, doing magic tricks. Soon he would send a sea of flames down to Earth, she'd said, to destroy all those who lived wrong and prayed too little. Those who'd done things right, he would spare. They'd be lifted up in his cupped hands and turned into happy souls forever.

Grandma must have been sitting in her bed when the fire took hold, the hungry flames coming closer and closer. She'd kept waiting for the mighty Jehovah to swerve around her. Grandma prayed away. When the fire started chewing the corner of her sheet, she would have liked to put out the flames with one of her folded hands. But prayers couldn't be interrupted.

Then the beams began raining down on Grandma's head. This seemed strange, but it was probably just Jehovah, building a beautiful bridge for her, high above hell. Grandma smiled and stuck out a forefinger so she'd be ready to point down at all those who wouldn't get to join her.

Then the flames began eating their way toward the feather-stuffed comforter. That was okay; it was just Jehovah, whispering.

Grandma leaned toward the voice and the flames. She squinted her eyes and silently scolded her legs for refusing to obey. It felt like the room was spinning around.

The flames grabbed the sleeves of her nightgown. It hurt. This was something no one had ever told her about. Her clothing burned away in no time. The hairs on her arms simmered and stank. She began flapping her arms. Perhaps Jehovah would make her into a bird. Yes. Grandma kept on flapping and flapping, but the bed only squeaked. Grandma never took off. She just sat in her bed and died.

When me and Dad got back to Rakkeby, Mom was sitting in the living room with the TV turned up so loud, it had actually moved. Closer to Mom. There were tracks in the rug. Mom had sucked the television right up to her.

Dad's whole head was filthy. So were his hands. All that working on the bench had changed him into a black bastard. Dad rubbed off on everything he touched. Mom looked at the dark spots he left on the white coffee cup. She switched off the TV and put both hands in front of her mouth. Now she was ready for the bad stuff.

Dad launched into a description of what had been seen in Hørmested. He said all was peace and quiet as usual. It hadn't been as awful as he'd expected. And it had happened fast—that's for sure. The flames weren't choosy and Grandma hadn't felt a thing.

Mom nodded; she kept nodding. Dad nodded, too, but only three quick ones in a row. Then he turned on the TV. A smiling lady was standing in a kitchen.

Mom pointed at the screen. At the smiling lady who was slicing tomatoes.

"It's Betty," said Mom. "She always makes such exciting food."

Dad's stomach started to rumble. It was way past dinnertime.

We couldn't hear any food sputtering or bubbling. We'd bicycled for hours. Dad went out to the kitchen. He came back quickly, empty-handed, and sat down on the edge of his seat, where he never sat. With his hands between his legs.

"Wow, that was quite a trip," he said.

"Look at this," said Mom. "Betty's going to make shellfish salad. Just like the time our own Anne Marie was to get her King Constantine. The prince and Grace were also supposed to attend. They were the guests of honor and were going to sit at the same table as Anne Marie and Constantine. The night before the wedding Grace happened to eat a portion of shellfish at the finest hotel in town. The shellfish had gone bad. Terribly bad. Grace was in bed with a bellyache all week. She missed the entire affair. She didn't even come out on the balcony so we could see her. But Queen Sirikit of Thailand, she came, feeling fit, even though they have such strange eating habits down there. She was wearing a snow-white gown with diamonds sewed on. I know exactly what Grace was thinking, the time she had the accident. She was thinking about that wedding in Athens. She was sitting there, kicking herself black and blue for having eaten shellfish. Then she just drove off the road."

Mom looked at Dad, confused. Dad didn't look confused, just tired. He got up slow. So did I. We went out to the kitchen. The kitchen wasn't big enough for both of us. We kept bumping into each other. I wasn't hungry anyway.

Dad heaved such a heavy sigh, the salt flew out of its bowl and sprinkled itself all over the kitchen counter like snow.

Next morning Mom made some terrible soft-boiled eggs. The eggs were runny and transparent. They slid off Dad's spoon like tiny, smooth jellyfish and onto the tablecloth. To no purpose whatsoever.

Luckily Mom didn't see it. She was washing the floor somewhere. We could hear the wet rag mopping.

Dad poured the liquid eggs out the window and placed the empty shells back in their eggcups. Then we sat awhile. Dad scratched his beard. He was probably wishing he had a good job to go and do, but Dad didn't have much work anymore. After the destruction of the playhouse, folks had quit calling.

In a way, me and Dad had become equally unemployed. Except for, in my case, Leftover had let me know he'd put a bullet in my head if I ever got near him again, even though I'd handed him all the money back, minus the folding chair.

Mom came in with the floor bucket. Dad got up.

"Well, I better get going. Ride up there and clean things up. I guess it's my responsibility, dammit."

Dad was on his way out. Then he stopped.

"What about you, kid? You coming?"

I followed in Dad's tire tracks. I didn't care where we went. Dad cycled out in the middle of the road again, the morning traffic honking in our backs. We bicycled for a long time until finally we were back in God's Hørmested. Standing before the little charred hills and the new bench.

Dad sat down and opened a beer. He looked out over the field, pipe moving from one corner of his mouth to the other. Flies burned themselves on his forehead. I went around poking a stick in the rubble.

A little after noon an old green car came chugging down the twisty gravel road. I recognized it right away. It was Grandma's Chevy. Chevy stopped in front of the bricks. The window was rolled down. Out came a hand with fat, dirty fingers. The hand fumbled after the door handle.

"I swear to you…she wouldn't let me fix the door, only the muffler…by all that is holy."

A little man finally got out of the car. With a blue cap and clothes that were nice and dirty.

"Oh-oh-oh-oh-oh," said the man, gazing out over the little black mountains.

Dad fished a beer out of the rolling toolbox and went over to the man.

"Here you go!"

The man looked at the beer like it was something totally incredible.

"What in tarnation?" he muttered. "Could it be, you aren't even members of the family of…?"

The man stopped.

"The holy terror," finished Dad.

The man squinted hard at Dad, as if he were trying to squeeze the truth out of him. Then the little man slapped his thigh, threw back his head, and laughed so much, his cap fell to the ground.

The man said he was the only mechanic in Hørmested. He'd had Chevy in his garage. Grandma had complained about how it sounded. It reminded her of a whole motorcycle gang on the march.

"It's sure enough a shame, all this, but one thing's for certain: the Chevy is now the lucky owner of a new muffler."

Dad liked the mechanic. Conversation was easy and beer number two quickly saw the light of day. The mechanic stood up and plucked a pink slip of paper out of his breast pocket. Taking his time, he tore the paper into a thousand strips and offered them into the Hørmested wind in a kind of ritual.

"There's no damn way I'm going to take money from a phantom motorist," he shouted.

Already the same day me and Dad were cruising from Hørmested to a garbage dump in the middle of nowhere. Dad and the mechanic had welded Chevy in its ass, rolling dice while it cooled off. Now Chevy was humming along the country road with a trailer bumbling along behind, exhaling a dark cloud of ash from the burnt boards and soot from the brick rubble.

The mechanic had told us we were doing both him and the rest of the population of Hørmested a great favor by cleaning up the mess ourselves. He knew plenty of folks who would immediately hire a bulldozer and a flatbed truck. The mechanic had no time for those kinds of people, and besides, vehicles like that were too high to fit in his garage. We were doing the only right thing, and if the car broke down, he'd gladly come and patch it together again. And bring a few beers.

"Take the wheel for a second!" said Dad.

I grabbed the steering wheel. Dad wanted to fill his pipe. We drove over a bump in the road. The beer between Dad's legs splashed.

"Oops, dammit."

Dad finished packing his pipe and took a quick gulp. He set the beer back between his legs and took the wheel with one hand while he coaxed a match out of the matchbox with the other. Using only two fingers, he struck the match, then ducked his head so the flame could find the fresh tobacco.

When we reached the dump, we both had to roll our windows down to stick our hands out and open up from outside. That's how the front doors liked to work. The back doors wouldn't open at all. Chevy had grown old.

We got out. The garbage dump looked like the world's biggest scarecrow, but it didn't scare off a huge fleet of seagulls that were screaming to high heaven.

"Look up there," said Dad, pointing. "It's a king seagull. They're rare as hell. This calls for a beer."

I watched for a long time. All the gulls looked exactly the same. Dad went back and sat in the car, legs sticking out. I took Dad's shovel.

"Shall I just shovel this shit off the trailer?" I said.

"No, son, the bricks need to have a look around first and decide if the dump's good enough. If not, we drive them back again."

I put down the shovel and kept looking at the seagulls. Then I heard Dad laughing in long bellows.

"For Christ's sake, kid, of *course* you should dump the shit."

I took the shovel and banged it into the rubble. I hit the hardest brick of them all. The shovel bounced back, and me with it. I was shaking; I was getting mad. I took a new stab at the hill.

"I think it would help a lot if you got the shovel in *under* the bricks, instead of attacking from above," said Dad.

Then Dad started laughing again. I chopped straight down with the shovel so I would be sure not to get anywhere. The trailer load could take forever, for all I cared. I wasn't in a rush. I was standing out in the middle of nowhere, feeding Grandma's leftovers to the rats. Sweat ran into my eyes. The wind blew dust and ashes straight down my throat. I chopped and chopped, couldn't see a thing. I went by sounds: bricks hitting the ground, rubble hitting Chevy, rocks I wouldn't mind having hit Dad in the mouth and make him shut up about the right way to use a shovel.

The skin on my hands began to get tight. Blisters were born and managed to deal a couple of blows before they popped, just like that, my hands spraying everywhere.

When the trailer was finally empty and all scratched up, Dad stepped out of the car and swept the rubble off Chevy's roof.

"This isn't just for fun, you know," he said. "This is a burial ceremony. It's taking a long time—an incredibly long time—but, goddammit, this is the closest we'll ever come to burying your grandmother. You get it?"

CHAPTER TWENTY

DAD SAT ON THE BENCH. I was lying on the ground, chewing on a blade of grass. We'd been hauling loads for a few days. Twelve loads so far, and you still couldn't see we'd gotten anywhere.

Each morning, as Dad was pouring Mom's runny eggs out the window, I thought he was going to say enough is enough, and that now we'd done our duty. But no. He told Mom it was going great out in Hørmested. The place would wind up looking beautiful.

Mom hadn't said anything when we came home with Chevy. The car frightened her. Dad had had to tell the story about the mechanic again and again. He made a big deal out of the bill that had been torn to shreds. It didn't make the black circles under Mom's eyes go away, but the next morning she made lunches for us.

"Well, I guess it's lunchtime," said Dad, sticking his hand down in the earth's icebox.

Dad had built a fridge right next to the bench. A hole in the ground. Two shovelfuls down.

Dad spread Mom's chow out on the bench. Three with the works, with salami. Dad lifted a slice of salami and rotated it like a rare coin.

"What're you doing?" I asked.

"Checking the thickness."

Dad raised the slice of rye bread to his nose and sniffed.

"What're you doing now?

"Smelling to see if there's butter. I do believe she's given us a taste. How about checking yours?"

Dad handed me my lunch.

"I'm not hungry."

Dad shook his head and started eating. Two men appeared above the hilltop. The men were old and dressed warmly. They had two black cows in tow.

When they reached Dad, they let the ropes fall. The cows stopped on the spot, as if the men had turned them off.

"Looks tasty," said one of the men, nodding at the food.

Dad stood up, went over to one of the cows, and patted it on the forehead.

"So, you all are out taking a little stroll, eh?" Dad asked the cow.

The men said nothing; they looked around, especially at Dad's bench. Dad raised a beer from the hole in the ground.

"No, thanks, we only drink in the a.m.," said the smaller man.

"A little stiff one to get the day rolling," said the bigger one.

"Hallelujah," said Dad.

Now the earth's icebox had caught the men's attention.

"That's the good thing about Denmark," said Dad. "Doesn't matter where you dig. The ground's always 45 degrees Fahrenheit if you go two shovelfuls down. Beer won't have it any other way. But men of the soil like yourselves know all this."

The men looked at each other.

"Well, we better get going," one said. They turned around to go. The cows they let stay.

"Hey, didn't you forget something?" said Dad.

The bigger of the two men turned his head.

"The mechanic called yesterday and said you were the son-in-law. Right?"

Dad nodded.

"Then you just inherited two cows."

The men plodded off and disappeared back over the hilltop like they'd never been there. I stood up. The cows had already made themselves at home. They were munching grass.

I lay my hand carefully on the back of one. Could it really be them? Could they really be Grandma's holy Christian cows? I put my ear down to the cow's mouth. It sounded right.

"Take a look at this, Dad!"

I kneeled down and lay on my back. I closed my eyes, then scrambled my way in under the bigger cow's belly.

"What the hell you doing, kid?"

I opened my eyes. The cow and I were navel to navel. Above my face was blue sky. The cow's black skin was wet with sweat. Its muscles jutted like rocks. The cow didn't move; it stood stock still, like only a moment had passed since last time. The tail was slinging flies away. That was all.

"Now stop that fooling around."

Dad took my arm and pulled me out and way back. Then Dad walked to the hilltop.

"Wait'll your mother hears this," he shouted. "First the Chevy. Then two real-life cows. Correct me if I'm wrong, but I believe it won't be long before there's butter on the table. And the snoring. Goddammit, I believe your mother will sleep tonight."

Dad sat with his nose right up against the windshield. Outside it was pouring down and the wipers were broke. We sailed along toward the garbage dump with load number seventy-six.

"There's one thing you have to remember when you get a driver's license: never honk when it's raining. Motorists like to fall asleep when it rains. Then there's a good chance your honk will cause sleepyhead to wake up and make a stupid swerve right into your lane. But in any other kind of weather you can honk to your heart's content. Remember that!"

I nodded. Dad started humming with his pipe drifting back and forth from one corner of his mouth to the other.

"Shall we see if there's anything good on the airwaves?" said Dad.

He turned on the car radio, skipped quickly over talking and singing. He was searching for an accordion. He did this every day.

"It's damn incredible, actually. Radio Denmark has its own, whole symphony orchestra. Over a hundred musicians, ready and waiting for instructions from the director general. And every single time, it's the violins he asks to get cracking. Unbelievable."

"Are you sure they've got accordions in a symphony orchestra?"

"Jesus. What a dumb question. They've got every instrument in the whole, wide world. It's Radio Denmark's duty. Hell, they even have an Australian diggetydoo and a tuba."

Dad turned off the radio and knocked out his pipe against the dashboard. I lit a cigarette. Chevy didn't have any ashtrays. We used the floor. Dad said we could always ask Mom to vacuum when she was feeling better.

The survival of the cows hadn't been as good news as Dad was counting on. Mom was glad to hear they still existed, but she was even gladder to hear that the two old men still did, too. They were brothers and Mom had gone and gotten eggs from their place when she was a kid. The brothers were as good as the day was long, she said. In wintertime the brothers drove out in their field and scraped the ice off the ground. It was for the pheasants' sake; they deserved having some earth to peck around in. This Mom remembered very clearly. But the cows we had absolutely no space for in the freezer. In our county-owned house there was only room for four pounds of ground meat at a time. If Mom wanted to make more room, she'd have to take out a lot of rye breads that would go moldy before they got eaten. This she preferred to avoid, she said.

Later that evening Dad drank himself drunk in the cellar. Next morning we walked all the way up the hill, down the other side, and across the field, each of us leading a cow. The cows were chiming because I'd hung little iron bells around their necks that I'd found in the rubble. Seeing the bells had made me glad. They'd gotten totally black, but just as soon as I'd given them a spit bath, they looked like their old selves. Once they'd been on Grandma's footstool, one on each end. I used the footstool when Grandma was sleeping. Then I rode out across the prairie on Buffalo's back. And if I rode hard enough, I could make the bells ring without touching them. It was a good sound and now it was going to live on, around the necks of the resurrected cows.

The earth was soft and my shoes kept coming off. I'd used the laces to hang the bells from. Dad shook his head. He thought it was all one damn mess, and it didn't make things any better when the brothers told him Grandma's livestock were much too old in the flesh. If you threw them on the frying pan, their meat would be so tough, it would have to go through a reaper before you could get it down. But the brothers wouldn't mind buying the cows, they said, and let them be at pasture until they pitched over peacefully from old age. Dad could have a hundred bucks, here and now. And so it was. Dad didn't say thanks, but the cows were glad. They didn't like the idea of living on a rope by Dad's bench.

We reached the garbage dump. Dad opened the car door, popped open a beer, and sat with his feet out. Dad was never in a hurry. My hands were itching to get started. The shovel was fitting better and better. I could empty a load in no time.

I was sure the shovel had taken part in building Hirtshals more beautiful in the old days. Maybe I'd even tried holding it myself. I wasn't tall enough then, but now I could stand in a garbage dump in the middle of nowhere and feel how the shovel turned into a piece of furniture—a sofa, a hammock—for all good workers who deserved a rest. It was nice, standing totally still with sweat or rain dripping off my nose tip, and seeing Grandma's sad remains grow smaller and the dump bigger. Then the seagulls would float above me with lumps in their throat, ready to hit the brakes for fear of me building a mountain that reached the sky. Which might well happen. We weren't even close to being done. And maybe other farmhouses would manage to burn down. The region around Hørmested was full of firetrap farms, just waiting for a knocked-over candle.

When the trailer was empty we drove back after load number seventy-seven.

Dad and the mechanic were throwing dice. Outside the window a pink pig was going around among all the sick cars that were waiting to be fixed. It looked like the pig was considering buying a Ford Taurus. I would rather buy the old boat that was standing out there. It was named after the mechanic's wife. *Gertrude.* The name was painted with big black, tarred letters.

Inside the mechanic's office fishing poles hung all over the place. There were also a lot of pictures of the mechanic holding fish that were always bigger than he was. They'd been caught over along America's coast. The mechanic was always trying to tell Dad about his voyages and his catches, but Dad preferred to just roll dice.

"Four threes," said Dad.

"Four fours," said the mechanic, and raised his hand so we could see where he was missing a forefinger. Once the mechanic had dropped a car on it. The jack slipped and it was ow-ow-ow-ow-ow. The mechanic's finger hadn't been good for much when he got it free from under the car, so he'd told the doctor to clip it off quick. The mechanic had rolled a ton of fours ever since.

"No way," said Dad, lifting his leather dice cup.

The mechanic jumped up backwards out of his easy chair and waved his cup.

"I've got them all myself!"

Dad couldn't believe it. He stuck his nose right down to the table. Dad wasn't nearsighted, but there was so much oil on the dice that it was hard to see what they said. They said four fours.

Dad nodded and folded a beer cap in half between two fingers.

"Your finger sure as hell went to a damn good cause. What kind of car was it that gave you a squeeze?"

"An Audi 100," screamed the mechanic.

Every time Dad lost, they had to go through what happened to the mechanic's finger and the car. Each time was exactly the same, but they howled with laughter anyway. Then there was a knock at the door.

"Just a minute!" shouted the mechanic, and sped over to his calendar where a naked lady with big breasts said we were somewhere in September. The mechanic turned the calendar around. On the other side was a photograph of a gray-haired lady. She had clothes on because it was the mechanic's wife.

"Come in."

The door opened and Gertrude said a farmer had gotten himself hopelessly stuck in a stubble field by the church.

"That's fine," said the mechanic.

"Our meeting here's just about finished anyway," said Dad.

"My words exactly," said the mechanic.

We got into Chevy and headed for Rakkeby. The windshield wipers still weren't working. That was supposed to have been the reason why it was so vitally important we stop in at the mechanic's. But now it wasn't raining anymore, and Dad could tell from his right elbow that the next two weeks would be sunny and cloudless. Every time Dad had been throwing dice with the mechanic, he could tell what the weather was going to be.

Dad started whistling with the pipe all the way in one corner of his mouth.

"I'm the only one who can smoke a pipe and whistle at the same time. Did you know that?"

I acted like I hadn't heard him. I stared out the window. Me and the shovel weren't satisfied. There hadn't been enough loads today. Then Dad decided to start telling about a man. His name was Roger and he could imitate the voices of all birds. Once Dad and Mom had been to a concert with Roger. Dad could remember it like it'd happened yesterday. Roger's best song was a titmouse. Afterward Dad had found Roger in his dressing room. Finding him was easy because Dad had built the concert hall himself. Roger was sitting smoking a pipe. Roger had asked Dad if he wouldn't like a little stiff one and a pipe, in peace and quiet. To this Dad had said no, thanks, even though it hadn't been easy. Mom didn't like being alone in a town as big as Aalborg, and one mustn't ever park a wife somewhere she didn't like to be. Then it was better never to invite her.

My ears heard everything. It was always like that, even when I didn't want them to. Dad couldn't make the tiniest sound without my hearing it.

We drove through Sindal. A mother was holding her little girl by the hand. Dad put on the brakes and waved them gently across the road. He used the pause to open a beer.

"Why'd you total that playhouse in Rakkeby?" I asked.

"Which playhouse?"

"Have you destroyed other ones, besides the insurance man's?"

Dad pulled off to the side of the road and went out to piss. He didn't have the wind with him. Dad turned around and pissed right in front of a man who was walking his dog. The man stopped a couple of feet from Dad. Dad stood where he was until he was finished.

We drove a few miles in silence.

"I'd just painted Brandon Sax's roof," Dad finally said. "Brandon Sax was standing down on the ground, watching. He was on vacation. He spent his vacation standing and watching. When I was done, he said he'd like to have his daughter's playhouse painted. He'd bought it ready-made. Cheap, flimsy wood. Not worth shit. Brandon Sax said his daughter was going to choose the new color. The daughter wasn't home, but he wanted to pay me to wait for her. And when she came home, he wanted me to crawl into the playhouse. And sit with her. And talk about colors. That's what he said, swear to God. Completely serious. Me and an insurance man's little daughter, sitting and discussing colors… That's how it was."

CHAPTER TWENTY-ONE

I WENT AROUND RAKING. The black mountains were gone. We'd lifted, driven off, and said farewell to millions of bricks. One hundred forty-four loads, to be exact.

I walked over to Dad. He was sitting on the bench with his back to the sun. He made room for me. I stayed standing.

"How old are you, actually?" said Dad.

"Fourteen."

"Fourteen! Why the hell didn't you say that before?"

Dad unbuttoned a beer and held it out to me.

"Cheers!" he said.

I stood with the beer in my hand for a long time. My tongue was growing, filling my whole mouth. I couldn't get any words out, but I could sit myself down and drink.

I followed Dad's swallows out of the corner of my eye. It was best that our gulps were the same size.

"Hey, listen," said Dad. "Can you hear the foundation over there?"

"Nope."

"Sure. Just under the surface of the ground. The foundation is screaming that it wants its body back. The fire baked it good and hard. If we give the foundation another house, it will stand forever."

Dad had plans for the place—this was something I knew. He had already paced off a new house. And written down a whole bunch of figures.

"If you give the foundation a new house…are we gonna live in Hørmested, then?"

"Hell no. Are you kidding?"

"Then who'll live here?"

"A flock of seriously raunchy, un-Christian folks. It's Hørmested's only hope. The mechanic can't do it single-handedly. And he doesn't play the accordion, either."

"Where's the money supposed to come from?"

Dad laughed and pointed at Chevy.

"Why do you think your grandmother drove around in that hurdy-gurdy? Because it got 250 miles to the gallon. And why do you think she froze down all those sad-ass chicken carcasses in little bags and saved them to make soup of? She did it because she was the world's stingiest Jehovah's Witness. And now one toppled-over candle has sent all her savings and a hell of a nice piece of property home to your mother. Who's just as stingy. There's a lot of things you can say about Our good old Lord, but a sense of humor—*that* he's got."

"Does this mean we're not poor anymore?"

Dad looked at me like someone had slapped his face. He shook his head and knocked out his pipe on a bench leg.

"We've never been poor, dammitall!"

I got off the bench. I couldn't keep up. I walked around with my beer. Dad was mad. Now he was sitting there, thinking about the days when he and Alexander came home from topping-out ceremonies. When a new house had been born. They sat in the garden. In pitch darkness. Sharing a smoke. They were playing with ideas, new plans, new holes in the ground that would shoot up like castles in no time. They said nothing but knew everything. They just went out and built. With Alexander sitting on the peak of the roof and Dad running around on the ground, spitting Five-Inch and the Cement Baker in the right direction.

But now, as I walked around on the freshly raked earth, I couldn't imagine a house rising up out of the ground. I'd never used a hammer. I'd never knocked one single nail into anything.

I went up on the hilltop and looked out over the grazing cows. I sat down, put the beer between my legs, looked at my hands. The blisters were gone. Instead I'd grown small, tough humps of skin at my finger joints. It was almost like my hands had gotten muscles. If I rubbed them together, it made a cool sound. I'd gotten the hands Gina wanted. Mink farmer hands. Sore and worn, too tired to hit with.

Gina had called one time. I'd gone to bed, totally worn out and sleepy in a way that made the blanket feel like an old friend. Mom called me downstairs. A girl, she whispered, and handed me the receiver like a present that was going to make me glad. The phone cord wasn't long enough for me to get away. I was standing right in the middle of Mom and Dad's evening cup of coffee.

Gina sounded wrong. Cars were driving past the spot where she was standing. I saw her by a freeway. In another country. The man with the fat moustache, waiting in his car, gunning the engine impatiently. They were on their way to Paris. To buy fur coats.

Gina asked if it was me who'd set up a folding chair beneath the wall hole. I'd forgotten all about it. It was nothing. It was merely the chair I was going to sit on while I looked up at her. It was okay for her to know that. I would never touch her again, but it was all right to talk about the chair.

Gina was in a hurry. Through the whistling line, she asked whether it was me who'd been up in the attic. And I should tell the truth, she said. It was something she had to know. Was it me who'd taken the board away? Had it been me who'd opened the way out the heavens? This wasn't how she said it, but she should have. Because that's the way it felt in the morning when I stood there, pissing in a great arc and letting in the light. And behind me, able to make out a body, lying in wait. It was us. That's where we lay. Slept together, shared a mattress. We tried sharing everything we could.

I wanted Gina to call again later. After Mom and Dad had gone to bed. We had to be alone. I hated her. That was also something she ought to know. And Alexander. Gina should know about him. We had to share him, too. Gina could take it. Gina threw shirts around and socked her mother to the floor. Gina let hedgehogs die of thirst because they weren't her problem. Gina knew about evil. Gina was a natural when it came to hearing about Alexander. We were never going to get married. We were never going to see each other again. But she was going to hear about my big brother. All of it. I wanted her to get him out of my mouth and throw him away.

I stood there in the middle of evening coffee, leaning over the vase with the knitting needles and the cookie tin, full of party songs. With Dad muttering and the TV scolding me from behind in a sharp, impatient voice.

"Yes," I said into the receiver. "It was me. And I saw everything."

We were quiet at the dinner table. Mom had made pea soup. Dad was slurping and smacking his lips.

"How is the mechanic doing?" asked Mom.

"Fine," said Dad.

"And his missus?"

"Just fine."

"Didn't he have anything at all exciting to tell about?"

"Yes," said Dad. "They're getting a new traffic roundabout in Hørmested. To serve all the town's seven residents. It was the county's idea. The mechanic wants to make a roadblock out of used cars. Without wheels. By the time the county's done removing them, he figures they'll have used so many man-hours that they'll shelve the whole roundabout idea."

Mom looked at me like I could help her understand what Dad was saying, but she could forget all about it. We were done with our work. We'd made Grandma a fine burial place. The fire had been turned into a lovely spot. Now Mom and Dad could take a drive in Chevy and check it all out. Then Mom could think back on her childhood in peace and quiet. And when Dad lost his patience, he could pull up Mom's sweater and draw a new house on her belly for all I cared.

"And the dice. How'd that go?"

Dad looked up with the rear end of a sausage hanging out of his mouth. The way it was tied off at the end helped make him look extra fierce. Mom shouldn't try discussing games of chance. She didn't have the slightest clue when it came to gambling.

"Alarmingly well," said Dad.

We kept on eating. Mom turned to me.

"How many loads did the two of you make today, Karl Gustav?"

"Five. A lousy five."

"And now you're all finished?"

I nodded.

"So how many trips have you made, all in all?"

It wasn't so much Mom's question that bugged me; it was more that I had the number on the tip of my tongue. Like a little trophy I wanted to show off. To someone who would understand how goddam many bricks had passed through my hands. But for Mom, the figure would just be one more sound, whizzing in one ear and out the next.

"A hundred and forty-four," I said, to get it over with.

Mom bit her lip. She went pale. She grabbed my hand and squeezed it.

"What did you say? What was it you said, Karl Gustav?"

Mom's fingernails were pointy, the fingers flaming warm. I looked at Dad, confused. He'd also come to a halt, spoon in mid-flight.

"A hundred and forty-four," I mumbled, trying to tear my hand away.

"Say it again!"

"A hundred and forty-four."

Mom's eyes grew. They were on their way out of her head. Then they shrunk again. Mom's whole face went soft. The mouth opened.

"'And they are singing as if a new song before the throne and before the four living creatures and the elders; and no one was able to master that song but the hundred and forty-four th…'"

Mom got silent.

"'The hundred and forty-four th…?'" said Dad. "'Th' what?"

"Thistles. The Revelation of St. John the Divine, chapter 14, verse 3," said Mom, looking at the tablecloth.

Mom let go of my hand and stood up. Silently she glided to the window out to the road, facing toward heaven. Mom leaned back her head.

"And no one was able to master that song but the hundred and forty-four wonderful thistles that have been bought free of the earth."

CHAPTER TWENTY-TWO

WE SAT IN CHEVY, each of us with a beer between his legs.

"You know what?" said Dad.

"No."

"The curse on us has been lifted. From now on there are only good days left. I can feel it."

"Where? In your elbow?"

"Yes, but mostly here," said Dad, pounding his chest a couple of times.

There were still remains of egg yolk in his beard. Dad had gotten up to three soft-boiled eggs. Each in its eggcup. Mom was wearing her party dress and lipstick. Dad had his robe on with its own ventilation system. This was because bits of lit tobacco had a habit of lifting off from his pipe bowl like tiny fireflies and making holes in all his clothes.

Dad looked at the eggs in anticipation. Three eggcups—that was something new. Mom had pulled out all the stops. Dad's fingers quivered as he picked up the little spoon. He paused. Then he gave the first egg a blow to the top of its head. The blow was so soft, it stopped halfway into the egg. Dad leaned all the way over and raised the spoon with the greatest of care. His eyes were squinted shut, expecting the worst. But nothing ran out. The egg was firm.

Dad hurriedly laid the top of the egg on his plate. It would have to wait. Then he stuck the spoon down into the firm, white egg meat and made a little hole. The moment he pulled the spoon out again, yellow yolk trickled out.

Dad almost fell off his chair.

"Perfect!" he cried. "The egg's perfect!"

Without sampling so much as a drop of yolk, he attacked the next two eggs, this time without caution, chopping off both their heads. They were just like the first one. Dad was beaming. Mom's feet were doing a little dance under the table.

Dad dug up a whole egg onto his spoon. Carefully balanced, he led it to his mouth and stuffed it in. Like a bowling ball that was going to barrel down the throat lane and scatter all memories of the runny, useless eggs Mom had served all the mornings when she couldn't sleep at night.

"Aaahhhhhhhhh," Dad groaned, eyes closed.

He sounded exactly the way I did when I'd just learned to masturbate. It was easy to recognize. It was a sound that meant something was too good to be true. A sound that came from suddenly realizing there was hope and relief to be found within your own body. Though with Dad it was different. He got it all from a soft-boiled egg.

Mom went over to the bookshelf. Clutching a little parcel in her hand, she sat back down at the table.

"I don't believe it," said Dad.

Dad plucked the package out of Mom's hands and started tearing it open. Cigarettes cascaded out like little white party favors. Dad grabbed one and stuck it between Mom's lips. Then he struck a match and hovered over the table with his medicine. Mom sucked it all up. Her cheeks popped. All color left her face and she leaned back. The smoke escaped like a whispering moan. Out of both mouth and nose. It sounded like a sigh of relief. I'd never heard her make a sound like that before.

Still hovering above the table, Dad yelled:

"I've got it! We're driving out there to build a house for the bench! Now! This instant!"

So we were on our way, sitting in Chevy with a beer between our legs.

"You're going wrong, Dad. Hørmested's that way."

Dad laughed.

"Hell, we're going to Hirtshals. Down to Olsen's. Dealing with anybody else would be stupid."

When we reached the hill into Hirtshals, Dad put Chevy into neutral.

"Look! If the traffic's with us, we can coast all the way down to Olsen's."

We rolled past Deadeye's light blue board house by the side of the road. That the wind had peeled most of the paint off. A lifesaver ring hung from the front gate. The grass was six feet high.

We reached the bottom of the hill.

"No!" shouted Dad. "A roundabout. And shark's teeth! In the middle of my town!"

Dad put on the brakes and knocked out his pipe bowl on the gearshift.

"And what kind of horror show is this?"

In the middle of the roundabout stood a granite dinghy. The dinghy was upside-down, as if all hands had been lost.

"Hirtshals is the city with wind in its sails. That's the town motto. What the hell's the point of a capsized dinghy? This world is infested with bungling artists. Couldn't they just have gone and built themselves a soap-box racer, dammit?"

We made it to the lumberyard. Dad went and lit his pipe under a sign that said NO SMOKING. Then he walked in. Big steps. Dad called for Olsen. A thin man came toward us.

"Get me Olsen."

"Jacob Olsen?"

"Yep."

"He's dead. He died a couple of years ago. Is there anything I can help you with?"

More big steps, Dad looking to the left and right, babbling away.

"We've started building again. I just need to know if this is where we're going to spend our cash. Or whether it should be someplace else. Well, whaddaya say?"

The thin man was having a hard time keeping up.

"Hey," said Dad. "That reminds me…are we going to use wood or stone? What's your opinion?"

Dad was looking at me now.

"Uhh…"

"No. Uhh-houses, that's something the county builds. What do you think? Wood or stone?"

A half hour later we were on our way again. Heavily loaded with yellow bricks, cement, and mortar.

And we hadn't put so much as a dollar down. Dad told the thin man we'd pay after the topping-out ceremony.

The thin man had asked Dad what he meant by that, but Dad hadn't had time to explain. He just said it had been much easier dealing with Olsen in the old days. There wasn't nearly as much haggling over money. And the thin man was more than welcome to call Olsen's widow if there was more he needed to know. No, there wasn't, but the thin man would have to find his boss right away.

On our way out of town we passed Deadeye's house again. This time he was standing in front of his gate, stabbing with his cane.

"Hey, that was Deadeye," I said.

"No, kid, it sure wasn't," said Dad. "That was the Legal Beagle in all his glorious blindness."

I was sure it was Deadeye. We argued for a few miles. I wouldn't give in.

"All right!" said Dad. "We'll turn the old tub around and drive the Legal Beagle to the harbor."

I smiled. Finally. Dad was really going to get put in his place. There were a lot of things I knew nothing about, but Deadeye I could recognize a hundred miles away. And it *was* him. Deadeye poked at the trailer, the bricks, the sacks of cement, and Chevy's trunk and roof. It may well be that Deadeye fumbled his way through the world, but to my ears his tapping was the sweet sound of triumph. I was one up on Dad this time.

I crawled over onto the backseat. Deadeye climbed in and sat down.

Dad said nothing. But Deadeye did.

"If a ship's in distress, the captain is obliged to do all that's in his power to preserve it, and he may not abandon ship as long as there's hope of its salvation. Mine's named *Sylvia*. Be so kind as to convey me to her."

"As you wish," said Dad.

I stuck my head right in front of Deadeye. There was curry on his breath. Maybe that's why he hadn't smelled me right away. I breathed in his face. Deadeye's nostrils went into action. He sniffed me onboard.

"I detect Finlandia Avenue," said Deadeye.

Dad laughed.

"That's about as close as you can get. We lived on Norwegian Way. But we've been gone for some years."

"Yeah, yeah," continued Deadeye, "but there's also beer in the car, something tells me. I believe I catch a whiff of Carlsberg. Correct me if I'm wrong."

"Right as rain," said Dad, letting Chevy steer itself. So he could open a beer on the seatbelt buckle.

"Cheers, Legal Beagle," said Dad.

This didn't confuse Deadeye. "Cheers," he said back, and made himself comfortable in his seat.

"You get one more now," said Deadeye. "As thanks for the refreshment. It is the captain's duty that the vessel be in seaworthy condition and that he take sufficient time in seeing to it that the ship is well fitted out, competently manned and provided with victuals and beer, as well as coal and other necessities, in the event of the vessel being a steamship."

Deadeye heaved a sigh and took a giant gulp of Carlsberg. I couldn't wait anymore.

"Deadeye, it's me. Karl Gustav."

"Yes, yes, I know. And you're carrying bricks. And our chauffeur is Buffalo. You're on your way across the plains…I'm not slow-witted, you know. Cheers to Buffalo and son."

"Cheers, Legal Beagle," said Dad.

Sylvia was down in the harbor, waiting. Dad got out and opened the door for Deadeye. A little boy was standing on the wharf.

"How many do you want me to get today?" called the boy. "I'm ready."

Deadeye calmly led his cane toward the voice. When it hit the boy's feet, he let it rise. The cane went all the way to the boy's shoulder, where it took a rest.

"I think we'll have three today."

Deadeye found some coins for the boy, who made off for the grocery store. Dad followed the boy's eager legs with his eyes and laughed. Deadeye leaned against the car.

"Take care of yourself, Buffalo. Let me know if there's something I can do for you."

"Fine," said Dad.

Dad drove on, humming his way through Hirtshals. Dad waved to every single person we saw.

"Well, wasn't I right? Was that not the Legal Beagle? Hell, I'd forgotten how great he is. The man doesn't have a nickel to his name, and then he pays for a lift with quotes from maritime law. That's not only great, it's Hirtshals at its best, goddammit."

I didn't answer. I was thinking about the kid. Deadeye had found himself a new beer boy. And a whole other name.

"Did you hear Mother's snoring last night?" said Dad. "I'm telling you, I was lying there, reading the Revelation of St. John from one end to the other—what a lot of mumbo-jumbo—but your mother just snored on like a dream. And you know what?"

Dad waited for me to ask what. He had nothing but time. Dad's world was sweet just now.

"What!" I yelled. "Mom's name isn't 'Mom' anymore, maybe? Has she changed names, too?"

"Nonsense. Now pay attention. This stuff's important. In the Revelation of St. John, it doesn't say a word about thistles. And that number...the hundred and forty-four...the real figure is 144,000. Your mother swallowed the last three zeros and spit them out as flowers instead. Do you follow me?"

"No."

"Your mother bent the Bible. For the first time in her life, she bent the words of the Bible. She made the words her own, just like you're supposed to."

Dad made a sharp turn that the heavy trailer disagreed with. The load of bricks shifted. Dad stepped on the brakes. The wheels squealed all the way to the edge of the road. It sounded like all the bricks were going to come sailing through the rear window. Then it was quiet. I looked back. The trailer and Chevy were standing at right angles.

Dad turned to me.

"Yesterday your mother said goodbye to the Jehovah's Witnesses. She lied for the first time in her life. It's wonderful. Don't you get it?"

CHAPTER TWENTY-THREE

I was looking up at the sky. The clouds were busy. Maybe something was happening over in Sweden they wanted to check out. I hid the sun behind my bricklayer's trowel when I heard Dad. I had a look. He was busy crawling around the foundation, huffing and puffing. With his pipe, some nails, and a carpenter's pencil in his mouth.

Now he was pressing a long nail in between the bricks he'd just smacked together. He made a loop with a long, white string and tied it to the nail. On his hands and knees, Dad unraveled the string all the way to the far end of the foundation, where he stuck in another nail and made a new loop. Satisfied, Dad stood up and looked at the long, straight string, stretched a little bit above the ground. It looked pretty important.

Dad went and stuck his finger into the wheelbarrow, into a mixture of cement and mortar that I'd mixed with a shovel. His finger didn't get far.

"More water," called Dad. "More water!"

I took the two pails and walked over the hilltop. The cows were grazing down on the other side. Hens and geese were running around the two old brothers' farmyard, laughing their asses off. On top of the farmhouse roof, instead of a weathercock, stood a weathercow on sturdy legs. It was black and white and had an arrow in its forehead, pointing the way forward. The brothers were top-professional farmers, and here I came, with two empty pails that were supposed to end up with a house.

The brothers were laughing, too.

"So there's a topping-out ceremony this evening, or what?"

I set a pail under the faucet in the yard and turned on the water. The brothers were named Mortimer and Elmer.

When the pails were full to the brim, I handed Mortimer a dollar.

"We don't want your money," he said.

"Dad'll only have your water if we pay for it."

"Then keep your dollar."

"But I don't want it."

I stuck the money in Mortimer's shirt pocket and nodded to him.

Back in the wilderness Dad was still down on the ground by the foundation. His shirt was sopping with sweat.

"We have to mix up a new batch," he said.

"Does that mean a beer?"

"A new batch always means a beer. And remember to smoke while you're mixing. Minimum one cigarette."

I took a shovel full of cement and threw it into the wheelbarrow. Then I emptied a sack of mortar on top and poured water in. I opened a beer and lit a cigarette. I took a slurp and tried to suss out how to get the least smoke in my eyes. Paddling with the shovel and smoking at the same time wasn't easy, but necessary. It was how you timed yourself when you worked with Dad.

Dad had promised it would take at least six million batches. This was batch number two. As I was mixing, Mortimer came driving his tractor over the hilltop, pulling a flatbed trailer. Behind him came his brother, driving a machine with a lift in front.

Dad acted like he didn't see them. The brothers started emptying the flatbed. It was full of blue sloshing barrels. The crane heaved the barrels into the air and let them down right next to my wheelbarrow. Eight barrels in all.

The brothers turned off their machinery and stood next to each other. They took off their caps and pulled combs out of their back pockets. They combed their hair and replaced the caps.

"Rainwater," they said. "All it cost was patience. Good luck with the work."

Then the brothers left again. Dad got up and wiped the sweat off his forehead. He went over to a barrel and cupped his hands into the water. He splashed rainwater on his face and even drank a little of it.

"What'd I tell you? The curse has been lifted. Just wait until Mother hears about rainwater that appeared in the sunshine. But they damn well could have asked first, whether it was something I was interested in. This time they were lucky."

Dad stuck a finger into my mixture.

"Give it a mouthful of rainwater, then it's ready."

I leaned up against our first wall. I gave it a quick shoulder tackle. Unbudgeable. I gave it a loving pat, releasing a cloud of dust from my hand. I was gray all the way to my elbows. Gray like the wall. Every single brick was colored by my hands and my new buddy, my trowel.

We'd made the wall different this time, given it a new face.

One day I'd asked if the house really had to be yellow. It was an ugly color. Dad agreed, which meant the house had to be washed with cement right away. Dad claimed that cement washing was the finest sport in the bricklaying profession.

When you cement-washed a house, it suddenly became old-looking. And since we'd decided to build our first house in the wilderness, it couldn't just stand there, a screaming yellow building competing with the sun for attention. No, the house had to look old and wind-blown, as fast as possible. So there was only one solution: a luxury cement bath.

I'd prepared myself for some new, shitty, slow work that constantly had to be measured with a yardstick and a plumb on a string. But that's not how it turned out. For a cement washing you simply took the trowel, jabbed it down into the cement and mortar, and smacked the shit onto the brand-new bricks. Then you spread all the stuff out, making sure there was an even layer. There was no measuring. No doubts. You didn't have to think at all.

Already on the first smack—where the goodies splattered all over, including my face—I could tell cement washing was a good idea. I kept hurling the goodies onto the wall; it went faster and faster. The shovel was smiling. On a good day I used up a couple of tons of cement and mortar.

Dad was busy, building and measuring, steadily raising the white string. The idea with the string wasn't as dumb as it looked. It helped Dad keep his balance in the late afternoon. Building walls was thirsty work.

When we quit for the day, I took my trowel and washed it clean in one of the water barrels. Then I unbuttoned myself a beer. It was my duty, Dad said. One must never go home before admiring one's day's work.

Before we took off for Rakkeby, I uncoupled Chevy's trailer. Its tires were just about worn through; there was no sign of tread anymore. The mechanic had offered to change them, many times actually, dangling two free beers into the bargain. Dad didn't mind the idea of drinking the beers, but he didn't want new tires. The trailer was going to be allowed to wear its tires out all the way.

In the car on the way home we talked about the lunch Mom had made. With remoulade on the salami. And deep-fried, toasted onions.

"Sometimes miracles do happen," he said. "Think, if you'd said a hundred and forty-five loads instead of a hundred and forty-four. It could just as well have been. Grandma's old cast-iron stove actually counted, too. Then it would have been a hundred forty-five. That number could have been a catastrophe."

"Did you count the loads, too?"

"Sure I did. One always counts one's loads. What else are you going to do when you're standing at the Pearly Gates and Our Lord and Hans Peter are there, asking if you've been diligent?"

"Who's Hans Peter?"

"The cemetery caretaker in Hirtshals. He died last week—a good, thirsty man, Hans Peter. He had a shack full of funeral beers, right next to the church. That's where I went when I visited. It was a good place to be. Much better than, well…anyplace else around there in those days. Now Hans Peter's stationed at the Pearly Gates, handing out beers up in heaven. No doubt about it."

We drove past a market that had a special deal on hotdogs. Dad backed up and went inside. He came out, still talking, with a pack of red hotdogs and two crates of beer. The grocer closed the door behind Dad, so he had to yell the rest of his story through the shop window. Something about Mom's lunch and the deep-fried, crispy onions.

We drove on, now with hotdogs in our mouths. We made it to Rakkeby. Dad took the old country road. He began packing his pipe. I took hold of the wheel and steered for a while.

Sometimes Dad wasn't in such a rush to get home. We took a lot of after-work drives through Rakkeby so Dad could take a look at all the new houses shooting up.

Dad shook his head a lot. The new building sites used big cement mixers, where you just had to pull a hose up to the wall and a flood of goodies oozed out. A totally worthless device.

Dad took a turn out of Rakkeby. We drove by my party shirt in the ditch, past all the mink farmers. When we passed Gina's farm, Dad glanced at it. Little Horsey wasn't standing out front. The folding chair was gone, too, and the board was in front of the hole.

I remembered the time we took a walk in the wet grass and I told Gina all the things I was going to do to the farm when her mom died from drinking. Now I could actually do something about it. I could cement wash. The farm needed it. The spaces between the house bricks were big as mail slots.

"Dad?"

"Yep."

"What happens to a house that has a hole in the wall?"

"A hole where?

"Up by the attic."

"Top or bottom of the attic wall?"

"Bottom."

"It will fall apart within two years. Less, if there's a really hard winter. And if the house has a dad who doesn't know where he's supposed to bed down for the night, then one ought to leave the house alone. Because all the inhabitants are stone dead anyway. Especially the daughter."

I didn't notice the sea before Chevy had come to a halt. Dad got out with a hotdog in his mouth and bare feet. Waves were forming way out in the water and foaming all the way in. I was thirsty. I climbed out, too. The wind was cold. Big drops of North Sea hit me in the head. I opened the trunk and lifted a whole case of beer out. I wanted it to come in and sit with me awhile on the backseat. I tried forcing it in, between the seats. In over my shovel. There wasn't room.

Dad took the case out of my hand and set it on the sand. On his side of the car.

Dad opened a beer, handed it in to me. The mouth of it banged into my teeth and I spilled beer onto myself. Dad's door was still open. The wind was howling through Chevy.

"Will you close the door, dammit?"

Dad stood on the beach for a couple of moments, like he hadn't heard me. Then he got back in the car and slammed the door, heaved a sigh and stretched out his legs. He packed his pipe. Then he started telling a story.

"Back when your big brother was six or seven, he wanted a playhouse in the garden. I'd promised to take a couple of days off so we could build it together. Alexander had made a drawing of the house. It was supposed to be a mini version of Little Norway...that's what he called our house, you know. Anyway, a couple of days came along where I didn't have much work to do. We bought hotdogs for the topping-out ceremony. And found a mustard that was sweet enough that he'd eat it. Late that evening I got a phone call, to come out and see an exciting new piece of ground. With a toppling-over ceremony afterward. You know, some hands of cards and a lot of beers. I didn't come back the next morning, or the next couple of mornings either. When I did come home, no one was there. I went out in the garden, and what was standing in the middle of the lawn? One playhouse! With insulated windows, for Christ's sake. I went inside. The playhouse smelled like only something made out of new timber can smell. It smelled of Olsen's lumber. Solid wood. The real thing. There was a pot on the floor with hotdogs still in it. The jar of sweet mustard was full of flies. High up on the wall there was a shelf. Lying on it were all the tools he'd used. And the diamond he'd cut the glass with. Which he wasn't allowed to. Not at all. The cross-cut saw was lying there, too. With its blade that could have stolen all his fingers.

A saw like that he was never even allowed to *look* at…but what really took the cake was the shelf itself. He hadn't just decided to use a board and leave it at that. No, he'd made a whole box of it. With molding around the edges. Why the hell had the kid gone to so much trouble, I wondered. Well, I eased off the top strip of molding and… You know what was inside the box? I'll tell you what was inside the box. A whole layer of insulation material. The kid had god-help-me insulated the shelf. Later, after I'd given him the world's biggest bawling out, I asked him why he'd insulated the shelf. Sure, he said. His tools weren't going to just hang on a cold wall like mine did. His were going to stay warm and cozy all year round. Yeah, but all the tools are mine, I yelled. Alexander looked me right in the eye, and said: Not anymore. That was the only thing he said."

Dad shook his head. He opened the car door and spat out onto the sand, reached down, and pulled two more beers back inside. We drank and looked out over the sea. I thought about Alexander's bawling out. About how bad it had been. And whether it had included a slapping.

The sun was about to go down.

"Can you swim, Dad?"

"Everybody can swim."

"I don't think *you* can."

Dad laughed.

"It's a shame you can't drive a car. Then you could pop over to England and pick me up. There's always been something special about swimming from one body of water to another."

"You're full of shit. You can't swim at all."

Dad emptied his beer. Got out and took off his clothes. His shirt blew up on the dunes. The workpants plopped to the ground. Dad's shorts were small and white, with little Danish flags. Then Dad strode off toward the North Sea.

The sun was pulling the light into the sea with it. The water was blue only way out; the rest was dark. Dad stopped at the edge. He took the pipe out of his mouth and studied it. Then he turned around, crouched down, and scooped together a little mountain of sand with his hands. He hit the peak with the flat of his hand.

Dad took a puff of the pipe, plowed a parking space in the sand with two fingers, and set the pipe down to wait. Then he waved to me and turned back to the sea. He ran out and threw himself into the first wave he met. The sea shrank back—fast. As though such a big chunk of Denmark falling straight into the sea had scared it. Dad started swimming out. Lay on his belly on the waterline and waited for more water, new waves. He paddled eagerly with both arms, trying to dig his way out to the deep. A wave washed over him. Dad tackled it with his head, water spraying into the air.

I sat with my nose pressed against Chevy's windshield. Finally Dad stood up in the water, satisfied, arms crossed, looking bigger than the North Sea. Dad caught a last glimpse of the sun, sinking. For Dad it was easy enough. He could tell me things about Gina that I didn't want to know. He could speak about Alexander without breaking down, then take a swim in the North Sea and return to his pipe. The pipe was still alive.

Dad came back to Chevy. Took two beers, climbed in, and sat down on his seat. He was bleeding from his forehead.

"Those damn trick waves. There's no way you can know where they start and where they end. But it was actually nice. There's nothing better than crawling. Of all the ways to swim, the crawl stroke's the best, don't you think, son?"

The mechanic climbed out of his car with six beers and shouted good morning. I was cement washing but managed a quick nod. Dad didn't have time to. He was on his knees in front of the bench. It had been painted white. By Dad. He wanted to have a better surface for his large drawings of the house.

The mechanic walked quietly over to Dad, bottles clinking. But Dad didn't turn around. He sat there, chewing on his carpenter's pencil.

The mechanic put the beers down in the earth's icebox. He stood watching awhile, then crouched down next to Dad. I kept washing walls, listening to Dad tell about how life would be in the new house.

"And here we have the living room, with a little peephole out to the kitchen. Incredibly practical. So the wife can stand out there and keep track of when the men need a bite to eat while they're playing cards."

"Or rolling dice," added the mechanic. "It could just as well be dice."

"Yeah, yeah. That's enough outta you," said Dad.

When Dad had given the mechanic a tour of the entire house and described the good, un-Christian things that would be happening in all the rooms, he invited the mechanic up for a sit on the roof.

"Can you feel the ridge of the roof?" said Dad. "That's where the kid'll be sitting. With a view of all Hørmested and beyond. And a hotdog in his mouth with mustard on the end. The topping-out ceremony."

The mechanic nodded. I did, too. I gave the trowel a little rest. Instead I dipped a shaving brush into the pail of water. The shaving brush was a tool you simply couldn't do without when you were a master cement-washer.

If you just smacked the goodies up on the wall, the surface got muddy and uneven. It looked okay, but not beautiful. To get a beautiful surface you had to dip the shaving brush in water and shake it out two times on the grass. Not three times, not once, but two times.

They had to be firm shakes so there wasn't too much water left when you used it. Dad himself had shown me how it was done.

When I used the shaving brush exactly right, all the lumps disappeared. The wall's surface became nice and even. Old and beautiful. Dad said the shaving brush gave the finishing touch. All good craftsmanship always ended with the finishing touch. I needn't make a mental note, Dad said, because once you'd learned to make a cement wash beautiful, you'd never forget how.

CHAPTER TWENTY-FOUR

ME AND THE SHOVEL SHOVELED SNOW, but our hearts weren't in it. The night had dropped a thick layer over everything, at least in Rakkeby. The TV weather forecast was choosy. It never said how the weather was out in Hørmested. It tucked the whole of north Jutland beneath one big snowflake, leaving us to go around, pissed off, not knowing a thing. The snow wasn't real work. It fell and was dead on arrival. If you scooped it up, it weighed too little. If you let it alone, it disappeared sooner or later anyway.

The county's snowplow came rumbling by. The driver waved as though we knew each other. He felt we ought to stick together. We guys who worked in the cold and never knew when the work was finished. I spit after him for good luck.

Mom came out and thanked me and the shovel as she walked her bicycle over the black earth we'd just scraped free. Mom was on her way to the rest home. She'd become a member of the board of trustees. They sat around drinking coffee and eating buns, with Mom knitting away through it all. She was allowed to turn in a blank ballot when they voted on important issues. Mom preferred not deciding anything, but she loved going to all the meetings. She said it was just like knitting in the Danish Parliament.

I checked out the cellar window. Dad was down there, sitting. We hadn't been to Hørmested for weeks. When the snow started falling Dad said one must never build or wash walls if flakes were landing in your pipe. If we worked in below-freezing weather, all the bricks would be wobbling come springtime. Our house would start cracking. As perfect as my cement-and-mortar mixture was, it couldn't stand the frost.

So Dad had decided to sit down all winter. It wasn't something he announced, but it's what he did. Every morning he disappeared down in the cellar. He didn't even stop to eat Mom's soft-boiled eggs. Dad sat in the cellar until dinnertime. Then he came up and sat at the dining table. Not hungry at all.

One evening Mom had asked Dad if he was sick, if he could feel something wrong in his body. Dad didn't get mad. Without making a big deal, Dad said he'd caught a cold. It wasn't a normal case of the snif- fles. It was pigheaded. The cold was so damn pigheaded that he took off his hat to it. Mom didn't like the idea of Dad taking his hat off to a cold.

When he had gone to bed, Mom said that Dad had never been sick. Never, ever. Mom could only remember one time where Dad had been in the danger zone. It was the time a doctor had poked his balls around to see if Dad was available in the event of World War III. He was, the doctor had said, and then Dad spent months in a military jail cell because he wouldn't walk in step. Mom didn't mind this at all because it gave him time to write her letters. She'd kept them all. Mom said they were letters full of longing.

When the driveway was cleared, me and the shovel started mak- ing a path between the trees. The pond wasn't exactly the North Sea, but you never could tell where Dad might want his beer.

I built a path that lined up square with everything. Then I went down to Dad. He wasn't sitting at his spot. I could hear him out in the john. Standing, rocking back and forth in his tattered slippers. Dad's pissing had gotten full of pauses. He could even put a pause in the middle of a perfectly normal leak-taking squirt.

Dad came in and sat down.

"I cleared a path between the trees."

Dad nodded.

"There's no way you can go wrong."

No response. I got up and looked out the cellar window.

"Are you sick, Dad?"

The quiet continued. So quiet, I could hear the spit washing my dry mouth.

"All right. Listen, Karl Gustav."

Dad was packing his pipe. That was a good sign. He was getting warmed up for a story. We'd be laughing soon. Dad put the pipe in his mouth and his hand in his back pocket. He pulled out his wallet and found ten dollars.

"If you happen to be going by the grocer's, you can buy me some tobacco. But only if you're going that way. I've got guests, you see. Nasty guests, hungry for rib roast. Morning, noon, and night. Rib roast. That's the only thing they'll eat. I'm in the process of smoking them out. Give them so much smoke, goddammit, they'll choke to death. You understand?"

I nodded, but stayed seated until I was sure the story was finished. Then I took the ten bucks and went to the laundry room. I pushed my bike up from the cellar without making a sound.

Out on the road I tried to think if there was anything else Dad needed. I wanted to go back and ask, but that would be dumb. Dad was just going to have to sit a while, thinking about how he'd begun asking people to do things for him.

It wasn't a white Christmas. It started thawing just at the beginning of the holidays. The grass was peeping up—a little pale, but green. Every single Christmas song on the radio was about snow. This didn't confuse Mom; it made her glad. Now she could get to all the church services without having to walk her bicycle to keep from slipping. She could float into church and sit an hour, praying to Dad's cold, for it to go away.

I didn't look to see how the weather was. I cycled to the grocery store. Out in front was Gina's moped. It was easy to recognize because someone had jabbed a knife through the seat. The foam rubber poked out like spongy weeds.

I went inside. Gina was at the checkout stand. She was buying milk, cigarettes, and caramels. I stayed standing at the door. Now we were practically the same height.

"Hi."

"Hi."

The grocer didn't say anything. He just stood there. Like me.

"I'd like to get by," she said.

I stepped aside. As she passed, I smelled after her, got pulled along outside. Gina put her things in the green box on the back of the moped. She was busy.

"I thought you'd moved away. Far away."

"I thought you were on your way in to shop."

Gina wasn't glad. She could hear I was lying. She knew I'd been by her farm, way out by the road, looking in her windows. Just like everyone else. Gina knew she lived on the farm that smelled the worst to the long-noses. She was used to all the looks from people trying to see in the windows. People in cars, on bikes, by foot, all straining to cop a peek. Gina lived inside a TV set that anybody could watch, see how it looked on the farm where awful things happened. Where a father had once laid down in the wrong bed. And enjoyed it so much, he kept on doing it. Sometimes the father disappeared, which was when Gina said he was dead. But he wasn't. He came back. I'd met him. Through a keyhole. He'd wiggled his big toe and knocked me out.

"How about Little Horsey? Is he okay?"

"Just fine."

"I'll try and come by and break up the ice in his..."

"No, don't. I got engaged. We're getting married in a few weeks. Just as soon as mink season's over."

I nodded. Gina took off. Maybe she was lying. Maybe it was true. Maybe Gina was no lady at all, just a girl who went around saying she couldn't even remember the last time she'd been sorry about anything.

The rissole was steaming; the potatoes were pure white. The brown sauce wasn't too thin, wasn't too thick.

"It's so nice, eating down here. Strange we never thought of it before."

Mom lit a bunch of little candles. Dad stared into space. He hadn't touched his fork yet. There was still a swallow of beer in his bottle.

While Dad had been off peeing his damaged stream of pee, I'd torn off the corner of the label on his beer. To keep track of Dad's refuelings. I went out to sit by the pond. When I came back, three hours had gone by. It was still the same bottle.

Dad was sitting with piping-hot cheeks in the middle of a face turned gray. Mom started going on about all the events at the rest home. Many of the residents had been sad at Christmas. It was the roast duck's fault. The bird had been served at twelve noon. This the residents couldn't understand, since it was still daylight. Mom looked at Dad to see if he had an opinion. Dad didn't. So Mom looked at me and said the personnel didn't have arms and hands enough in the evening, because many of them went home to their own Christmas dinner. Timing the roast duck had been the only item on the agenda at the last meeting of the board of trustees. They hadn't reached an agreement.

Mom picked up the knitting in her lap. The needles began twining around each other. Dad's tools hung on the wall behind us. Mom was knitting in Dad's cellar. The county-owned house was shifting.

"I'm just so thankful that I'm allowed to turn in a blank ballot. Deciding about that duck is impossible. One wants to make everybody happy, of course. It's easy to understand how politicians wind up with a case of nerves and health problems. They have to think about a thousand things all at once. Just like our own prime minister. He seemed to be doing just fine, and suddenly…no, thanks. I've had enough of this job, he said. Time to move to the country and grow old gracefully."

Dad coughed; his eyes watered. Dad stood up with the entire county-owned house on his back. Shuffled out to the little john, the john that was his, alone. Out to do more coughing. To see if it was possible. To get rid of those damn guests that had moved in. If he couldn't smoke them out, he'd cough them away. That was Dad's mission. All alone.

The sky was wall-wash gray. Ruth was smoking a cheroot. She wasn't at all mad that I'd called in the middle of the night. It was part of her job, she said. Ruth's taxi spun down the road at a hundred miles an hour. The clock said the time was 4:56. Dad was scheduled to be operated on at seven.

I looked at Ruth. Her cheeks were much fatter than I'd remembered. She had rings on all her fingers. Maybe things were going better down in Hirtshals. Maybe the fishermen were taking taxis more.

"Do you still live in the yellow apartment building?"

Ruth nodded. She'd told me Axel was home, in bed, sleeping like a log. Axel had been to the all-Jutland weightlifting championships.

He'd come in number three and was sleeping with his lovely medal around his neck. Ruth said Axel had been perfectly satisfied being number three. She also promised Axel would laugh for sure when he heard his old birthday present had come into favor. That's what Ruth called it: "Come into favor."

"Axel was a damn good goalkeeper, I can tell you that."

Ruth nodded.

"Axel was the fucking best goalie in all of Denmark, I can tell you that."

I leaned back in the seat. I felt like saying a few other things about Axel. I felt like driving all the way home with Ruth and heaving him out of bed so we could go down to the beach and eat sand crackers, and Axel could play goalkeeper and never catch a thing. Not one single kick.

But now it was nighttime. We were on our way to Aalborg. I didn't know why. Something just happened while I was sitting down in the cellar, drinking all of Dad's beers. I couldn't take being alone. Mom was asleep upstairs. Mom was able to sleep because Dad had promised her he'd come home again. That's all Mom wanted to know. Dad had called from the hospital and told Mom we shouldn't worry. The operation was no more than a little cut in his back. Dad would be coming home more fearlessly erect than ever. He promised.

I'd been sitting there in the cellar, wrecking the beer's taste with hands that made the bottles much too warm. I couldn't stay there. I emptied my wallet of its coins and old knackered bits of paper that were hard to believe had once been important. In the middle of the pile, I'd found a little orange slip. I couldn't remember ever seeing it before. In the middle was printed TAXI, plus a telephone number where the last digit was worn off.

I'd crept up to the living room. Then I'd woken up some people I didn't know, but when I reached the number 7, I heard a voice I recognized. It was Ruth's, the perfect mother from Hirtshals who wanted to drive me all the way to Aalborg and not take a dime for it.

"Axel was a damn good goalkeeper. The best."

"Axel is a good boy," said Ruth.

I nodded and settled further into my seat. The taxi was big as a bed.

"Ruth?"

"Yes?"

"You said once that it was a major pain in the ass, that business with Dad and jail."

"I did?"

"Yes."

"Don't worry about it. I give all men a hard time. It's something that comes with driving a cab so many years."

"Dad didn't do anything."

Ruth nodded. She rolled the window down and tossed the cheroot stump into the darkness.

"Did he tell you that himself?" she asked.

"No, why should he? When you haven't done anything, you don't have to tell anything."

The hospital was tall. At the bottom sat a lady behind a plate of glass. She'd only talk through a little porthole. The lady was afraid of catching all kinds of things, but she didn't mind telling me where Dad was. He was up on the ninth floor. That was all the way at the top, she said.

I went into a large white room. There were no stairs, only a lot of elevators. The hospital had plenty of cleaning ladies, I could see. The floor was so shiny, it made me dizzy. I took off my shoes and got into an elevator. It was a quick trip. I stepped out into a new, big white room. Now I could see out over all of Aalborg. The houses had gotten little, the cars, even smaller.

I stood there a moment, looking out the window. I hadn't seen Dad since the night he was hospitalized. Mom's running down the stairs had woken me up. She'd sounded like a hooting child. A couple of seconds later she was running back up the stairs, even faster, yelling louder.

I snuck out into the hall. I listened. The door to their bedroom was open. The light was on. I stuck my nose and left eye in. Mom was on her knees in front of Dad. Between Dad's legs she was holding the dishpan.

Dad was sitting up, bent over the side of the bed, his beard reaching below his belly button, legs and arms limp. Sweat dripped in big pearls from his hair, dripped down on Mom's hands, dripped into the dishpan. The ones that hit the pan sounded like they were much heavier than any other kinds of drops.

"Won't you let me call?" asked Mom.

It was the only thing she said. Over and over again. Dad didn't answer, he only made sounds. A deep rumbling that seemed to come straight out through his body. It was the impatient rib roast guests, sticking knives and forks in Dad, screaming for food.

I put my mouth right up close to the window facing out over Aalborg. I made everything foggy. Then I started down a long hallway where there were no names on the doors, only numbers.

Dad was lying in a room all by himself. It was dark. He was sleeping and wasn't in pain. His mouth just needed the pipe to look fine and dandy. I sat myself on the edge of a chair. Dad was lying on his back. In a little while he'd be lying on his front, so they could reach the right spot. Or maybe they'd hoist him up so they could get at the heart fast if it stopped in the middle of everything.

I remembered a class trip with Rakkeby School. We were going to a slaughterhouse to see how hotdogs came into the world. At the slaughterhouse they hung the pigs up on big hooks. The hooks were remote controlled. Someplace you couldn't see, a man was driving the pigs back and forth and all around inside the building. Driving them through flames. Tim was there, too. He got sick. He threw up in a bag he'd brought along.

When we'd seen how the pigs were driven through hell and cut into slices, there were free hotdogs. It was a strange tour. First death and destruction, then food. Tim never made it to the finished hotdogs. He went and sat out in the parking lot with one of the teachers. I missed Tim. Suddenly I missed him so much, I went over to the window and pulled back the curtains to look for him.

"Where is your mother?"

I turned around.

"Back in Rakkeby."

Dad sighed.

"At least the two of you take turns losing your minds. How'd you get out here?"

"By bike."

Dad closed his eyes a while.

"No, you didn't. And why are you standing there with your shoes in your hands?"

I looked at my shoes. Dad was right. I was standing there with my shoes in my hands.

"I took a cab...with Ruth. It was free. Axel... D'you remember him? Axel, my old..."

"You damn well bet I remember the black bastard. It was you who hammered that ball into the net while he flopped around on the ground. You knocked Hirtshals clean out of Rakkeby Stadium. You copped the trophy."

I stood there, not sure what I was hearing. Of course I remembered the match. And the kick. It was a roller, the weakest kick in the world. Axel just let me. What was Dad talking about?

There was a knock at the door. A man in a jogging suit stuck his head in. He asked Dad if he was awake. The man must have been close to blind.

"Good morning. I'm the one who's going to be operating on you."

"Not in those damn clothes, you're not," said Dad.

The man looked at Dad, confused, then looked down at himself. He slapped his forehead.

"Oh, right. Sorry. I always run in the morning so I'm fresh. Don't worry. When we get going, I'll be in uniform."

"Are you one of them there joggers?"

"Yes."

"Jesus Christ."

"You are perhaps not a jogger yourself?"

Dad shook his head.

"I'm ready," he said. "Just give me the weather forecast."

"The weather forecast?"

"My legs. Are they coming back? What are the odds? I assume you've tried this before."

"Yes, of course. I'm sorry."

The man in the jogging suit looked down at me like I wasn't welcome.

"The kid's come all the way from Rakkeby. He deserves to hear the weather forecast, too. Just let me have it!"

The man nodded.

"Two times out of three, it goes well. The third time, not so well."

Dad was studying the ceiling.

"You married?"

"Yes."

"Can your wife make a fricassee? Can she? Big chunks of beef, swimming around in thick brown sauce, but not too thick? The meat melts in your mouth. You have to look up to heaven to keep back tears of joy. Can your wife make food like that? An honest-to-God fricassee?"

"No, I don't think she ever has."

"Fine," said Dad. "Then you can get the recipe from Mother when she comes."

CHAPTER TWENTY-FIVE

A LONG-HAIRED BOY WAS STANDING IN TIM'S YARD, throwing up. It wasn't Tim. I walked past the boy and into the house. The door was open. Music was blasting. A thousand bottles stood on the kitchen counter. There were also overflowing ashtrays and bowls of potato chips. In the living room silly girls were dancing about. Two boys were sitting on the sofa, blowing on a stack of cards that were balanced on top of a bottle.

I continued on to Tim's mom's pottery workshop. Two lit candles stood on the floor next to Tim's old mattress, on top of which two people were fumbling around. One of them was Inga with the glasses. The other I didn't recognize. Inga's eyes were far away. Her breath smelled.

"You know where Tim is?"

Inga giggled. The boy stuck his tongue in her ear. I went back in the house and knocked on Tim's door. No answer. I opened the door. It was pitch black inside.

"Just leave me alone," I heard.

"It's me, Big Ox."

It was quiet.

"Whaddaya want?"

"My dad's about to die."

Tim got his bedside lamp lit. He sat up, hair a mess. He rubbed his eyes.

"Is your father about to die?"

I nodded.

"Of what?"

"Cancer, somewhere or other."

"Where?"

"A little bit all over, but mostly in the protestant."

"I don't think that's what it's called."

"You have to find it in one of your books. I need to know about it."

"Do you want a beer?"

"Yeah. I'll get it."

"Would you mind bringing me a glass of water? Cold water. Ice cold."

I put my finger under the faucet and waited till the temperature was right. I filled a whole pitcher and stuck a clean glass in my pocket. I threw a dishrag over my shoulder so Tim could clean the glass if he figured my pocket was too disgusting. Tim had a lot of his own rules.

Tim had thrown off his blanket. He was perched on the edge of the bed in an orange shirt covered with yellow flowers. Tim had started high school and begun wearing weird clothes. We didn't see much of each other anymore.

I handed him the glass and the dishrag. Tim polished his glass. I poured for him and sat down on the floor.

"Where is your father?"

"In Aalborg. But he's coming home tomorrow."

"So everything's probably gonna be all right. They don't send a dying man to Rakkeby."

I nodded toward Tim's bookshelf. The one that was full of medical science magazines and books.

"Take it easy, I'll look."

Tim started searching. Now some progress was being made. Now Tim was going to tell me whether Dad was going to get back on his feet. Tell me what the metal plate in his back was for, since that's what the operation was all about: getting the metal plate inside to where the cancer had eaten everything no man could do without.

When Dad woke up after the operation, he could wiggle his toes. Grinning, he'd showed us how. As if a little life out in his toes was a big deal. Life, and happy days for the toenails. When Dad was done grinning he said me and Mom should hurry home and make some fricassee because it was a hundred percent sure he'd be wanting some a little later. And now we ought to leave, Dad said. Which we did. All the way down the elevator to the bottom of the hospital, where Mom sat herself on a bench in the middle of everything and took out her knitting. Mom didn't want to go home. She wanted to sit and knit awhile.

Mom was talking. About the time I was born. Dad had driven Mom to the hospital in Hjørring but stayed in the car, so Mom could go up and give birth without too much fuss. Dad didn't like births. He didn't like sitting still in a car, looking at a hospital, either.

When Mom came out to the parking lot with me in a bundle, Dad had disappeared, along with the car. Dad had gone to a bar in the neighborhood. And that's where he was when he called and asked the whole hospital how it was going with Mom.

When Mom heard Dad's voice on the line, he immediately bellowed "free drinks" to all the bar guests. Mom was still a little mad about that, because she was sure Dad didn't know anyone in Hjørring. It would have been much better if he'd driven to the inn in Hirtshals, because at least there he'd be giving away beers to people he knew.

I fell asleep and woke up with my face against Mom's shoulder. We sat there in the bottom of the hospital until it got dark. Then Mom went up alone to say goodnight to Dad.

When she came down again, I asked if Dad had been mad about her coming back up. Mom shook her head. Of course not. Dad had known all along that we hadn't gone home yet.

Mom said her and Dad had a habit. A good habit, a wonderful habit. They never parted without saying a proper goodbye. In the old days in Hirtshals, when Dad came home in the middle of the night from the inn, he always woke Mom up to say goodnight. Then she'd lay awake awhile, listening to the house. The house only sounded right after Dad had come home.

Mom could only remember one time things had gone wrong. It was the day Grace Kelly died in Monaco. Mom never got to say a proper goodnight to Dad, but that was only because morning was already peeking through the window and the voice on the radio had made her sad. There were days like that in all marriages, Mom said. Disasters out in the great, wide world were something one had to learn to live with.

"Here it is," Tim said finally, holding a thick book under the lamp. "Your dad has cancer in his p-r-o-s-t-a-t-e. I remember that one. I thought I had it myself once. It's a male sickness."

"Just like the male bats?"

"Exactly."

I took a sip of beer and tasted the word.

"Sounds right to me," I said.

"Why's that?"

"They just removed Dad's nuts."

"They did?"

"Yeah. First they banged a metal plate into his back. That was the metallizing. Then a couple of days later they chopped off his nuts."

Tim lay the fat book on his bed. He got down on the floor.

"Sounds like your dad's really sick."

"How sick?" I wanted to know. "What do you think? Just say what you think."

"I've got this friend. He's a head doctor at the National Hospital. We exchange letters. I can ask him, if you like."

"Why do you write letters to a guy like that?"

"He's a good researcher, the best in Denmark. I research his research. Plus he has a hole in his heart. We're members of the same association. He's gonna be fifty-one in April."

"Does he research his own heart?"

"Of course. But he knows everything about diseases."

"Then write to him. Soon as possible."

"Okay, I will."

Tim took a gulp of water and held it in his mouth. Then he stuck a pill in between his lips and threw his head back.

"Did you see Inga around?"

I shook my head.

"She's a dumb bitch."

Tim unbuttoned his flower shirt and tossed it into a corner. He stuck out his chest. I looked at the long scar. Yes. Tim had gotten a slash, too. And he was still living.

Tim sat there, living so much that I patted him on the knee.

Dad was trying to reach the cellar. I was already sitting at the table, waiting. Dad took a step. I could hear him slapping the pillow. First he had to get it wrenched free from under him, before he could get it onto the next step. Dad had given the pillow a name. Its name was Buttman. Buttman wasn't that big, but no matter where Dad sat down, Buttman had to be underneath.

Dad had been home two days. The man in the jogging suit had tried getting Dad to Løkken where there was a physical therapy center. The place worked wonders, the jogging-suit man claimed. Dad didn't believe him. Dad had once bought a piece of land in Løkken. The ground looked just fine, but two shovelfuls down Dad discovered the earth was full of tar because once upon a time fishermen had stood there, treating their nets, spilling tar all over the place. It was a mess and Dad had refused to set his foot in Løkken ever since. He'd rather come home to us.

Now Dad's feet were coming into view on the stairs.

"Go get a beer and count to a thousand."

I went out to the beer storage room and ate an apple while I counted to a thousand. I could hear Dad's feet dragging themselves across the floor. Dad had the most strength left in his right arm. It supported his cane and the rest of him. His legs were like a long pair of flapping socks.

"Go get Buttman."

I rushed to the stairs.

"Watch the beer, goddammit."

We sat, each with a beer. Dad packed his pipe. On the wall we could see how erect Dad would be the rest of his life. It was an X-ray of the metallizing. Dad had gotten it from the man in the jogging suit when the operation was finished.

Dad's ribcage looked like bars on a jail cell turned sideways. He had bent them a little so it was easier to breathe. Behind Dad's ribs you could see the metal plate, like a wall.

"That metal plate is an incredibly cool color," I said. "It's wall-wash gray."

"Huh?"

"Nothing."

Dad started shifting in his seat. He was about to begin a new journey. Out to his little john to squeeze out some drops. Dad looked at me. I did what he asked. I went out in the yard and counted to two thousand.

Valdemar was trimming his hedge.

"Pssstt," he said.

"What's the 'pssstt' for?"

"How's it going with him?"

"Perfect. You can just go down and drink a beer together."

"Yes. And I will, too. Soon. For sure."

"Have you seen any UFOs recently?"

"No. Damn things are gone."

"I'm on my way down to Dad. Wanna come?"

"Maybe a little later. I have to finish this."

I nodded.

"Valdemar?"

"Yes?"

"If I were you, I'd keep seeing lots of UFOs."

CHAPTER TWENTY-SIX

I CYCLED OVER THE HILLTOP, hoping they were there. The sky was low, but the fields were empty. The cows hadn't been let out yet. My bike was out of breath. I hopped off and pushed it the rest of the way.

Mortimer was watching his brother work. Elmer was sitting on the tractor, steering its big shovel. He was pushing a mountain of dirt down in a deep hole. When he was done, there was still some left. Elmer didn't like that. He pounded the shovel up and down on the bulge until it was banged flat.

"What are you doin'?"

"Burying a cow."

"Right there?"

"Right there. But don't worry, your bell cows are doing just fine. This one here was just pestiferous."

"What's pestiferous?"

"The plague. Come, we're going in for coffee."

We took off our shoes in the pantry. Mortimer combed his hair. Then he went to the kitchen and hauled a platter out of the fridge. It was full of already-buttered slices of bread piled with rolled meat sausage, gravy jelly, and onion rings.

Mortimer took a bottle of schnapps out of the freezer.

"I thought you guys only drank in the morning."

"When a cow catches the plague, you owe it to yourself to take a wee nip."

Mortimer set two glasses on the table. Elmer came in and nodded to his brother.

"Whaddaya think, Elmer?"

"The kid, too. It was a good cow."

Mortimer nodded and took another glass. He poured all the way to the rim. The schnapps made great fumes. The brothers didn't say cheers or anything. They lifted their glasses and downed the stuff in a gulp. I did the same.

The schnapps was gasoline. When it all hit bottom, it lit itself. Smoke came out of the brothers' ears. I stuffed a slice of bread into my mouth to keep from catching on fire and wiped smoke and gasoline out of my eyes.

"So, how're things at home?" asked Mortimer.

I chewed a bit.

"Perfect. Dad's just been back in the hospital again, but that's only because the man in the jogging suit forgot to empty his bladder. It had puffed up just like the balls on a bat. They had to stick a hole in it so the piss could come out."

Elmer nodded.

"We all need to take care of our dung tanks. Those goddam environment bastards think it's the end of the world if you take a leak in a creek. Show me the frog who isn't overjoyed by a stream of cow piss. Show me it. It doesn't exist."

Elmer pounded the table with his fist to prove it.

"What about the house building?" said Mortimer. "Have you discussed that?"

"Yes, I'm building the house myself."

They didn't believe it, I could tell. Elmer even shook his head. I was done eating. I biked back to the building site. The pedals were heavy. I had to stand up and tramp on them.

I cycled past our one finished wall. I'd actually been thinking I'd mix a good batch and lay some bricks. It wasn't so much in order to build the house bigger as to get to cement wash a little. Dad was the bricklayer; I was the cement washer. I didn't feel like being both.

I turned off the road at Hørmested. The mechanic was home. He was down in his hole in the garage floor, arms reaching up into the bottom of a car. I sat down on a stack of tires. The mechanic kept working. It was nice. All I could see were his legs. I told them everything. How Tim's friend in Copenhagen thought Dad would die within a year. The cancer had spread. It was growing. Sometimes you could be lucky if it was all in the crotch, but when the back had to have a metal plate, it meant the cancer was too powerful.

I told the mechanic about how Dad went around in the living room. In the middle of the night. He couldn't sleep. He hurt all over. He was forced to take Buttman and make the trip on his ass, all the way downstairs. These were long journeys. Sometimes Mom came along. It was an outing. Dad had a little beer; Mom drank coffee.

Mom had also cut Dad's hair at the hospital. In the room for smokers where all the other cancer people were. They sat there in their white, sick pajamas, blowing cement-wash gray clouds. The window was open, white curtains dancing for the patients, but most-ly for Dad. Dad got his haircut. In Mom's beauty salon that she'd assembled out of the blue, Dad's hair blowing all over the place.

In the middle of the room sat a man with no legs. He had a strong cancer. Two stumps stuck out like elbows. They just managed to hold his underpants up. The man had his cigarettes and matches inside his shorts. He complained about the pajamas having no breast pocket, but the rest of the time he told jokes. Dirty ones with na-ked ladies and everything. The man was an old seaman. Mom stood there, face turning as red as the little Danish flag she'd brought along with its little base so it could stand by itself. Dad laughed at the sailor's jokes. His laughter rumbled past Mom's flag and out the window. I sat on a sofa, watching and listening to it all, next to a man who wasn't laughing. He wasn't missing any parts. He had all his arms and legs, but his sense of humor was gone. He never said a thing.

As I was telling stories in the garage in Hørmested, a black, greasy hand occasionally stuck itself out of the hole and passed me a beer. I drank them fast. It helped. I said that Dad was training. That was why he got up in the middle of the night. He was training his legs so they could walk out to Chevy again and drive us to the building site. Out to our Little Sweden. So I could mix perfect batches of cement and mortar.

Dad's nighttime training was really incredible. It was better to stumble in the dark. Much better than in the light, because everyone stumbled in the dark.

I wanted to tell more stories—some of the good ones—but then came a crappy one.

I told about Dad's blue pail in the cellar. It was an empty old paint pot. It had never been used for anything but tobacco remains and pipe cleaners. Now it had started smelling like piss. It wasn't Dad's fault. He just got so weary and he had to go all the time. And sometimes when he made the long journey out to his private john, he left again with nothing to show for his efforts.

So it was much better to totter over to the workbench, with the old shavings still smelling real good. Here he could support his whole body while he tried hitting the blue pail.

"Hold on just a minute…"

The mechanic's head popped up.

"Oh-oh-oh-oh-oh. Time for a breather. Cheers, kid!"

The mechanic scratched his chin.

"Do you know what I'm standing in?" he asked.

"You're standing in a hole."

"No, I'm standing in a grave. That's what it's called. With both legs, too. But now…" The mechanic swung himself up and stood in front of me.

"Now it's just a hole. And it's the same with your father. He's still far from the grave. Let me get the dice and we'll drive home to your dad. And then, lightning strike me down if I don't roll so many fours he'll forget about all the rest."

I got up, dizzy from schnapps and beer, and especially from the mechanic's plan. It was a good idea, but it wouldn't work. Dad would flip out if me and the mechanic came waltzing in. It would look like we'd lost our minds, I said, standing there, shoes in hand. Dad would look at us like we were two beggars. The mechanic shook his head.

"Twaddle," he said. "That's a load of nonsense, but I wouldn't be surprised if you're right. It's just like the tires on the trailer. Am I ever going to get to change them in this life? No! And it's *my* damn trailer!"

The mechanic wiped his black hands. Then he asked where Dad's blue pail was. He wanted to know exactly. I said it was right under the picture of Dad's ribs.

The mechanic nodded and went out to his car. He opened the trunk and started trying to stuff my bike in.

"Don't," I said.

"Say what?"

"I'm not going with you. I wanna ride my bike."

"Where?"

"Home. To Dad. To the cellar."

"Yes, but…why, by hell's hubcaps, don't you just ride with me?"

"I wanna ride my bike."

When I reached home a couple of hours later, the mechanic's car was parked next to Chevy. I listened through the cellar window.

I couldn't hear anything, but then came the sound. The totally fantastic sound of dice hitting a bare tabletop. No tablecloth. I pictured how Dad had flung it off so the dice could dance and make all the noise they were supposed to.

I took the inside stairs to the cellar to show Dad I had no idea what was going on. Mom was sitting on a chair right by the door to the cellar. With a cup of coffee, the knitting lying at her feet. She smiled.

"They're quarreling away just fine down there."

We listened through the door. It was true. A mess of curses floated up the stairs.

"Go on down there to them."

Mom got up, moved the chair, and opened the door. I flew down the stairs. Dad was sitting in place, back straight, on top of Buttman. Down by Dad's feet stood a flock of empty beer bottles, hugging the table legs.

"What the hell…? Here's the kid, by god," cried the mechanic, shaking the leather cup over his head.

"Fetch us three cold ones, would you?" said Dad.

I did. And opened them.

"Four fours," said the mechanic.

Dad lifted his cup. Just a tad. The pipe bobbing up and down. Dad had his winter jacket on. Plus his thick scarf and wool cap. The cancer had wrecked his temperature. All winter he'd sweat like a horse and now it was spring and he was freezing.

The mechanic waited for Dad's dice. Which took their time. Dad began fidgeting in his seat. That meant it was time for a trip, I could tell. It wasn't good. Dad had to pee.

"Oh-oh-oh-oh-oh," said the mechanic.

I tried to kick him under the table. Nobody was allowed to mention Dad being in pain.

But then the mechanic got up out of his chair, teeth clenched.

"Gotta go again, goddammit!"

Swearing like mad, the mechanic took a couple of sorry steps. Bent over, he stomped over to the picture of Dad's metallizing. A zipper was unzipped. Right above Dad's blue pail. A second later came the sound of a good spurt with no pauses. He shot so hard, the pail almost tipped over.

"Listen to this. You aren't going to believe it," said Dad. "While I've been sitting here all winter, locked in mortal battle with rib roast guests, our friend the mechanic has been flat on his back in the hospital in Hjørring. With gallstones, for Christ's sake. Untamed, nasty gallstones. Now his piss plumbing's all out of whack. When he's gotta go, he's gotta go. No ifs, ands, or buts. So it's damn lucky there's an old pail just sitting around that isn't choosy. Ain't that right, old boy? Sometimes one's just so damn thankful to have a pail."

The mechanic was finished. The zipper zipped up. Then it was Dad's turn. Afterward they kept rolling dice. New beers appeared and were popped open; arguments flared up and died down.

Even Dad's ribs on the wall joined in. Through the clouds of smoke I could see them bending, piled on top of each other. They looked exactly like a stack of smiles.

CHAPTER TWENTY-SEVEN

THE OLD LADY WAS STILL AT HER POST inside the glass doors of the rest home, frozen in the middle of a somersault, reading with her magnifying glass. I said hello. Dad's room was at the end of a long hallway. The door stood open. Mom sat on a chair with a view of the parking lot. She knew all the people walking by. She told Dad who they were, where they lived, who they came to visit, and how often they came.

Dad was in the corner with no view. He preferred just sitting and looking at Mom. The radio was on. It was somewhere between stations. It sounded like the North Sea, raging. Mom acted like she didn't notice. If Dad wanted to listen to a raging ocean, it was up to him.

I sat down and looked at the radio sitting on the coffee table. I leaned over the table and took one of Mom's cookies. At the same time I managed to turn down the volume. The North Sea almost disappeared.

I leaned back in my chair.

"I'm listening to the radio," said Dad, rotating his body slowly.

Dad turned up the volume again, this time louder than before. I went out and stood in Dad's new bathroom. It wasn't a bathroom, it was a machine room with strange machines that were supposed to help keep Dad in one piece.

I looked at myself in the mirror. I was sweating. Couldn't keep up. The cancer had changed direction. From one day to the next. It wasn't going to settle for living in Dad's stomach and back anymore. Now it wanted to move into his head.

There was an afternoon when I'd gone down to the cellar. Dad was sitting on Buttman. He didn't say a word. I sat down with him and looked at the ribcage. It had gotten dusty. It looked good. It was something we could talk about. I turned toward Dad. The one half of his face had sunk. His right eye stuck out and up. It looked like Dad's eyes had had a major disagreement.

"What is it?" said Dad.

I'd run upstairs after Mom. It was back to the hospital for Dad. He'd gotten a blood clot someplace in his head. It happened a lot when the cancer wanted to be really evil. Then light bulbs and blood clots started popping all over the place.

Dad woke up at the hospital with a patch over his eye. He had to keep it on, day and night. Or else the eye would dry out. Dad said it was a fine patch. Now he could set sail for the Seven Seas and rob all the ships he wanted and empty them for rum. Mom nodded. I nodded, too, only Dad didn't even like rum. Dad's stories were beginning not to make sense.

Maybe that's why Dad had suddenly said he didn't want to go home to the county-owned house. Either the hospital was going to let him keep lying where he was, or else they were going to have to find him a place somewhere else. He wasn't going home to Mom. So that's what happened.

Now Dad was living at the rest home. He sat still in his chair and waited for the radio to give in and serve up the accordion he'd wanted to hear for ages. If the radio ever did, he wouldn't be able to hear it. Of course I could go visit him and pretend. Yell into his ear that finally this was the moment; finally they were playing the happiest accordion the world had ever heard. Dad would just look at me and twist the radio dial some more.

I flushed the toilet and went back in. I bumped into Mom. She was in a hurry.

"Where are you going?"

"Fashion show. It starts at one," said Mom.

I decided to go with her. I didn't like being at the rest home. All the people there were ancient. Some of them just sat, drooling. Some laughed and cried at the same time. The somersault lady was easily in the best shape of any of them.

Mom walked into a large, bright room. A lady was seated at the piano, ready to play. Old people were sitting around with thermoses of coffee and plates of cookies. Mom went over to two other ladies. Then she started taking off her clothes and putting other ones on, in incredible colors. The piano started. Mom was determined to go for a walk. She went in a straight line through all the old people, all the way to the end of the room, where she executed an about face.

"Here we see Anna in a smart silk top. Please notice the cut. It is incredibly elegant. The silk top costs only $34.99. Now Anna will promenade one last time. But don't worry—she'll be right back. In gorgeous new spring and summer creations."

The words were spoken by a red-haired lady whose face was a layer of makeup. She was talking into a microphone. Mom was changing clothes again. She was in the middle of a fashion show. Mom had the leading role.

I flew down the long hallway. This was *exactly* what we needed. Then all the accordions in the world could pack up and go home.

I banged through the door into Dad's room. It was hard to see if he was sleeping. The eye with the patch never closed. The other one wasn't completely shut, either. I jostled him. Waited. I jostled a little more, took my hands away quick. Then the good eye opened up.

"Dad! Mom's going fancy. Mom's going Grace Kelly!"

It was night. Dad lay absolutely still. His breath was with a pause in between. I stood by his bed and looked at the eye patch. It was brown, but transparent. Little tiny golden beads were living on the inner side of the patch. What could they have been made of? Sweat? Steam?

A little burp came up out of Dad's mouth. A couple of beads broke. The eye smiled. Dad was lying there, thinking back. He was probably sitting on the bench outside Little Norway. A new house had just shot up out of nothing. Alexander was sitting next to him. They were drinking beers and sharing a smoke. Something like that, you couldn't forget. Something like that popped up again when it was all about to be over. Like tiny golden beads inside an eye patch. The ocean of beer Dad had drunk in his life was now starting to emerge from his head.

"Dad?"

Dad was in the middle of a pause. I looked down into his open mouth. White threads of spit crisscrossed like a spider web. I stuck a finger into Dad's mouth and removed the net, cleared the path. I began telling a story into the darkness.

I told that Alexander had been swimming out in the North Sea. Up alongside the coast. Cutting through the water. We were just on our way home. We'd gotten an ice cream cone at the beach hotel. I was cycling with Alexander's watch in my hand. There was a hard wind. I was getting tired. Somewhere out in the North Sea was the red buoy. It lived out there, never said a thing. But now it was shouting that everybody should take a break. Everyone should stand stock-still and look at it. I stopped. Alexander kept swimming. Just a little ways. Then he stood up in the middle of the North Sea. And got mad. He bellowed that there wasn't a record in existence where anyone had taken a break. I pointed out at the buoy. I yelled that it looked like a cherry. The finest cherry in the world, much better than the ones in our garden. I yelled that I bet he couldn't reach it. He couldn't even get close. Alexander looked out. He shook his head. He wasn't going to do it. He just wanted to get home. Then I screamed he was chicken. That he couldn't do it. That he was a shitass. This was too much for Alexander. He lost his temper. He wanted to fight. Not with me; I weighed nothing. No, my big brother wanted to fight the North Sea. He was going to trample it underfoot, swim out to the buoy and knock its block off. That's what he was going to do. Alexander swam out. Alexander got smaller. I shouted with joy. The waves were big. They tried to knock him down. Alexander clambered over them, painting foamy white lines. Like an airplane in the sky. Everyone could see who he was: he was Buffalo's son. Out there somewhere the foamy white line broke; there were parts missing. It got full of pauses. I jumped up and down, joyous and excited. Alexander's feet had stopped; he was only using his arms. He waved. I was winning, I could see it. Then he disappeared. And came up again. Now only his head was left. Then he took a long break. He was gone completely. He was resting, gathering strength. His nose was sticking up—I just couldn't see it. I looked at the watch. I lifted it up to the sky. I took the time. It was my job; I did what I was supposed to. My eyes were watering. Suddenly I couldn't see anything, nothing at all, only hear. I could hear the wind. And the waves, crashing. The North Sea was really pissed off. I waited. And waited. And went out in the water with my shoes on. And my bike. We went out in the water, me and the bike. As far as we could. We held onto each other. And the watch, it couldn't get one single drop on it. And when Alexander came back, he'd see how dry it was. Bone dry, with a new record. I let go of the bicycle with one hand and threw the watch out to my big brother. I threw for all I was worth. Now Alexander could scoop it up. Like a treasure on the ocean floor. He'd be glad. In just a little while. Then the bike froze; that's as far as it would go. The wheels sank. My shoes were getting sucked down. I had to help the bicycle and my shoes get up again. All the way up. To where the sea wouldn't come after us. The bike couldn't swim; I had to get up on it to make it work again. We started bicycling. We had to make it back to Hirtshals. So I could tell the whole town what had happened. That my big brother had broken all the records. He'd swam out in the North Sea and never come home again.

The cellar was quiet. Three soft-boiled eggs stood before Dad's empty spot. They stood there every morning. The eggs prettified the table for a few hours, then disappeared. I never found out what Mom did with the eggs when they'd dressed up the table long enough, but we never ate them. Maybe Mom just didn't want to stop being Dad's clock.

Mom put down her knitting and looked out the window. She'd been ready a couple of hours. With a blue scarf over her hair and woolen sweater. On her feet she had high-heeled shoes.

"Mom?"

"Hmm."

"Don't you think rubber boots would be better?"

Mom smiled and shook her head. And kept looking out the window.

The mechanic was on time. Mom stood up when she heard his car and bolted outside. Nothing was said as we drove. Dad had said we should ride with the mechanic, that Chevy wasn't going anywhere. That Chevy's Good Old Days were over.

Down in the harbor *Sylvia* was rocking all by herself. All the other cutters were out working. Deadeye was already standing at the wheel. He was staring into space, but I could see he was listening with his ears and nostrils.

I didn't know whether Deadeye and the mechanic had become friends, but in any case they'd held a meeting to discuss the funeral. They'd also shot dice. The mechanic told me how the game had gone on and on. Deadeye hadn't only toyed with each roll; he'd also toyed with each of the dice. All the eyes had to be counted with a slow forefinger.

The mechanic said it was hard work, shooting dice with a blind man, and in the end Deadeye had wrecked the whole game when his hand suddenly lost its temper and threw the dice into the harbor. The mechanic thought that was a pretty rotten thing to do, but what was worse was when Deadeye broke into song. The mechanic had never heard anything like it, he said. It sounded more like a list of maritime rules than singing.

The mechanic hadn't been too sure as to whether Deadeye had all his marbles, so after Deadeye had toppled over on *Sylvia*'s belly and was fast asleep, the mechanic checked out *Sylvia*'s heart. There was no doubt: *Sylvia* was capable of sailing Dad out where he wanted to go.

I jumped out of the car and opened the door for Mom. She led the way along the wharf, carrying Dad. I brought along Mom's basket of cold beers, cookies, and knitting. Mom stopped at the gap between *Sylvia* and the wharf. She looked down in the water. I knew Mom was missing the church. Instead, she had to go out in the North Sea to say farewell. This was something she'd never dreamt of doing, but all marriages were like that. One had to deal with the worst situations. She'd said so herself.

The mechanic sprang onboard and offered Mom his hand. Mom didn't want it. She jumped. She landed on *Sylvia* with Dad in her hands. Mom gave a screech. So did the high heels.

Deadeye's ears grew.

"High-heel shoes," he shouted. "This is a first for *Sylvia*! A hearty welcome to you!"

Mom wasn't in a talking mood. She sat right down, as close to land as possible. She asked for her knitting and that I hand out beers and cookies to the men. I was also supposed to tell them it was okay to start up the boat right away, because Mom could tell the weather might easily turn bad. Dad had always had a fiery nature and she wouldn't be surprised if it had come along for the ride.

I did as Mom said. Deadeye asked me to stuff four cookies in his mouth so he could munch on something while he steered us safely out of the harbor. It was not impossible that the mechanic's eyes would have to help us a little bit, but no one knew Hirtshals' harbor like Deadeye. There were a lot of sneaky traps we could get caught in, he said, and it was incredibly important that we wait to make a toast to *Sylvia*'s health until we were clear of the breakwater.

After the sea opened up before us it started getting windier. Mom held her scarf tight. She sat looking back toward Hirtshals, ignoring the knitting. The beach was deserted. Dad was silent, clenched between Mom's legs.

It was my job to spread Dad's ashes. Dad had said he wanted me to. I was the only one who could spread him in the right direction. I was the only one who knew the spot.

EPILOGUE

I STOOD AT THE BUILDING SITE WITH A GOOD GRIP ON DAD'S BIKE. I checked out the rolling toolbox. It was looking fine. I'd emptied out all the tools I couldn't see any point in bringing.

Now all I had was a pile of bricks, a pail, a sack of cement, a sack of mortar, my shovel, and my trowel. I took my time. One must never dive right in.

I poured a splash of water into the pail and began making a perfect mix. I didn't have the wheelbarrow. It was back in Hørmested. My shovel wasn't too good for mixing in the pail. There wasn't enough room. I had a smoke and thought the situation over.

I decided to give the shovel some time off, even though it complained. Instead I stuck the trowel down in the pail to let it try something new. This went real well. Then I unloaded the bricks and lined them up nicely next to each other.

I took another break and drank a forty-five-degree-cold beer in small slurps while I looked up at the hole in the attic wall. I couldn't reach it. I needed a ladder. I nodded at Little Horsey and knocked on the door. Gina's mom opened up.

"What the heck… Is it you?"

"Yes. Do you have a ladder I can borrow?"

"A ladder?"

"Yes, a ladder. It doesn't have to be that long."

"You can have a look in the stable."

Gina's mom followed along. In her pink slippers. She smelled like schnapps, but she was doing all right.

"Gina got engaged, you know. She doesn't live here anymore."

"Uh-huh. Then you have the whole place to yourself. How's it going with the hedgehogs?"

"Fine. They're doing fine."

Me and Gina's mom found a ladder. It was standing up against the stable wall. It was made of wood and was missing some steps, but that's how it always was at a building site. Sometimes you had to walk an incredibly long way to fetch water and other times you had to use a ladder that was missing things.

Out in the yard Gina's mom was curious about the tools I'd brought.

"What is it you're going to do?"

"Close the hole. It's already been like that an awful long time."

Gina's mom looked up at the hole.

"Yes, but the board's doing the job nicely," she said. "Gina nailed it on herself."

I shook my head.

"You're never supposed to drive nails into bricks. That's a real bad idea. Nails only get along with wood…I think. But it doesn't matter. The farm'll fall down if I don't wall up that hole. And that's what I'm gonna do."

I collected my gear at the foot of the ladder. There were a lot of things I had to get up to the hole. The bricks were heavy and took up way too much room. There was only one thing to do. I turned to Gina's mom.

"What's your name, actually?"

———

A couple of hours later I bicycled off, out in the world. The weather was great. I had a tailwind all the way. When I got to Hørmested I said hi to the wheelbarrow and told it how much it had been missed. I also told it the building project in Rakkeby had gone much better than expected. Gina's mom's name was Lilly. She'd been good at helping. Lilly didn't have anything at all against standing down on the ground, handing me up bricks, one after another.

We'd taken a lot of breaks. Then we sat with Little Horsey and drank beer and schnapps.

While I bricked up the hole, I thought what Gina would say about my work. I was sure she wouldn't care. For her it was a hole that could never heal. For me it was a great tale, gone to pieces.

Nobody would ever look at those bricks and be able to hear an "I'm sorry" squirm out between them. But that's how it was with a lot of my apologies. They came all too late.

I sat down on Dad's bench in God's Hørmested and surveyed the site. It was quite a mouthful. Maybe building a whole house by yourself couldn't be done. How could you lay a roof without a nice lady standing at your side who didn't mind handing up the tiles, talking about her daughter who you missed?

In front of me stood the only part me and Dad had finished— the one wall. It looked pretty sad.

I tried using some of the steam I'd built up from patching up the hole in Gina's wall. But then I clenched my eyes. And swore. I'd been wanting to get to Dad's bench so bad, I'd forgotten the most important part. The luxury cement-wash. The finishing touch.

The wind started blowing. Blowing into my back. Over the hilltop came the mooing of cows. I listened for the sound of bells. I couldn't hear any. That was what I got for not finishing the job.

I leaned over the earth's icebox. It was empty. Just a couple of curled-up beer caps. Then I noticed the drawing Dad had made on the bench seat. The lines weren't so strong anymore; they were trying to erase themselves.

I stood up. Time to say so long and bike on. I took a last look at Dad's drawing. I saw something else next to the house, a part of the drawing I'd been sitting on. It looked like two animals of some sort. With bulging stomachs and matchstick legs. And something around their necks. Like bells. Sure, that's what they were. Cowbells.

I sat back down on the edge of the bench so I could see the whole drawing. I remembered Dad's words. That when the house was finished and beautiful, a bunch of raunchy, un-Christian people would move in. It wouldn't be bad if they played the accordion, too, at least one of them.

Now a storm of moos was blowing over the hilltop. It sounded like the whole flock was flipping out. Maybe one of the cows had caught the plague. Maybe all the healthy cows were screaming that Mortimer and Elmer should hurry up and come and get the sick one.

I ran to the top of the hill. I couldn't spot the bell cows in the swarm, but they all looked like they were doing fine. The whole flock was standing on all fours and mooing in unison.

Was it possible for cows to catch cancer? There was a good chance. At least the bell cows could, since they were so old the brothers would only give a hundred bucks for them. Before sundown they might catch cancer and the plague.

Maybe the brothers would bury the bell cows right away. Mortimer and Elmer were always so busy. They didn't have time to wait for me and the shovel. They didn't have time at all for beautiful funerals.

I bit my lip. The wind was making my eyes water. I went back to the bench, had to sit down a little. I looked at the wall. It seemed alive. I walked over to it, patted it all the way from one end to another. The wall went straight into nothingness. Six bricks were lying scattered on the ground. It looked sloppy.

Down on my knees, I piled them one on top of another, then shoved them up against the end of the wall to keep them out of the wind. I walked back to the bench to see if it looked better. It did. Much better. It almost looked like the beginning of a new wall.

I took a few steps further back. It was like a beginning that was growing all by itself. Now I could see. This was going to be the back wall. But it'd sure look pretty dumb with two walls just standing there, each headed in its own direction. Maybe I could build a whole other third wall. One that was like the first one. Then everything would be dead flush. It would take time; maybe I'd never get finished. But if it ever worked, there'd be an entrance. A big wide one you couldn't miss.

Then I'd just need a roof. A major task, but I was sure the bell cows wouldn't care how the roof turned out. They wouldn't care about the bathroom, the bedroom, the kitchen, or the living room either. That was one big advantage—maybe the biggest advantage a building project could ever have.

I nodded while I tried to figure out the roof. Maybe some boards lying across, on top of the walls. Maybe that would be enough. Why not? All they had to be was watertight.

I walked back and forth. Then I ran. Up the hill to the top, toward the singing of the cows. I poked around in my pants pocket. There wasn't even a quarter. But hell, the idea was worth its weight in gold. The brothers would agree. They'd say congratulations. And every day I was sure they'd be by in the tractor to see how things were going. Would it work? Would the kid ever wind up building the finest flat-roofed barn in all of Hørmested?

That was the plan. To start with I had to get the bell cows back. Maybe they weren't particularly un-Christian, but they sure were raunchy.

And when that day came—when we all celebrated the topping-out and ate hotdogs and grass—I'd be surprised if by then I hadn't bought myself an accordion.

Yes, that's how it was gonna be. I could see it, hear it, taste it all. Now the barn just needed a name. Before I had a chance to think, the name fell out of the sky.

No doubt about it. My barn was going to be Buffalo's House.